STRANGER,
FATHER,
BELOVED

STRANGER, FATHER, BELOVED

TAYLOR LARSEN

GALLERY BOOKS

NEW YORK   LONDON   TORONTO   SYDNEY   NEW DELHI

G

Gallery Books
An Imprint of Simon & Schuster, Inc.
1230 Avenue of the Americas
New York, NY 10020

First Gallery Books hardcover edition July 2016

GALLERY BOOKS and colophon are registered trademarks of Simon & Schuster, Inc.

For information about special discounts for bulk purchases, please contact Simon & Schuster Special Sales at 1-866-506-1949 or business@simonandschuster.com.

The Simon & Schuster Speakers Bureau can bring authors to your live event. For more information or to book an event, contact the Simon & Schuster Speakers Bureau at 1-866-248-3049 or visit our website at www.simonspeakers.com.

Manufactured in the United States of America

10 9 8 7 6 5 4 3 2 1

Library of Congress Cataloging-in-Publication Data

Names: Larsen, Taylor, author.
Title: Stranger, father, beloved / Taylor Larsen.
Description: First Gallery Books hardcover edition. | New York : Gallery Books, 2016.
Identifiers: LCCN 2015040917 (print) | LCCN 2015050809 (ebook) | ISBN
Subjects: LCSH: Middle-aged men—Fiction. | Families—Fiction. | BISAC: FICTION / Literary. | FICTION / Family Life. | FICTION / Coming of Age.
Classification: LCC PS3612.A7733 S77 2016 (print) | LCC PS3612.A7733 (ebook)
  | DDC 813/.6—dc23
LC record available at http://lccn.loc.gov/2015040917

ISBN 978-1-5011-2475-4
ISBN 978-1-5011-2476-1 (ebook)

TO MY MOTHER, HARRIET,

A GREAT READER AND LOVER OF LITERATURE,

AND TO JAIME AND JAMIE

STRANGER,
FATHER,
BELOVED

CHAPTER ONE

With the tops of the trees around the house lost in fog, Michael and Nancy James prepared for the last party they would ever have, though they didn't know it at the time.

In the planning of the party, the house was filled with an atmosphere of seriousness. Careful consideration was given to each decision, as if they unconsciously knew then that there wouldn't be any more parties. Everything mattered all the more. They chose each dish, each appetizer with such care—quiches and salted ham on tiny rolls—and consulted each other obsessively about every little thing. They were united in this endeavor only. Nancy would follow Michael into the bathroom while he brushed his teeth and discuss her plans for decorating the tables, and they hashed and rehashed the options for hours until they were sure everything would look just right. Should they trust the weather? Should they set up tables with food outside or inside? Early May could be temperamental, and this spring was a cold, rainy one, but in these last few days the season seemed to finally be coming out of its depression.

It was as if they were both aware, on a plane so deeply imbedded and subconscious that it would seem to hardly exist, that this night would forever change their lives, but they were not sure in what way. In the hours before the party began, Michael felt desire curdling in his belly, desire for something different. It seemed that something was already changing. At the beginning of the evening, he felt an electric charge being around Nancy, as if she were a girl he had just met at a party instead of his wife. As they let guests into their house, he knew that the guests, too, could feel that things were different. They were giddy, the two of them, giddy and youthful, and Michael observed that Nancy, in her long green silk dress, had, through some means of feminine sorcery, transformed herself into a beauty. She seemed to glide across the room, and her bones possessed a confidence that she deserved to live in this huge house; that she was not a bitterly unhappy wife advancing toward old age but a young girl, with her whole life ahead of her and a light in her heart that had not yet been put out.

Michael had been becoming aroused frequently, and he experienced erections not directed toward anyone specific or for any particular fulfillment. At the party, he got one of those erections and excused himself to go to the bathroom. When it happened, he had been eating some smoked salmon on dry toast with capers and staring at a painting on his living room wall while his gin and tonic rested in the palm of his hand, cooling it. The painting showed a simple scene of an open field with lavender growing under a darkening sky, trees lining the perimeter of the field in the distance. Even though he had seen the painting a thousand times, today he was awed by it, and he momentarily forgot where he was. When he brought himself back to reality, he found he had a strong, pulsing erection, and he laughed without thinking and made his way into their small bathroom underneath the staircase. After he locked the door, he sat down on the toilet and sipped his drink as he waited for it to grow soft. He ran his tongue over the lime wedge in his drink. He had begun to feel so sensual recently. He wanted to touch and taste everything he could see.

When Michael emerged from the bathroom, he found his old college friends out on the lawn and joined them. They were in the same way he was, he felt, the drink had them, too, and they had all forgotten their age. They kept looking up at the sky, which, because it was cloudy, reminded him of the sky in the painting he had just seen. His old friend Ben brought Michael another drink, and they sat on the stone wall at the side of the yard and talked about their days at the university. Big hydrangea bushes, full and blooming, caught the eye. Two light blue ones sat on either side of the patio hugging the back of the house. Three bushes with violet-colored hydrangeas sat around the far edges of the lawn, contrasting nicely with the bright green grass. The gray-shingled Cape Cod–style house stood impressively behind them, charming in detail and grand in proportion. He could see two neighbors' houses from the backyard, but they weren't close enough to be too oppressive. Their gray sides blended in with the green of the pine trees all around. One house had a tree house, and a skinny young boy stood up in it, watching the party.

Michael, now forty-two, could act freely with many of these party guests, for they had known him as the brilliant scholar at Yale University, the winner of prizes for outstanding academic achievement, so many years ago. Nancy stood deferential and bashful when the lively group engaged in their academic talk, as she had been only a nanny for Michael's favorite professor and had never attended college herself. Michael was glad she was not around at this moment, so he would not have to see her downcast gaze and smiles. All of his friends from college accepted Nancy, but their talk changed around her. They tolerated her, though they must have all been secretly shocked at his choice of a marriage partner when he was a younger man. Before he had switched to business for graduate school, Michael had been an academic star in philosophy and political science. Everyone had thought he would have ended up as a tenured professor at the university because of his former interests and talent.

Michael stood by Will Campbell, his formerly shy classmate who had now blossomed into an extrovert, perhaps because of his marriage to a likable and talkative woman from college, Mary, who had brightened him up over the years. He now stood next to Michael, vodka in hand, talking to him conspiratorially, with an arm clapped over Michael's shoulder. Will lived a five-minute drive away on the Peninsula but worked as a full-time professor at a community college on the mainland of Rhode Island.

"Michael, Alex got in touch with me a month ago. He asked me to read an essay he wrote. I'm trying to help him get it published. I have some connections in Massachusetts at university presses . . ." Alex Woodson had been Michael's best friend at Yale, but the two had drifted apart over the years.

"Oh, is he still living in Massachusetts?"

"Yes, he's still there, has two beautiful little girls. Even though he works in finance, he started taking courses for his master's degree in literature a few years ago, very on the side, and now he teaches one course a semester as an adjunct at some obscure little college. I think it makes him happy to have an oar in the academic world. His essay is, of course, brilliant, but we've been having a little trouble getting it placed. Would you consider taking a look at it?" Will asked. "You always gave such great critiques . . . I already ran it by Alex, and he seemed eager to get your feedback as well."

Michael was deeply flattered by the request, but he tried to hide the extent of his feelings from Will. "I would love to take a look at it," he responded.

"Great, I brought a copy with me. My wife has it in her purse. Remind me to give it to you before we leave."

Michael had not been a part of academia for so many years, yet the thought of it still gave him a charge of excitement that nothing else did.

Michael looked up and saw the dear face of his sixteen-year-old daughter, Ryan, staring down at him from the window. She had refused to come down for the party. When his eye caught hers, she turned away abruptly from the window, and his heart ached at the disappearance of her face. He had forgotten for a moment that she existed, and then there she was, her hair messy around her face, her gaze curious and then immediately guarded.

He went inside and up the stairs to her room, thinking that maybe they could make up from the fight they had had earlier. He and Nancy had, though futilely, tried to insist Ryan should dress up and come down to the party. It had been a sticking point—he felt that she absolutely had to be there, but in the end, they couldn't force her to be a part of it. In her usual fashion, Ryan had slammed the door, after yelling "You can't make me do anything anymore. I can't wait to get out of this house!" Nancy had knocked firmly on Ryan's door and even raised her voice a little, and then Michael and Nancy had stood silently in the hallway, their arms helplessly at their sides. Now, hours later, Michael stood outside her room and placed his ear against the wood.

"Ryan, you could come down for a little bit, huh? You've got to try the food. Your mom got the best." He was referring to the salty Virginia ham that he knew Ryan loved. Nancy had had a leg of the ham shipped to their house for the occasion.

There was no response from within, but he knew she was listening.

"If you come down and apologize to your mother and me, then we'll forgive you." There was still no answer. She might have had her headphones on, lost in a world of dramatic music.

Teenage behavior, he always told himself as comfort. Teenage behavior, not related to him. She would have acted this way with any set of parents, he would muse to himself, but these days, he secretly wondered if this was true. His daughter had become increasingly unhappy the older she got and the more beautiful she became. Morose posters littered her wall, black-and-white stills of various singers slumped against walls, pale-skinned women and men, looking up at the camera either as a challenge or as an erotic invitation. The posters had suddenly appeared one month, Michael supposed, as his daughter's music interests changed. Two posters were of the same woman, a singer with full lips and a low-cut tank top staring at the viewer as if in challenge. The straps of her tank top were close to falling off her shoulders, almost exposing her breasts. He had been disgusted by the belligerent and blatant sexuality it professed and the anger burning in the young woman's eyes. He did not want his daughter to see sexuality as a challenge, as a threat to unleash onto others, as these posters suggested. It was absurd, really, their beautiful, traditional Cape Cod–style house, the epitome of good taste, strewn with posters unashamedly celebrating women's anatomy. What was next, tattoos, motorcycle rides, acid trips?

Michael turned and left the vacuum of the second floor, space that lacked the life of downstairs and threatened to pull him back into his heavy fear, that mental state related to his faulty wiring. The walls were painted robin's-egg blue, and he had bought two paintings from a famous local artist, Bill Clopher: one that depicted the ocean at its wildest, the tops of waves twisting in a white rage over its glassy green middle; and the other that depicted the ocean at its calmest, containing the murky forms of thousands of glittering-eyed creatures with tasks of their own, making its slow, almost indecipherable crawl under the moon's instruction.

Before rejoining the party, he looked out the window by the front door at the street beyond. A family raced by, all on bikes with different-colored helmets on their heads, the bright flash of them making him want to retreat into the cool, silent darkness of his basement. He slipped his right hand into his pants pocket and curved his palm over the bottle of pills. He could take one if he needed to, if his mind began to turn over the wrong thoughts, thoughts of panic and paranoia that he didn't need as his companions. He had options. When he began to worry that a party guest was staring at him because his joke wasn't funny, or if he felt all eyes were watching his back when really they weren't, he could take a pill. If he did not take a pill when the first paranoid thoughts emerged, they began to worsen. The people around him must know he had pills in his pocket, this person before him assumed there was something wrong with him and was hell-bent on finding out exactly what, people were going to go home and do research on his background and try to find out something bad about him. These kinds of thoughts went on and on.

He had to go to the bathroom. He went down to the room under the stairs and pulled hard on the handle. It was locked. He stood back a few paces and examined his hands. The nails were clean, but he saw that his fingers had gotten fatter over the years. Then the door opened, and a man who was almost exactly Michael's height and whom he had never met stood before him. The man's eyes were large and brown, and his expression was somber, reflective.

"Enjoying the party?" Michael asked. "I'm Michael James, and this is my house—great to meet you."

"I just got here. I haven't met too many people yet. I'm John. Your neighbor Mrs. Keller invited me," the man replied bashfully.

"Let me get you a drink." He walked with the man to the bar and got him the same drink that he had. It did not occur to him that the man might not want what he had. Then Michael found Nancy and had his hand on her back and things seemed to be starting to spin, which he knew was a bad sign. He knew he would have to sober up. Nancy would say something to him soon, a quick, nonconfrontational suggestion that he shouldn't be drinking for many reasons, especially considering that it mixed poorly with his medication, a fact he already knew.

He went down to the basement to gather himself and sat counting from one to ten, letting the freezing cold, dead air tingle the side of his face. He opened a bag of potato chips he found next to the case of ginger ales and began to eat them and drink a soda. He lay back for several minutes of spinning and then finished the bag of chips. When he got up, he was much clearer in the head.

When he returned to the first floor, he walked past the man from the bathroom, whose formerly tense face had softened from drink and who was talking with his neighbors. Their eyes met again, and Michael observed the man's old corduroy jacket and khaki pants. He wondered, was he affiliated with the university? Perhaps.

He found himself standing with Molly from the HR department of their company. Michael had been in the upper management of a software development company, Phairton, which had done so well that they had been able to sell it to a larger publicly traded company; in the sale Michael had been asked to stay on as a consultant for the new company, an offer that showed its management's admiration for him. He still had his office and secretary at Phairton, but no one watched his hours. He had been integral in making a fortune for the original company and continued to bring in profit, and though he was still young, the high-profile title had worn him out in a span of years, and he was happy to be in a less pressured situation. The work had been interesting during the first couple of years to some extent, but it had never truly challenged his mind. Now he found it hard to focus fully on his work at all. Two paths had been presented before him at a young age: one, working in academia as a professor, which would have fulfilled him immensely, the other, this path that, while making life comfortable, daily drained him of his strength. Molly had worked with him for years, and ironically, even though she was not a people person, she was efficient at her work and quiet in her affairs, and no one seemed to mind her heading HR. She was one of the antisocial guests at the party, so Michael felt he had to attend to her. There she lolled, a skinny woman, her back slumped against the wall near the sliding glass door to the yard. She had a special liking for him, which he had never quite understood. She was quiet, yet tightly wound, and her nervousness was infectious.

"Molly, so glad you could come. How are things going for you?"

She appeared relieved to see him and stepped closer. He noticed that her face had a distinct line where the layer of foundation ended along her jawline. The skin on her neck was paler and less alive but more real. Women seemed to love Michael's height, just over six feet, and his thin trim frame. Many, upon meeting him, would glance up at him, take him in, and their eyes would gleam with instant respect. He had a full head of hair, large eyes, and delicate features. By no means considered universally handsome, he was also not considered unhandsome. He was not mentioned as one or the other, which left it all open to interpretation.

"It's good to get out. You know how it is," she replied.

Michael nodded. He pitied her, standing there in her olive-green dress and slightly worn-out black shoes. Those must be the shoes she always wore to parties, every year for God knew how long.

"Where's your daughter? I've always wanted to meet her after seeing her photo on your desk."

"She's in hiding—you know how teenagers are. They never want to show themselves." Molly was unmarried and seemed resigned to her fate. Desperately, Michael thought of what else he could say to her. His daughter was in hiding, and his severely asthmatic six-year-old son, little Max, was already asleep. There was nothing else to say about either one of them that he could think of.

Michael felt as if Molly were forever searching his face for something. She was one of those mysterious women who was drawn to him and sought him out for some reason he could not identify. She repulsed him, but just because he could, he began to flirt with her, listening with his full being, talking sensuously, lightly touching her arm. He knew those attentions were delighting her, as they were so different from his normally cold demeanor. Just when he had her excited, he excused himself.

Then he was back outside in a dark yard. Nancy had lit little candles, just as they had planned, and the air was lovely and warm, the lighting flattering to everyone, equalizing them all in an image of God's beauty. All faces could bend and slant into something nice to look at if just given a kind and delicate light. Michael's friends were young men again in this light, and the women were dangerous beings, deliciously different from them, whom they loved to watch glide around. His wife was not among the nymphets, so he went inside to find her.

Michael found Nancy sitting on a chair in the living room talking earnestly with the man from the bathroom. The man sat across from her on a yellow armchair that matched hers in color and fabric, and they both had wicked grins on their faces. They sat next to a small table with a delicate blue glass lamp on it that cast a soft, intimate glow on their faces. The light seemed to separate the pair from the world around them. Michael thought of going up to them and entering their pleasant conversation but then thought better of it. They were speaking in such a way as to stop him in his tracks.

Time was moving slowly in their corner of the room. Nancy was leaning comfortably forward on her elbows. Michael saw that his wife was grinning with an ecstatic happiness, and he knew he had never before elicited from her such a response of unrestrained joy. She appeared to him a different woman from the one he had married. The man was studying Nancy as she spoke, clearly amused by her, his lips parted ever so slightly, hanging on her every word, as if they were sharing a secret. Nancy would occasionally laugh with her head cocked back, a wild gesture Michael was sure he had never seen in her before. He was amazed to see her so animated, so unself-conscious. A stab of jealousy coursed through him, and then just as quickly it vanished, leaving only a sense of wonder.

The weight that normally coated Nancy's face seemed to have miraculously left her features—they were sharp and bold, and a sense of preciousness clung to her, surrounded her. Her hands seemed more delicate, her mouth and eyes more alive, more passionate. Michael was sure that she had never looked like this, never once, until now. He watched her and the man, whose own features, in their preciousness, seemed a mirror of Nancy's. They both had happy, well-cared-for faces.

It was at that moment that Michael realized, without a doubt, that this was the man Nancy should have married. The energy around them was electric, and as he watched them he felt a strange shaking sensation rising up from his legs. This realization was immediate, could not be explained, and could not be refuted by anyone. He had never in his life been more certain of anything. Their two bodies were meant to be joined. It occurred to him that perhaps they were the reason for all of his erections. Their coming together, a process that must have taken much time to come about, had finally arrived, and the sheer magnitude of its power descending on the house had been arousing him for weeks.

Michael knew that *she* didn't know that. She was not the kind of person to open herself to such forces. She could not see that the man before her was more closely related to her romantic destiny than her own husband was. She was unaware of the force of change that had descended upon their house, slowly, bit by bit, over the course of their miserable years as a family. A force sent to free them.

To her credit, Michael was sure that the man was someone she had just met and toward whom her intentions were totally inno-cent. Yet he still saw it. At that moment, something restless that had been previously undefined began to crystallize inside Michael. He could feel his molecules realigning. As people shifted around him, mingling and murmuring, he kept his eyes focused on the two of them. It was really quite beautiful to witness such a match perched before him. He drew in his breath in a trance and watched as they chatted casually, completely oblivious to their obvious, deep compatibility.

Michael wanted secretly to clear out all the guests, tiptoe to the door, and lock it behind him, sealing the two of them in a private world they could explore together. He knew if they were left alone in a timeless realm, they would go on talking forever, or at least late into the night until they fell asleep together. And their sex would be beautiful and innocent, like two teenagers having their first time on a bed of sheets and covers they made in the woods.

Michael stood transfixed, smiling at the thought.

———

At the party's end, Michael stared outside at the lamppost, which lit up a section of the driveway and left the rest in darkness. It was getting colder; the spring nights still had their chill. Stray fog was drifting through his yard as it always did; he could see an occasional flicker as it blanketed the light post. The clouds moved quickly out here over the rocky coasts and dark, cold waters surrounding their peninsula; the sky was constantly in motion with charged gray matter—above, a mass moving purposefully forward; below, playful swirls of mist skipping over the houses and trees, causing mischief. Some of Rhode Island was tacky, but this little strip of land was positively wild and elegant, he felt, like an old English marsh. If he got too caught in his head, he knew to come outside. The cool, wind-filled air always dissipated his anxiety, the paranoia that had marred his life. It was like an evil growth, a malignancy that clung to his side and made thoughts arrive in his mind at a different timbre from regular people's.

The paranoid brain was fast and often perceived an innocent look or comment as mocking or cruel; hints were amplified and meanings distorted. Talking with other people could be a horrifying experience, though Michael could usually pass for normal. Most of the pain was internal, a private hell that his silent, brooding twin offered up daily tickets to. To make matters worse, the older he got, the less his medication seemed to work. It still put a sheath over about thirty-five percent of the anxiety, but the rest stayed strong and functional, doing what it did best. At work, though he was admired and had made it into senior management, nothing to worry about anymore, he still had to flick a switch when talking to other people. That clicked on the full smile and the easy handshake, which banished the dark thoughts and lit up his eyes, creating the impression that the person before him was the most important person in the world. The autoswitch clicked off once he left the conversation, and the great swell of tension returned and claimed him again.

But coming outside seemed to free him from the dark mass and the dark mind, and the elements of wind, water, and earth pulled him away from himself. There were the pine trees, the sea-misted air, the sounds of the water on stormy nights, all the little animals and birds, hawks and owls that moved around the outside of his house, securing shelter and adapting to the moods of the atmosphere. In a sense, it was unnatural to live in a solid house that was never affected by the weather. If he had been an animal or lived in a house that was not sealed with sterility, his mind might have been freer and less paranoid. The salt air would soothe the malignancy, coax it away into the night.

———

In his study, Michael could hear Nancy cleaning up in the kitchen and could not bring himself to go and help her. Looking out into the hallway, he could see the blaze of lights at the other end of the hall. Nancy always cleaned with every single light turned on, so that each square inch could be scanned and no detail missed. The overheads were blaringly electric and hurt his eyes. Nancy was very good at keeping house, and her diligence with cleaning allowed Michael to relax when he moved through one orderly room to another. When he needed a snack later, the kitchen would be serene and spotless, a small lamp left on in the corner of the room to allow him to get his late-night snack in relative darkness.

Michael knew his wife was avoiding him, as he could turn hateful from drinking. Or, he thought, maybe she wanted to be alone—maybe she was thinking of the man she had talked with at the party. He closed the door to the study and settled into his burgundy leather chair. He pulled out his secret bottle of scotch and poured some into the glass he held, which still had ice at the bottom. An excitement tinged with anxiety burned in his stomach as flashes of Nancy talking so flirtatiously with the other man lit up his mind. He would give her this gift for so many of the wasted years she had spent as his wife. He could deliver her this man as a prize for enduring the years of disappointments. Though he was excited, the alcohol slowed his mind down with each sip. He had Alex's essay in his lap, but he was too disoriented to begin reading it tonight. He reached up and snapped off the standing lamp next to his leather chair. The room was mostly dark. Miraculously, he found himself going in and out of dreams. More miraculous still, his wife had gone to bed, had not rap-rap-rapped on the door to see what he was up to.

When he awoke from a deep sleep, it was three in the morning. That was quite an accomplishment, sleeping for a few hours. Out of habit, he stood from the chair and made his way to the stairway to the second floor to join his wife in bed. Perhaps he could get one or two more hours of sleep; his mind was foggy enough to allow it. Sliding face-first onto the massive bed, he stretched out on his half of the mattress. She knew not to come to his side.

CHAPTER TWO

From her window, Ryan observed her parents standing in the yard. They both seemed at ease, satisfied with the evening, as they stood on the lawn waving. It was a rare moment of unity between them. Her father was standing a couple of feet from her mother on the grass, saying good-bye to the last of the guests. He never stood too close to her. They were watching their friends Gayle and Todd get into their car. Her father held a drink and was no doubt sad to see this particular couple leave, as they were old university friends. Her window was open, and through the screen she could hear bits of their conversation on the lawn. She could hear her father rambling to her mother about a certain joke that so-and-so had told, a joke that was probably way over her mother's head anyway. She felt there was nothing sadder than to hear him babble about all his achievements and awards won. It was pathetic to watch her mother remain silent, listening, as she, having no such track record, simply could not relate.

When she looked at her father lately, she knew in her heart that something was wrong with him. She had seen her mother whisper hushed concerns to him when he made himself a drink, and she had seen the pill bottles. Yes, there was most likely something wrong with him. She had tried several times to get her hands on one of his bottles to see the label, but she had never managed to find one. They were well hidden, wherever they were.

Ryan watched with irritation as her parents came back toward the house, both smiling, but for their own reasons. Her father always held his body stiffly, his shoulders unnaturally hunched toward his ears. He had unusually long, thin limbs and long, almost feminine fingers. Her mother had never been a beauty, and her figure had suffered from childbearing. Standing next to her tall, brittle-boned husband, she looked even shorter and rounder. As Ryan looked down upon them, they appeared to be mismatched.

———

That night, Ryan focused her thoughts on the fact that she would be having dinner the following evening at Jill's. For more than a year she had been going to her friend Carol's house after school, but these days it was to see Carol's mother, Jill, not Carol, who was present in the house, sequestered in her room.

Growing up, Ryan and Carol had been inseparable. They had played together in grade school and middle school and slept over at each other's houses on weekends. Their houses were in the same neighborhood, and they'd used to race to find each other after school, but at the beginning of high school, two years ago, they had begun to drift apart. Jill's house sat on the edge of the forest, a hybrid of the small local workmen's homes on the outskirts and those of the giant houses hidden within the forest. Many of the houses on the edge of town or outside had aluminum siding and squat, boxy shapes. A lot of local fishermen and plumbers lived there, as well as the family that mowed their lawn. Jill's was not a Cape Cod–style house, just a regular one, painted bright yellow, of medium size, neither impressive nor meager.

Back when Ryan had ventured down the road almost every night to spend the evening at Carol's house, she would pass the large beautiful houses tucked away behind their driveways, flowers overflowing in fuschia, yellow, violet. She passed homes with bursts of roses growing along wooden weathered gates, red, white, and pink roses, a preview of what was to come a hundred feet behind them in the dazzling gray houses with clean walls, happy pets, and well-fed children. She sometimes saw hummingbirds zoom up to the feeders that held the syrupy golden liquid they swallowed with true zeal. A little further down, she began to pass houses that had fewer flowers, whose lawns were more scraggly, and that were closer to the road. The structures became less and less magical until they became downright oppressively the same. Right before that point, where all turned ordinary, stood Carol's house, still among the cheery and cared for, to some degree.

Ryan would arrive out of breath, and usually she and Carol would heat up the microwaveable Betty Crocker chocolate cake with frosting and then eat it with either milk or orange juice, depending on what Jill had in stock. Then they would run up the stairs together and read magazines. She could remember the bizarre children's games they had played together. One of their favorites was called "college"—a role-playing game where they put tennis balls in their training bras and walked around the bedroom bending over in front of imaginary suitors and talking about parties. For some reason, the game had been immensely satisfying. One night, they had played the game wearing their two-piece bathing suits, tennis balls stuffed inside the padded tops.

With several books slung under her arm, Ryan had sauntered around the room and smiled and waved at male students she imagined she was passing. Carol was stretched out on one of her twin beds, her legs slightly spread, coyly fanning herself.

"Janet, you are such a tease!" Ryan exclaimed. "Why did you turn down Bobby's offer to take you to his summer house? He is so hot."

"Stephanie," Carol belted back, "how can I go with him after what he did to Katie's reputation? He torched it." "Torching" was a term often used at their middle school; it referred to a moment when a girl was suddenly, out of the blue, humiliated or abandoned by the people she felt were *her people*. The old term had been "dropping the bomb" and implied surprising a selected girl by refusing to speak to her or acknowledge her presence at all, but, over time, they had grown tired of it, and instead preferred the tidy, efficient term "torching." Typically applied only to female friendship, the concept was taken a step further in "college," where Carol and Ryan created sexual torching, which they supposed involved humiliation of some kind between a man and a woman after they had "had sex."

Then it was Carol's turn to take a lap around the room. Rising from the bed dramatically, she walked as if drunk; deliberate in all her movements, swinging her legs. When she reached the corner of the room, she bent over a chair and rested one hand on each of its arms. These pauses were for the imaginary male audience that was always circling around them. After hours of endless flirting with made-up people, they collapsed on Carol's bed and began flipping through magazines.

They didn't know it yet, but that summer just before high school was to be their last with children's games of any kind. They began to lose their sense of humor. When they were younger, their light-heartedness had lit up every room they were in and every game they engaged in. They'd made up scripts for fake soap operas and used

Ryan's family's video camera to film the scenes. They had two soap operas; one was called *Teardrops on My Lingerie* and the other *The Young and the Chestless*. But, recently, with games like "college," the tone had changed, had turned slightly more serious, more studied, and although it had still been playful, there was considerably less joy in it for both of them. Things were shifting, changing, and though Ryan could hardly have articulated it at the time, looking back now, it was as if a dark cloud had settled over their little section of the neighborhood.

At the end of middle school, Carol hadn't fared well; she had emerged from puberty slightly ugly, Ryan thought. Maybe it wasn't quite ugliness exactly, but her face was large and her features seemed out of proportion. The skin on her cheeks was also continually glazed with little acne bumps, shiny red colonies that could not be rubbed off. However, that was not the full reason Ryan felt awkward around her. It was mainly because, through these unfortunate physical developments, Carol's personality had changed. The knowledge that she now had worse cards to play than when she had been a cute, goofy girl made her paranoid around other people. The changes in her were subtle, but she seemed meaner and more guarded in her movements. In the girls' locker room, she was careful about who saw her undress, and she no longer smiled easily. Along with this new restraint, the beginnings of an unshakable sadness hung around her.

Ryan could recall one of the pivotal days between the two of them when they were twelve—they were putting on their bathing suits to use the slip-and-slide Jill had set up in the yard for them. As Ryan was putting on her favorite red one-piece bathing suit, and before she pulled it up to her waist, the two girls looked at the traces of her pubic hair and the tiny buds on Ryan's chest. It came as a shock when Carol gave a short, nasty laugh.

"I don't know if that's how it's supposed to look, but it looks weird to me," Carol said, and almost immediately Ryan was ashamed. Carol was gazing intently down at the floor, her face burning red. She already had on her blue Speedo bathing suit, and her short, stocky body showed no signs of any of the desired attributes. As they had both been waiting for those signs of life to begin showing themselves, it had never occurred to either of them that one would start before the other or that one of them would fall short of the ideal. Carol seemed to be looking more and more like a miniature Jill; her body was thicker, her face was pudgy, and traces of her biological father, who had supposedly been a startlingly good-looking young man, were, day by day, getting lost in the shuffle.

"At least I have something going on. You haven't changed at all since last year," Ryan answered. She curled her fingers tighter over her small breasts, as if Carol could somehow take them from her or stop the growing process from continuing. At that moment, each girl felt possessed by a deep-seated wariness of the other, a feeling neither would ever be able to shake. Each felt the other capable of harm and the one to blame should problems arise in the future.

At the start of high school, they tried to keep a friendly rapport going, even occasionally going out to a movie together at the local theater, but over the last year, as they had both turned sixteen, all attempts at connecting felt entirely forced, and they had stopped spending time together completely.

Now Carol was always staying after school for sports, field hockey, basketball, softball, so Ryan continued her habit of going over to her house to spend time with Carol's mother, Jill, instead of returning to her own home. It would be just the two of them for hours, and when Carol finally did come home, she would take her tray of food up to her room and shut herself up there for most of the night. Ryan, unsure why she kept going back there, knew only that she found Jill's presence soothing.

———

The next day, in the late afternoon, Ryan spread her biology books over Jill's kitchen table. The kitchen smelled of lemon, as Jill had cleaned it just before Ryan arrived. Ryan knew that Jill loved having her over and she was the reason the kitchen counters gleamed under the bright, cheery lights. Jill stood across the kitchen, making egg salad and, as usual, was completely caught up in her own world. She seemed to expect nothing from Ryan, and Ryan appreciated that more than she could express. Jill had a nature CD playing on the stereo. It was called *Distant Thunder*, and the rumbling noises and cricket sounds made the stereo speakers vibrate and hum as the waves of sound emerged and took over the room.

"Jill, I think the CD is meant to be played quietly to have a relaxing effect."

Jill smiled and poured some herbs into the egg salad. "I like it like this. It blasts through your system. Really stirs you up. Anything that stirs you up is good." But she went over and lowered the volume a little.

"Yeah, I guess you're right." Ryan sighed and looked back down at her books. She noticed that this new Jill was freer with her speech and seemed to have adopted an "it's all good" motto. Maybe all the self-help books she had read were finally making an impact. The old Jill had been shy and hesitating. There were only traces left of that insecure creature, Ryan felt. When just she and Jill were together, she felt the two of them had the ease that close friends share.

Until recently, she and Carol had always laughed at Jill, who had never married and so had raised her daughter by herself. They found it funny that she refused to dye her graying hair or shave her armpits and that she always seemed to be one step behind the times. She had a collection of glass mushrooms that was housed in a rickety wooden case in the corner of the living room. She always seemed to be embarking on some new, strange project that embarrassed the girls, such as growing sprouts in a little machine she kept in her bedroom, studying tai chi, or learning Portuguese from cassette tapes while she cooked meals in the kitchen. Back then, Jill hadn't seemed to mind that the girls were always giggling at her or rolling their eyes. She had taken it all in with generous patience and usually even laughed at herself or made a self-deprecating comment such as "I got to stay busy somehow, guys."

Jill had had a string of boyfriends, each of whom lasted for a few months. They would appear at the house, each of them slightly older than Jill, and hesitantly walk past the two girls playing in the yard on their way to the front steps of the porch. Three years ago, the procession of big-bellied men had stopped for some reason, and Jill had, without explanation, found herself permanently single. It was clear that she was somehow unlikely to date again—all three of them felt it intuitively, although each was unsure why.

The last beau, Robbie, had been the most likable of the bunch, although by the time he came around, Jill and her daughter were for the most part disillusioned with the idea of having a permanent man in their lives. Robbie had the bad luck of arriving in the aftermath of Andy, who had been the most hurtful of all. Andy's unpredictability had taken them all by surprise. Ryan had memories of Andy, who had been mild-mannered in his initial persistent pursuit of Jill, settling into a comfortable routine of having dinner with Jill and Carol and Ryan, and spending the night. But then, one summer morning, he had awakened to find that Jill was not in bed with him. She had just gone to get some groceries, and he had become enraged at her for not leaving him a note. When she returned forty minutes later, he had confronted her by screaming and throwing a chair against the wall, waking both Carol and Ryan.

Before Andy there had been Peter, whose main attribute had been his mind-numbing dullness. He had always seemed uncomfortable around Carol and, after getting drunk, would call her "little uggs." The only reason he'd gotten away with saying that for the first few weeks was that it was impossible to make out what he was actually saying. Jill and Carol had both thought he was saying "little one" until one night Carol had overhead him talking to one of his buddies on the phone.

"The little ugly one's in bed, so come on over and drink some beer with me," he had said and laughed. Ryan had seen clearly that Carol's heart had broken a little bit upon hearing that description of herself; her face had flushed and her eyes had gone wild with helplessness. Ryan had never thought of Carol as ugly before Peter said that, but now she saw it in her friend.

Later Robbie had entered the picture. He had been kind and a little boring but eager to give love to Jill and Carol, but the exhaustion that hung in the air had quickly dampened his romantic attempts. Jill was indeed exhausted and unable to take him seriously. The relationship had fizzled out until he had finally stopped coming around altogether.

As she sat in the kitchen with Jill, Ryan was distracted, as the house was full of memories; it was hard for her not to recall little moments that always involved Carol, as if their two happy little child ghosts were still roaming the corridors somewhere in the house.

On the page in front of Ryan, there was a drawing of a spinal cord and its little elephant-eared vertebrae stacked one atop the other. Taking a deep breath, she tried to focus on what the writing said and to block out the crashing thunder sounds coming from the speakers perched on the cabinet above her. Last time she had been there doing homework at the kitchen table, Carol had stood at the edge of the kitchen and watched the two of them, a quizzical look on her face. She had not come into the kitchen. Ryan wondered if she would do the same tonight.

Spinal reflex: involuntary, fast, predictable, unlearned, automatic, inherited response to stimulus.

She scanned the definition in confusion.

Withdraw reflex: withdraw from a painful stimulus.

"Jill, do you get this stuff?"

"What?"

"Do you understand the spinal cord and nerve reflexes? Can you help me with this?"

Jill put down her spoon and came around the counter. She leaned over next to Ryan, who could smell Jill's faint body odor and see the outline of her huge, soft breasts leaning her way.

The CD switched to bird sounds, and Jill said, "Oh, I love this part."

It was soothing to have a break from the thunder, and the birds' singing matched the sunny weather outside.

Jill ran her finger over the definition. Ryan noticed that her fingers were a little greasy. They left a tiny smear on the print. Ryan remembered Jill hadn't even been to college. Of course she wouldn't know.

"Yeah, I get it." She stood up straight and stretched her arms overhead. Her armpit odor was severe.

"Well, will you explain it to me?" Ryan said in exasperation.

"Here." Jill lunged at her chair, causing Ryan to gasp and fall out of it.

"That's the withdraw response."

Ryan laughed good-naturedly, though she felt mildly angry. She went up behind Jill and pulled on her bra strap, slowly letting it snap, because she knew Jill was embarrassed and helpless at the largeness of her breasts.

Jill laughed uncertainly and slowly looked over her left shoulder, keeping the rest of her body perfectly still. They stood there awkwardly; Jill had her back to her, while Ryan held the fabric of the shirt in her hands and with her index finger traced a small line along the edge of Jill's shoulder blade. She could feel heat dance under the cloth in her hand. Jill walked abruptly out of the room.

"I'll be back in a few minutes," she called from the stairway, and Ryan could tell she was trying to sound casual.

Ryan settled down again at her spot at the table and turned down the volume on the stereo, reducing the sounds of the birds, whose calls now sounded panicky. She felt a strange mixture of excitement, disgust, and power surge through her. At sixteen, she was blossoming and was coming to learn that there was nothing older people loved more than seeing beauty in its purest form, bursting forth in a newly sexual body. It was likely that she sensed a shift in others' behavior toward her, and it made her uncomfortable. Her body looked just like the bodies of the women in films. She now inhabited a space where boys and men became restless around her, and she was aware that she was entering a lifelong joke that she would never fully get but would always vaguely sense.

She thought of the kids at school and knew she was called a bitch behind her back. She was unsure who her friends were these days—she had been skipped over this year as the other kids had been forming their groups. She was sure people thought of her as the girl who couldn't take a joke, and that made her even quieter and more somber.

But she was growing more beautiful daily; she could see the popular girls eyeing her with alarm and perhaps interest. If she wanted to, she could make nice and be asked into their group. All she had to do was smile and play along, but she couldn't do it, couldn't stand to be groped by the jocks, to listen to the cheerleaders' gossip. The senior class two years above her was a particularly good-looking class, with so many brunettes with pale blue eyes and blondes with aquamarine green eyes, that just to walk down the hall was like seeing a wall of jewels against the lockers. Despite their being so pretty a group, the older kids still looked at her as if she might be one of them, should be one of them. If she smiled back, she would be obliged to go to parties, drink, and have sex with the mindless country club boys. So she stayed guarded and saw others' admiration for her pale face and long brown hair and thin, pretty body, an admiration that quickly turned to anger at her lack of effort to fit into the social hierarchy. The goth kids also looked at her with interest—she listened to their music, but she didn't want to go with them either. Eventually they, too, regarded her with disdain and she remained alone.

The school year was almost over, she kept telling herself. The summer would be easier. Until then, at least she could come here. She had this. There had been times, though, when something about Jill scared her, when she looked at Jill and felt she was viewing an alien— her long, gray braid, her slapdash grin, her skin speckled from too many hours in the sun.

She remembered one Saturday morning a month ago when they had driven out to the cliffs, a place, Ryan knew, where Jill used to do her partying when she was younger, and there had been a heavy expectancy and pressure for the two to connect. Since they had left before Carol had gotten up, their departure on this trip had felt illicit. It was still chilly, as it was April, so they had taken along jackets and hats to protect themselves from the cold wind that whipped around the rocks so close to the ocean. At the cliffs, they had had a moment of elation as they stepped to the ledge—the two of them grinning, bracing their hands against the rocks. Jill was being pulled around by the wind. Her loose-fitting shirt flapped around her body like a flag. She turned to Ryan and said, "You don't even have to inhale out here, the air just slams into you."

Ryan had laughed and closed her eyes as she lay on a long, smooth rock. The day was so bright and the wind so insistent. Nothing seemed permanent out there. The wind, the light, the water rushing over the shore and then sliding back into itself. She felt that the very rocks they were sitting on wouldn't remain long where they were. She could see herself and Jill crumbling into the ocean, an image that somehow didn't disturb her that much. In fact, it felt strangely right.

Jill had pointed at the water and said, "Look at it. It's like it's saying to me 'Come on in, I'll take care of you, I'll return you back to the shore.'"

Ryan had looked at the churning water and the way it swelled and then made little explosions of spray against the rocks and tide pools. "I don't see that," she had responded. "What happened to that tube of water you used to wear around your neck?" Jill had been wearing the tube necklace for weeks and this was the first time Ryan had noticed she was without it. It had mysteriously disappeared.

"I have a secret," Jill said. She was smiling too big, Ryan felt, and her overwhelming happiness had been unnerving. "I'll tell you what it is." Ryan suddenly knew she would not like hearing the secret.

Jill explained that she had ordered vials of spring water brought up from the depths of caves in New Zealand. This water, considered the purest of all the water on earth, had never seen the light of day nor been exposed to the air. It was completely unpolluted. It was flown over to the United States already sealed in the vials and sold at high prices in New Age stores and spiritual centers.

Jill told her she had inserted the vial into her vagina to purify that part of her body and was now keeping it in there until she felt cleansed. She said it as if it were the most natural thing in the world. Ryan smiled and looked away, trying to be polite, but she felt a painful clenching in her stomach, as if all the tectonic plates had just aligned in the worst possible positions for their little bit of land and the earth would soon start grumbling and offer up waves of hot lava. She'd had no idea that the vial had been nestled in there, in Jill's graying anatomy, and it bothered her enormously both that it had been there all this time without her knowledge and that she now knew of its presence. She imagined the poor little tube of sealed water, having to account for the purification of all that scarred female tissue, having to clean out an old passageway and erase confusion and disappointment. That was a big job for such a little vial, and it struck Ryan as blatantly unfair.

Jill's body seemed to Ryan a blueprint for failure—her sad eyes, graying strawlike hair, her feminine parts, which had been used and abandoned, the heaviness that coated all the curves of her body. Jill had that shocked look of one who has witnessed an awful accident and on whom the catastrophic image has imprinted itself indelibly. All the early years of drinking with her wild friends and the later years of disappointment had caused her organs to sit heavy inside. But Ryan had to admit that she loved her nonetheless.

Jill seemed to respect Ryan, and when Ryan was in Jill's house, she felt as though she could finally take a full breath and relax. In her own home, after her brother was put to bed, her mother usually went up to her bedroom alone with a romance novel or to watch a movie in bed before falling asleep early, while her father secluded himself in his study for the entire night. The house was segregated and joyless.

———

When it got late and the yard fully darkened, Ryan knew she would have to leave Jill's and return to her own house. As she walked out of the door, she heard the muffled sounds of the TV that Carol watched in her bedroom. She kept it on from the time she walked into her room until she went to bed, completing her homework over the course of a series of shows. Carol liked the volume on high, and little bits of light from the TV danced over the upstairs hallway walls in strange patterns. Ryan heard the laugh of the audiences of the game show and then the perky voices of the people in commercials as she shut the front door behind her.

When she got home, she entered her house quietly, so as not to attract any attention. She had been playing this odd cat-and-mouse game with her parents for weeks—they would not acknowledge that she did not come in on time, and she would not bring it up either. At this stage, her mother didn't even leave a plate of dinner for her on the counter as she had in previous weeks. In the initial phases of the game, her mother had tried to ground her for missing three dinners in a row. But when Ryan didn't come home the next night, there were no real consequences, such as taking away her car keys. Her mother had had harsh words about it a second time a week later, and Ryan had apologized to her, but the next night she found that she just didn't want to stay home and even she didn't know why. The plate was now in the refrigerator if she wanted it. It was her mother's feeble attempt at saying she had noticed that Ryan no longer came home for dinner.

They had no authority whatsoever, Ryan mused. Well, if they weren't going to trust her enough to tell her what was wrong with her dad, why he needed pills and looked miserable all the time, then she wouldn't tell them when she was coming and when she was going—simple as that. She was not a child anymore. She could handle whatever it was, but they didn't trust her with the information, and being in the house not knowing was unbearable. She ate half of the plate, enjoying the sharply cold, dry meat of the chicken.

Ryan went up to her room, sat there for a couple of hours reading a book, and then attempted to get some sleep, but without success. Often when she couldn't sleep, she'd bring her books into her brother Max's room and read in there while he slept. He didn't stir when she walked in, nor while she sat in there. His room had been decorated very carefully, as if the soothing lavender walls, the nurturing pictures of animals sleeping under the moon and children curled in their beds would somehow cancel out the chaos within his troubled body.

She had a passage to read about the Vietnam War for history class the next day, and she set into the task of getting through the dull series of paragraphs.

Max lay on his side facing away from where Ryan sat reading on the floor by the night-light. Every now and then, she looked up from her book to watch him. He hummed like a motor, waking himself with little wheezes. She was flipping through pictures of men wearing camouflage outfits with their arms around each other in the Vietnamese jungle. Her high school was making efforts to have the students read "diverse" books about various wars, though this book seemed much more focused upon featuring the US soldiers than it was on portraying the lives of the Vietnamese people, which would have made it more diverse. She was taken with one photo of a soldier slumped against a tree who had a particularly boyish face and a thin, almost effeminate body. He stood a few feet away from the others.

She had found her mother's high school yearbook in Max's room, and she had it open alongside the other, examining the smile of each of the students. Toward the back of the book were the messages written by her mother's friends. One said, "I'll never quite figure out what you've done to me." She couldn't make out the name under the signature. That was certainly a very out of the ordinary thing to say, especially to her mother, who seemed incapable of sparking such a profound and enigmatic comment from another person. Jill had often mentioned to her that there are some people who lead lives in which they merely graze the surface of their potential. Her mother must be one of those people—untapped. What treasures did she have? Ryan could not imagine any, although, looking around the room at the tiny comforts provided by her mother, such as the blue cashmere blanket folded at Max's feet, should he need extra covering in the middle of the night, she was overtaken by a sense that there was something. It was clear that her mother had known the blanket's extra softness would calm his anxiety.

She saw a photo of Max and herself, her arms wrapped around him, which her mother had framed and set beside his bed. Her mother would never put a photo of herself and Max on display; she would consider that vain. Yet she had shown the yearbook to Max to entertain him. Maybe humility was both her mother's gift and her source of failure?

Along the same lines, Jill was always talking about how crucial it was to manifest one's potential and it was her best and worst trait. Ryan was sickened by a woman of Jill's age having so much ambition but nothing to show for it. All she had was her hearty laugh and dumb earnestness. And yet, if it were possible, Ryan would spend every free moment with her. She mattered to Jill.

She looked over at the shape of Max's body under the comforter. His right arm was extended out over his comforter, revealing the sleeve of his favorite red flannel pajamas. She recognized the vague outline of the green squares on the red background, even in the dark. The only time he didn't wear them was when they were crumpled in the bottom of the hamper in the laundry room. Seeing his tiny face asleep, a face that would be handsome if it weren't so tense and compressed, she felt love for him flow easily through her. She wondered if he was aware that she was there with him. Closing her eyes, she tried to imagine what he might be dreaming. It must be something rough, jagged but not scary, because she was convinced that nothing was scary to her brother, not because he was brave but because he was worn out. He seemed aged though he was so small and only six years old, as he lay absorbed in another world. He held his raggedy brown teddy bear to his chest as he always did.

But now he was sleeping. She was glad for him, grateful for these moments of peace, when she could sit with him in silence. She knew that the older he became, the more problems he would face. He would grow to be awkward-looking and scrawny and would suffer because of it. He would be unathletic because of his asthma—a painfully withdrawn, hidden person.

This was probably his best time. For with a child so many flaws were overlooked, pardoned. It was his family's responsibility to make sure these years were as joyful as possible.

Before leaving Max's room, Ryan peered out his bedroom window at the dark yard. The lights from the living room shone onto the lawn, illuminating patches of grass with yellow light. She looked for the skinny little lone fox that had taken an interest in their property and could sometimes be seen hanging around the bushes at night. He had killed a few of the wild rabbits that lived in the bushes. Ryan had noticed that even though he had managed to eat, the fox was quite skinny, and when she saw him, often at dusk, when the yard filled with shadows, he would stop and stare at her with those intense, electric-green eyes before disappearing fully into a bush. He walked as if his joints ached, and he held himself in a dignified way; there was something noble about his solitary life. He didn't appear that night. She would leave some fruit out for him in the morning by one of the far bushes in the yard. He would eat fruit if he came across it and perhaps the sight of those skinny ribs would disappear beneath a fuller body. He seemed to prefer to walk alone at night and keep to the dark bushes.

CHAPTER THREE

"The Peninsula," as both locals and tourists called it, stretched about twenty miles into the ocean from the mainland of Rhode Island. The Peninsula's nucleus was skewed, its only town located at its base nearest the mainland. If you traveled farther out onto it, you encountered only random shops and the occasional lonely bar or restaurant. Once you passed the town of Orin, the road stretched uninterrupted for miles and you entered a kind of wilderness. From the edge of the "highway," the main road that ran around the edge of all three sides of the Peninsula, you saw rocky coast and water on your left and woods on your right. The center of the Peninsula consisted of deep forest, and, buried within this forest, a network of narrow, winding roads led to a small number of privileged houses, maybe thirty in total, all of them large, enfolded within the privacy of the woods.

Property in the center of the Peninsula was hard to purchase, as most of the houses rarely went up for sale. Once people owned, they generally stayed put. Though it was wild and touristy, Michael liked to think of this little section of Earth as the most desirable part of Rhode Island. Sure, areas such as Newport were beautiful and full of wealth, but the peninsula known as Orin's Island was something special—the mix of the forest and the sea reminded him of what he thought rural, coastal Japan would look like, from the books he had read on Japanese culture back in college. Even other wealthy New England residents would venture here for a dinner out or a weekend by the ocean, wearing their finest.

In the winter, the Peninsula became a ghost town. The beach town of Orin shut down; empty ice-cream stands and towel and T-shirt shops remained in darkness until the summer. The north side of the Peninsula was especially cold and desolate during the winter months. Fog settled in most mornings, obscuring the roads, so every mile or so a deer carcass that had been hit by an unsuspecting driver lay decaying on the edge of the road. There were only three real beaches on the Peninsula; the rest was jagged rock and water.

Two famous writers, a man and a woman, lived on the north side of the woods, about five miles from each other, in extreme seclusion. Rumor had it that they would consult with each other every week to share work or take a break from their solitary lives. Every now and then, an entourage of friends and family would travel down the roads to the north side, sometimes in a gleaming town car, until they reached their destination. Michael had gone to a couple of the readings they held once a year. One was in a converted barn, Old Barn House, a historic site atop a hill by the ocean. Hearing each of them read from their novels while it rained and the wind moaned outside had created a magical evening, cementing his desire to be a novelist himself.

Five minutes down the road from the Old Barn House, farther away from the rocky dramatic coastline, Michael's home sat on one of the privileged plots of land within the forest and could be reached by the winding little roads to the east or, to the west from the mainland, by two short turns off the highway. After passing the local restaurant Sammy's, open year-round, about three miles down, a right turn brought you into the woods. One and a half miles later, a sharp left led to the driveway and past a grove of pine trees that afforded a bit of privacy, then to their pretty dark gray house. Though it was in the forest, he could still smell the sea on most nights.

Men who lived on the Peninsula commuted forty-five minutes to the city of Providence every workday. It took a good twenty minutes to get through Orin with its stop signs and slow speed limits. Once through, they were finally off the Peninsula and onto the highway to the city. The majority of women stayed at home and cared for their children.

There were many birds on the Peninsula, along with rabbits, foxes, and coyotes. The rabbits lived in the bushes that ran rampant over the land and would come out onto the lawn to nibble timidly before looking around with terrified eyes and scurrying away. In the past couple of years, there had been fewer rabbits, as builders were cutting the brush down to expand homes and yards. With no brush to conceal them, many rabbits were eaten by coyotes or foxes. They could still be seen from time to time, but their numbers were nothing like they used to be. When she was younger, Ryan would set traps for them with carrots attached to string under propped-up cardboard boxes. She'd hide out and wait for one to venture under a box. Coyotes could sometimes be seen scurrying to the side of the road with their loose-legged gait.

Michael was always struck by how silent his land was, as if it were waiting with held breath, waiting for some turn of events to take place. Sometimes he would see the place he lived as if he were viewing it in relation to a gigantic map of the country. The Peninsula would appear as nothing more than a tiny hair sticking out from the right side of the massive continent. This little stretch of land, isolated as it was, had a shore that trembled as the ocean crashed into it from three different sides. The heart of the land, the forest, was the stillest, as if it had once received a good beating and now knew better. The interior of the land was deathly quiet, and, although its summers could be bleached bright with sun, the rest of the year it was often shrouded in clouds and mist.

———

Since he found himself awake at dawn most mornings, Michael used the time to sneak to the guest room for a bath. It was his secret routine, one that he was embarrassed to admit to, so he would walk quietly to the other part of the house, confident that he pulled it off without anyone else knowing. But since the party, he had not been so sure. On his way to that corridor of the house, he heard a sound from within as he tiptoed past Ryan's room. He thought he heard her door close a minute later and perhaps footsteps outside the bathroom door, which he now had closed. Was she listening through the bathroom door, curious? Could she hear him as he ran the shower water and filled up the tub to make it sound like he was showering instead of bathing? Did she hear the tiny movement of him sitting down into the water and the absence of sound while he simply soaked there? If so, the fact that he went to so much trouble just to take a bath in secrecy must have disturbed her greatly.

He thought it over. Ryan knew of his insomnia and that it must be at least partially responsible for behavior like this, but maybe she was beginning to wonder if there was also some other reason. Maybe she was beginning to catch on that her father was mentally disturbed. Perhaps she had found his medication and asked a pharmacist what it was for? As she showered in her own bathroom, Michael thought that she must have felt ill at ease, knowing he was just sitting there in the other part of the house, naked and motionless.

Michael lay in the water with his face slack. Light was pouring in above him from the skylight they had installed in the guest bath. The pleasantly dim room began to shift to an insistent quiet illumination as the day emerged. He was once again confronted with the image of his body spread out before him—his long legs and bony chest, and his long, thin toes that had always embarrassed him. He looked at his reflection in the polished knob of the bathtub spout. Was he handsome? He could never be sure. There had been people in his life who had found him strikingly handsome, but the average person did not seem to have that reaction. His daughter was beautiful and resembled him, and that surely meant he himself possessed a source of beauty that had been distributed.

She was in this house right now, yet a whole day might go by without his seeing her. He reflected upon how irritating it was that she had refused to come down from her room for the party, in spite of the fact that everyone had been eager to see her. When she had scooted from her seat in the TV room and trotted upstairs to her room, Michael had noticed that her long brown hair was disheveled and she was wearing a light blue T-shirt that was several sizes too small. "I'll be in my room," she had said, avoiding his eyes. She knew the guests would have been eager to feast their eyes on her and thus considered herself rare and prized. She had developed a vanity that allowed her to deny others the right even to look at her.

He had noticed she had suddenly become a flirt and begun tilting her head to the side when she spoke to a man. Once, at a restaurant, the maitre d' had chatted with her as they waited for their table, and her physicality had instantly changed—she'd cocked her head to the side and balanced differently on her legs, and a playful smile had appeared on her lips.

Other times when men paid her attention, she would become sullen and glance distractedly at anyone and anything except the man speaking with her. She would refuse to indulge the man in any kind of exchange or would answer in clipped noes and yeses to questions. It would be horrible when she met someone she actually liked and toward whom she would unleash her full attention, her full arsenal of charms. The simple act of her pulling her hair loose from a ponytail snapped men to attention as the brown hair spilled over her shoulders.

People were less interested in his son, Max. He was adorable, as most little kids were, but apparently less fascinating than his pretty daughter. Max had been born with deep and chronic asthma of such an extreme nature that the doctors were amazed that he had not cried constantly as an infant. Now he could be heard wheezing all over the house, going from room to room in his little stick-figure body, taking exhausting breaths with a fierce patience other people would never understand. They had all gotten used to the sound of the snap and release of his numerous inhalers, and also to the sight of them littering the house in their candy pastel colors—soft blue, yellow, shy green.

Michael thought again of Nancy and the man from the party. What was his name? He felt sure he was about to remember it, and then it would evaporate into some distant room in his mind.

Michael had filled the bath with very hot water, so that his submerged skin was now a deep pink. He did so for a reason, though: the hot water made him tired; it sometimes even pulled all the energy out of him at first light and let him have a precious little nap. He got to his feet, dried off with a towel, then wrapped himself in a big robe and lay on the bath mat with his head on a little pillow he had brought in for such a purpose. He was drowsy, and today it might work. He lay curled up and remembered his wife's face during the party, lit up with an easy kind of laughter. In that moment, as she had looked years younger, a brightness and innocence had reappeared that had been present when he had first met her. These days, she was always so careful around him, so unnatural. Yet he could remember what it had been like at the beginning of their courtship and could recall the reasons he had married her.

Nancy had remained with him through hard times. When he had just started taking his medication, she had been the only person, besides his mother, whom he had told about his mental condition. At the time, after telling her that day sitting there in the living room, he immediately regretted it. He felt he had told her too much. Things had gotten worse from there. Exposed and irritable, he had begun yelling at her, and had even gone so far as to call her a fool. After he had caused a scene, Nancy had quietly stood up, gotten her coat and purse, and made for the door. She had left soundlessly, shutting the door gently behind her.

With horror, Michael had realized he might never see her again, that she could tell everyone that he was mentally unstable and that her brief fling with a brilliant student had amounted to nothing. She was only a babysitter and had never been to college—perhaps she had set her sights on another young student and was already beginning to forget about him? He had known it must be over.

Michael had berated himself for telling her such private things, of his being on the line between neurotic and psychotic, of the trouble the doctors had had in diagnosing him just a year prior. Carried away by her understanding nature, he had even mentioned his nervous breakdown and that he had gone to stay at a mental hospital for six weeks before sophomore year at college. On some level, he had felt it added to his mystique. It had been a relief to tell her, but then he could not bear her knowing. He could not bear to have his weaknesses so visible. Since he was only in his sophomore year, if it got out, he would have to spend two more years surrounded by looks that were pregnant with disapproval from the other students. He had opened a bottle of scotch and started on his first drink, knowing full well that he was not allowed to drink on his medication, and let his head reel at the memory of his horrible utterances.

But forty-five minutes later, he had heard a light knock on the door. When he had opened it, he had seen Nancy, smiling at him from his front stoop. He had stood there in shock as she walked in carrying a bag of hot food. She had gone to the kitchen without saying a word, and it was at that moment he realized how hungry he had been and hadn't even noticed. She had set before him a plate of warm chicken, potatoes, and green beans, and he had devoured it.

After making herself a cup of tea, she had sat down across from him and sipped it silently. Without either of them saying it, Michael had suddenly understood that she was his, that she would never leave him if he chose to take her. In the silence, he had been able to get his head clear, and he had been grateful to her for knowing what to do, for not talking, for her little kindnesses. He had begun to think it might be wise to align himself with someone who knew how to attend to the basics of life, such as food, with such care and ease. She was the wife—this was her domain, feeding, soothing, and tending to.

That night Michael had discovered that Nancy was someone who could be trusted with his secrets. He felt a strong compulsion to repay her, to give her the beautiful house and expensive things that she had never had, to take her devotion and build a structure around it. The people he had loved most in his life were those who knew when to be quiet, for in the silence, his mind could finally settle down to a peaceful rhythm as his thoughts sorted themselves out.

He needed the silence more than anyone else could ever comprehend. He *needed* it. He considered himself lucky that she did not mind that he was at minimum just a "neurotic" and might have "episodes" from time to time. A whole new set of options opened up before him that he had never seriously considered—that he could lead a normal life and have children and not always be so alone were wonderful ideas to consider.

Since college, Michael had had two other breakdowns. One had occurred two months after his wedding to Nancy. Obsessive, paranoid thoughts crowded his brain and he had dizzy spells. *I've ruined my life. I'm a fool. Everyone at work knows there's something wrong with me.* He felt he had married too soon in life, but it was too late; it was a binding agreement. He felt he could not bear to look at Nancy. He had taken a week off of work, claiming to be sick, and slept all day in his study with his door locked. He drank heavily during that time and came out for meals and the bathroom only. If Nancy were nearby and tried to help, he had sharp words for her, words that he regretted at the end of that week, and the regret had facilitated their reconciliation. Eventually, he left his office, went up to the bedroom, and put his arms around his wife. He said he would go to the doctor for a stronger dose of medication. Shortly thereafter, Nancy became pregnant with Ryan, which excited them both—it was something new to focus on.

The second breakdown had come after Michael's father had died, and that one had been a bit more disastrous. Nancy was due with Max in three months, and Ryan was a little girl very much attached to her father. It began right after the funeral. Michael found he could not sleep a wink and nothing would knock him out. So he was awake for four days straight and then cracked. He didn't want Ryan to see him storming around the house, so he went and stayed in a hotel, leaving

Nancy alone for two weeks. Finally, he got heavier sleeping pills from the doctor and slept for almost sixteen hours in his last night at the hotel. Then he drove home to Nancy and Ryan, carrying red roses and lying in their marital bed submissively, telling Nancy about his troubles. To his relief, she was not mad at him, just happy to have him back and be able to take care of him. He took a lot of his medication, so he slept a lot, and one evening he woke up to see Ryan, almost six, standing tentatively at the door.

"Want to watch a movie, darling?" And Ryan crawled into bed with Michael. Nancy joined them with popcorn, and they all watched an adventure movie together about a kid and his father who realized that the contents of an old treasure map were real. They defeated alligators and goblins in a cave. It reminded Michael that life was magical, that dreams could come true, and his little daughter snuggled into the crook of his arm was proof of this, as was his benevolent wife, who was carrying a second child. After the movie ended, he was able to fall asleep easily by taking a heavy dosage of sleeping pills while Nancy tucked Ryan in down the hall. When she came to bed, he held her and told her everything was going to be all right.

Now, many years later, here Nancy was, day after day, moving through their house, keeping things in order. Completing wifely duties like driving the kids to doctor appointments and picking up dry cleaning were chores that filled up her days, as she didn't want to or have to work. She did for others all day long and put out the meals with straightforward humility, rarely expecting thanks. In her pure, unobstructed clarity, he felt she was the void that hangs around the static. After they were married, he had made her promise that she wouldn't tell their children about his condition. He felt he must have loved her. For what else could that tenderness have been but love? It had gone so quickly, but it had once existed.

———

His head was cloudy from too little sleep, yet he couldn't drift off. Sleep was a kingdom to which Michael constantly desired access. Unlike other people, he was often awake in the stillness of the house. It was a time of strangeness, when the moon was out, and he would sit and read book after book, drawing more and more information into his already cluttered mind, more knowledge to separate himself further from the people around him, making himself superior and strange to others. He knew his insomnia exacerbated his condition; if he were only able to get to sleep at night, his mind would be less troubled.

Lying awake, in his mind's eye he imagined the room called sleep: through an open door he saw a bedroom with a night-light illuminating a sacred, magical realm. He saw a room with a big navy-blue bed, dark as the night sky, with soft pillows and a fluffy comforter, a red fire truck night-light, a soft breeze coming through the window. The moon shone in softly. Fish slept in a tank in the corner of the room, their bodies swaying slightly as the filter pushed the water out and took it in. This was the world anxiety did not let him access every night—one of tenderness and surrender.

From down the hall, Michael heard his son cough in his sleep. For no particular reason, he looked up to make sure the bathroom door was still locked. It was. Secretly, Michael felt his son was responsible for his being this way. One winter when he was a year old, his son's asthma had been especially bad at night and he had developed pneumonia. The night coughs were excruciating—for four months someone had had to stay up and keep watch to make sure he didn't cough himself to death. He lay in his crib, his face pitifully twisted and red, and cried through fits of coughing. Michael could hear the air catch on the phlegm that lined his inflamed lungs. He was not able to read while he sat by his son—there was little to do. Picked up or lying down, Max still coughed. It was difficult for him to imagine this tiny tortured creature becoming a man—he seemed genderless, small in size, and incapable of peace.

After four months, the night coughs became less frequent, and he and Nancy were permitted to sleep. But at the slightest sound, they would wake up and decide whether or not one of them needed to go to him. Nancy had recovered from those awful years and could now sleep through the night, but he had not.

During that time, they had seen many asthma specialists for Max's condition, and each specialist had recommended that they consider moving to a climate with less moisture and mold. There was even some suggestion that the asthma had been caused by the climate—that Nancy had breathed it in during her pregnancy. Michael had spent many nights contemplating those things and even thought about moving, but he ultimately couldn't get up the stamina to put the house on the market. How could he give up the one thing in his life that still gave him pleasure? If he left, he would have nothing.

He had done enough research on asthma to convince Nancy that moving would be futile, that Max would suffer wherever he went. They were both careful never to upset Max, as any upset could easily trigger an attack that would take hours to resolve and drain the day of its energy. So they would both tiptoe around anything he did wrong, and when he spilled something they offered him big smiles and animated happy faces. Michael often felt the absurdity of his own reactions to spilt bowls of cereal—he suddenly got happier and peppier when disaster struck. Meanwhile, his son, sheltered and cushioned at every step lest he explode into disarray, now slept deeply.

Michael tried lying on his stomach on the bath mat, with his arms around the sides of his face to block out the light coming in overhead through the skylight. Maybe this position would lead to sleep. The house had the stillness that only Sunday mornings bring—no work to rush off to, people could sleep in, children came downstairs and parked themselves in front of the TV still in pajamas.

Michael listened for any sounds in the house around him as he lay. He knew his wife would be getting up in the next hour or so and would get Max dressed and ready for the day, whatever that involved for the two of them for this particular Sunday. His wife and son were extremely close, and their intimacy often startled Michael when he would come upon it. Because of the effort that breathing required, Max would become tired after school and would need a pre-dinner nap. When Michael returned home from work, he often caught Max and Nancy locked in some moment together, and the two of them struck him as a portrait of old age, neglect, decay. Max's head would be on her lap as they lay on the window seat. She'd be looking out the window, one hand in his hair or gently on his chest as he heaved air in and out. The two of them were so separate from him in these moments that they might as well have been aliens. He found their separateness special, and it somehow freed him from his constant disapproval of Nancy. Seeing her there as a complete person, sitting with her child, mysterious and solemn, he wanted to reach out to her but resisted, as doing so would shatter the moment.

As Michael watched his wife with their son, he would be reminded of and amazed at her genius for knowing and addressing human needs. That quality had always defined her, as some quality always defines a person in the eyes of another.

They had been so different from the start that it seemed best for them to come together as a team and complete each other. But with each passing year, he found himself more and more unable to relate to Nancy. It became clear that, apart from the children and him, she had no real interests and none would be developed. She was a reminder that he had given up his calling to be a professor at his university. Her grounded, loving nature had not been enough to hold them in a good place, it turned out, though it had worked for the first few years of marriage.

Those first few years they had gone out on "wine" dates, which involved two or three glasses of wine during a meal. After those dates, they had gone home and had sex and laughed while watching a late-night movie. Nancy was an attentive, generous lover, so once Michael was relaxed enough from the wine, the sex felt lighthearted and effective. In bed, after they had sobered up a bit, they would talk about what their future would look like with children. It was a nice routine, one that worked for those early years. After the first baby came, they were sure to go out once every month or every other month, but the outings didn't always lead to sex. Soon the carefree feeling attached to nights out had departed. One of their last real "wine" dates had resulted in Nancy becoming unexpectedly pregnant with Max. After that second pregnancy, their sex life had slowly devolved to about once a season, if that.

Nancy had never met a man like him before, a man of class and refinement, and he had reveled in her rapt attention and respect. She considered everything he said for decisions large and small, for she knew he must know best. That worried him; as the years passed, he sensed, he might not know best. He just might not know.

———

After his bath and the unsuccessful attempt at a nap, Michael dressed and moved through the shadowy kitchen, following his morning routine. The water was about to boil in the little pot on the stove. It heaved and tensed every couple of seconds and then began to quiver in little eruptions as bubbles floated to the surface. Michael had read and reread Alex's essay. It dealt with the permissiveness of content that unreliable narrators allowed and examined this through three famous novellas, one of which was Thomas Mann's *Death in Venice*. Alex's piece was well researched and well written and had that clarity of expression he had mastered in college. But in places it had even been a little difficult for Michael to follow, which showed him how deadened his mind had become over the years. He had been up half the night, looking through his own old essays, papers, and photos. He was trying to rekindle within himself the intellectual fire he had had in college, but it had been dulled by working in management for so many years. When he read Alex's piece, the thoughts didn't come as rapid-fire as they had in college. He had to read a paragraph over several times to truly comprehend it. Perhaps being around Nancy for so many years had drained his mind of its brilliance as well—it was not as if he could have intellectual banter with her or discuss politics in any refined way.

Suddenly the kitchen around him seemed a wicked place that slowly sucked the voltage out of a battery. Michael could not recall the last time he had been alone in the kitchen, standing idly by. He was normally up and out of the house before Ryan or Max came down for breakfast. But today Ryan walked in, dressed in spandex pants and a workout shirt.

He wondered, doesn't she realize that she should not wear tight clothing like that? She no longer has a child's body, and she should know it by now.

She muttered a subdued greeting and made herself some tea.

"Why are you up so early?" he asked.

"I'm going running on the track at school," she said without turning around. "Don't worry; there's no school today, so you don't have to worry about me being late for anything." With that she grabbed an orange and headed out into the half-darkness to her car.

The refrigerator buzzed loudly and inwardly crunched out blocks of ice. Michael stood there, irritated, no, *angered*, by the little sounds around him. Ryan's car was growling to life in the driveway, and when she flicked on the lights, they shone in through the windows, hurting his eyes. He wondered if his daughter had adopted his insomniac ways. He often heard her up at night, pacing around her room like a cat. He knew that she would occasionally smoke cigarettes out her window at night, as the smell would drift in through his window.

He wondered why she was also having trouble sleeping. Would she adopt other undesirable traits of his? They had started in his early twenties; if she was going to inherit them, it would be only a few years before the signs popped up in her.

He looked around the empty kitchen, his head pounding from exhaustion. It was Nancy's domain, yet there were only small traces of her taste there. She would have liked more of her preferred style, an unrestrained expression of country craft and cheery fuzz. As it was now, she had only an occasional plastic apple set on a random shelf, when what she really wanted was to have a whole row of bright red decorative apples on the wall. Michael knew she kept it to a minimum for his sake, and for that he felt deep gratitude toward her. When they had first moved in, she had dared to place a large brown teddy bear on a little ledge in the corner of the room, from which it had reigned over them with its dead glass eyes. Michael had taken it down one day, and Nancy had asked no questions, for she knew it should never have been there. She should never have tried such a thing. Ultimately, she was guilty and self-conscious about her bad taste, because it exposed her for what she really was, a simpleton, an unsophisticated mother-nurturer. She was aware of the danger there, aware that the tacky power of such an object could rattle his nerves if he was forced to sit under it, day in and day out.

He wondered about the combination of Nancy's and his genes; two such opposite people would surely make for a mixed bag. He saw himself in Ryan. He felt they shared the same kind of intelligence.

It pained him to imagine his link to his son, as Max had never had an easy day in his life. He had allowed Nancy to name Max after her own father, Maxwell, who had been a factory worker in rural West Virginia. Michael had never met the elder Maxwell, for he had died young, before they were married.

There was a video of the beginning of Max's birth in the cabinet under the TV. They had stopped filming in the middle, as things had not gone smoothly. On the timeline of his life, the birth of his second child coincided closely with his own father's death, and he could not help but connect them in some cosmic way. Just a few months before Max was born, his father's body had hardened in the hospital, and his mouth had permanently formed an "oh" shape, as he gasped his last breath. The man who had judged so many others for a living now seemed stunned by what he saw coming next on the other side.

Three months later, Michael had stood next to his wife while she struggled through labor, struggled to eject the tiny being. Her stomach had been cut open, and from underneath her intestines, the baby had been pulled out. Nancy had not wanted the C-section, and he had felt humiliated for her, that she had not been able to birth the baby "naturally" but had been so rudely slit apart in places that were not meant to be opened. All this for a notion of love and family, an idea she believed in wholeheartedly. Michael had always felt that she should have been able to birth Max *her* way and it was some proof of their skewed chemistry that she could not. She had given birth to Ryan without the aid of drugs, and though it had been a hard labor, she had borne it with more dignity than most and had looked at Michael with such pride when she finally held the baby in her arms.

It was after Max's birth, as she had lain exhausted, emptied, that he had realized just how much she had been cheated. Michael understood that he had not been prepared for this, for any of this, that life was indeed grotesque, that bodies with their spasms of life and death were ripped open and buried, a process of endless upheaval. Nancy had stayed in the hospital for four days after the birth, Max as well, and Michael remembered these days as an excruciating series of hours. Walking through the halls and looking through the glass at Max, he had thought of his father—both lay in the most fragile state, in the most sterilized of places, in lifeless rooms and halls. The gore that had showed itself so clearly, twice, in such an empty place had haunted him—the swirl of colors after the birth, wiped up, gone without a trace; the yellow and purplish skin of his father's corpse in the hospital, and then nothing except the green of the earth and the blue of the sky over his coffin while he stood mourning with a very pregnant wife and a bewildered little daughter. Life was swift in the big events—quick to do its work and then move on, leaving silence and endless contemplation.

CHAPTER FOUR

It was an uncommonly bright Thursday morning as Michael sat in his car on the edge of the road. After spending a sleepless night puttering around his study, rereading all of his old essays, he could not bring himself to drive to work. He had left the house as usual, to fool Nancy, and had driven in the half-light toward the freeway, giddy from the secret changes to his routine. He had already, secretly, called in sick to his office.

Michael could not bear for one more second to think of Nancy and the man talking at the party. He had to get them into the same room again. Two weeks had passed, and the beautiful image was already growing stagnant. He feared that this dream, these plans, would dissolve if he didn't act on them. He had to meet the man to get some new image in his head, to move things forward. Nancy had the numbers of everyone who had been invited to the party on her desk in the kitchen. It was just a matter of waiting until she was out of the house, and then he could return and hunt around for the man's number. The idea of simply asking her his name was out of the question; mundane discussion would spoil everything. Michael wanted to surprise her, though he wasn't sure how or why.

With two hours to kill before Nancy would leave for her aerobics class and then book club, he sat on the side of the road drinking from a thermos of coffee and thinking about what a miserable wretch he was, as cars whizzed past him. All the forms in the cars were hunched over with expressionless faces. Michael mindlessly tapped out a beat on the steering wheel with his fingers, numbing their tips.

Anxiety clenched his heart, and the pace of his heartbeat picked up. There were some people in the world whom you fundamentally liked; for one reason or another, their essential nature commanded your approval. Even if they didn't deserve it, you just liked them. He felt such an acceptance for his daughter, Ryan. And he felt it for his old college classmate, Alex, who had power over him. Something about that big silent man produced in him the utmost reverence. Alex was blessed with refinement; some personalities had been put through the cosmic sander and had had all rough or vulgar aspects polished away, leaving only sophistication, intelligence, and quiet wisdom. Alex could have been friends with anyone at school, but he had chosen Michael. He could have been the head of a fraternity if he'd wanted, so handsome and solid was he. For all his beauty, though, he was not interested in the trivialities of life or in parading around with riotous egomaniacs. He preferred Michael's quiet company.

Michael thought of Alex's essay waiting in his study, and his mind began churning. He sometimes blamed his marriage to Nancy on an awful woman from Georgia whose company he had been subjected to since she was dating Alex. That spring during junior year in college, he'd noticed he was seeing less and less of Alex, who finally told him about his new girlfriend. He and Nancy had begun spending time with the two of them so they wouldn't lose touch. Meg had a pointy face and large round eyes that were a little too close together. She had a small frame, and everything about her was angular: chin, fingers, and nose.

Michael had disliked her from almost the first moment. She had an ordinariness to her, and next to the magnificence of Alex she seemed harsh and shrill. She possessed a lack of real intelligence or real insight, and her ordinariness was so carefully hidden behind a more colorful attempt at personality that he literally felt nauseated upon seeing her. She spoke often on just about every subject, and once she began speaking, it was almost impossible to get her to stop. He could not believe that such a person had been created—it seemed like God's cruel joke that she should have come into his life. Michael believed sincerely that if she hadn't, he and Alex would have remained close and they would both be esteemed professors at the university.

Michael would watch Alex and Meg together and always muse to himself, why are they together? Is it a sex thing? Perhaps great sex was clouding his judgment.

Her southern accent, general opinions about everything, and occasional subtly racist comments seemed to zap the spark out of everything. The fact that Nancy also disliked Meg was a great comfort to Michael. When the four of them were out at a restaurant, he would watch Meg's tiny little mouth motor away and then see silent, obliging Nancy sitting next to her. At such moments he felt proud to have chosen someone as stoic and dignified as Nancy. He was almost positive that his being subjected to Meg's company must have influenced his decision to want to marry Nancy.

Going home after those evenings out with Meg and Alex, Nancy and Michael had experienced genuine companionship. They would drive silently or exchange a few knowing looks or brief comments about the evening. Nancy would hold his hand, and it was such a relief knowing he had her to sleep next to when they got back to the dorm. They were united against Meg. When Michael spoke, Meg would look politely in his direction, but when he looked into her eyes, nothing seemed to be there. Once she had even rolled her eyes during one of his discussions about Foucault, rolled them when she thought he was looking away. But he had seen her, and his eyes had burned into her like two lasers, causing her to look down at her half-eaten spaghetti and blush at her mistake.

As Alex had gotten closer to Meg, Michael had spent more and more time with Nancy. During senior year, Michael and Nancy had gone to Alex and Meg's wedding, and they had all been polite and warm toward one another, but right after college, Alex had moved up to Massachusetts, near where Meg's family lived, and he and Michael had found it hard to stay in touch, until they lost touch completely.

The coffee had raced through Michael's system, and the effects of the caffeine were now dwindling. He decided to read over his novel and perhaps add a few lines that might unearth what the story was really about, get at its essence. He put on his sunglasses to protect his eyes from the sun and opened the window so the pleasant breeze would blow into and out of the car. He had started writing the novel a year ago and kept working and reworking the same thirty pages. The plot revolved around a young American man traveling around Europe. He was using many of the settings from his own travels to Europe during the summer between his sophomore and junior years. He kept a copy of the novel in a box in his car, and now he pulled out the set of wrinkled pages and reread them.

He had overheard Nancy bragging to people at their party that he was working on a "wonderful" novel. When asked what it was about, she had struggled to answer and resorted to the beautiful writing—"like poetry" she had said. That seemed to satisfy them, though they still had no idea what it was about. Michael had slunk off to get another drink when he heard the conversation taking place twenty feet from him. Nancy didn't know a thing about good literary writing, and perhaps neither did he. He could take it as a challenge to try to learn, though, to become a writer.

He wrote a few lines: "The man had traveled quite a distance with his carpenter bag. He didn't trust leaving it in his seedy Parisian hotel, so he kept it by his side at the café." That was an intriguing couple of sentences indeed and could lead to something. But he would have to figure out what was in the bag.

Eventually he began to get drowsy and could not turn down a chance, any chance, to finally get some sleep. He edged the car back onto the road and drove very slowly half a mile to the Exxon gas station, where he parked in its lot away from the pumps and fluorescent lights. Then he crawled into the backseat and easily fell back asleep in the quiet, lying on his side in a fetal position, wondering to himself why he didn't do this more often. It was such a nice, secret location for sleep.

——

When Michael awoke in the sun-heated car and sat up, the side of his neck was sore and rigid from holding its cocked position. The day was startlingly bright. The air was still sharp and cool, but summer was trying to come through the dazzling sunlight. Soon the days might be too bright, the air too lazy, but for now spring still hung on. Cars were streaming into and out of the gas station, and looking at the clock, he saw that he had only thirty minutes left until Nancy would be coming home.

Driving up the coast toward the turnoff for his house, Michael remembered the smaller home they had owned before buying this one seven years ago. Upon returning to that house at the end of the day, he had come upon it with dread. He saw it as compressed, squeezed into its lot, wedged in between the two houses on either side, its gray cement driveway sprawling out toward him like a deranged tongue, sick and hot. Michael had never been comfortable there, and he sensed that nine-year-old Ryan had felt the same as he did.

Back then he had fantasized about moving to a more expansive property, and when they had visited their friends Will and Mary out on the Peninsula, the idea of moving there became his obsession. They had drunk wine on the porch on a shifty, misty night. The clouds would occasionally expose a full moon. He was bewitched by the landscape, the weather, and the wealthy community nestled in the forest. Once he heard that two celebrated writers lived there, he became determined to move. He had inherited a good amount of money when his father died, and that, combined with his salary, allowed him to have more than enough money to move to this beautiful area. The move was seamless, and the first year it seemed as though the house itself were enough to keep them happy. The yard, the forest, the ocean, and the sense of seclusion, with no other house in sight, made the locale seem gothic. In such an elegant place, their peaceful cohabitation felt guaranteed.

Michael turned and passed a trail head for a hiking area. When Ryan had been in middle school, she and Michael had taken many hikes out into the woods by their property. They had made a rudimentary trail with some cedar chips and logs and built a fire pit for campfires in the backyard. They had often walked to an expansive pond that mixed fresh and salt water, with mussel shells that had been picked over by the gulls that glimmered light purple and black in the shallow water by the weeds. Ryan liked to throw stones in the water and watch them plunk across the surface and then disappear into the sandy bottom. In the summer, they'd swim in the pond, the water warmer than the shocking Atlantic Ocean nearby. They did go to the ocean, too, to swim, and Michael would hold Ryan while she kicked around in three feet of water, Nancy watching with her hand at her brow, squinting into the sun. After a day spent outside in the fresh air, at night Michael and Ryan read their books together in Michael's study. The ritual always included a mug of hot chocolate for her. She would sprawl out on the rug and flip through her books, occasionally glancing up at him to check if he was still reading. That little face—so trusting, so perfect. He had taken her into work with him several times on a Saturday because she wanted to read her books near him while he worked, didn't want to be separated from him. He had been so proud at how well behaved she was at the office, at her cheerful little face when she met one of his colleagues, and at how they gushed over her.

What a time that had been—his life had been full of purpose when he had been so adored in the eyes of his daughter. When she had hit puberty, it had all gone south. She had become sullen in eighth grade, losing the cheerfulness that he had assumed would always be part of her personality. For the first time, she didn't want to go out on her walks to the pond with him. That was the beginning of a series of bad moments between the two. She wanted to watch TV and requested one in her room. He said no, the living room one would do just fine, and she had refused to talk to him for days. Michael had always imagined that he would help her with her middle school and high school homework, as he was quite good at tutoring others, had done it in college, but when he tried to offer help, she scowled at him and slumped off to her room. He had felt a panic at those changes. She tried wearing dark eyeliner and cut her jean skirt so it was quite short the summer before high school, and he'd made her change her clothes and wash off the makeup. He didn't want her to attract the wrong sort of person; he didn't want her to grow up so quickly. Adulthood was serious, and sex had a disturbing edge to it. Beyond that, her moodiness frightened him. It reminded him of his own self. She was becoming different; she might not fit in, just as he had never fit in at her age. Where was the friendly, confident face of his beloved girl? Why were the shadows closing in on her too?

———

Michael found the guest list in one of the wicker basket organizers that Nancy kept on her desk in the kitchen. When he scanned it, he remembered being briefly introduced to a John Randolph and was fairly certain that the name matched the man whom he had seen chatting with his wife. John was an honest name, one that matched the personality of that soft-spoken figure. Since he had shown up to the party without a date, Michael assumed he must not be married. Why had he been invited? Michael certainly had never met him before that night. Wearing khaki pants, an old button-down shirt, and a worn-out blazer, he had been dressed much more casually than the rest of the guests, as if he weren't used to formal parties. A moment of suspicion crept through Michael as he wondered how Nancy knew him. Then he laughed about the whole thing. He knew Nancy's being devious was impossible; she would never have an affair. Michael felt he might like her better if she were the type of woman who had it in her to cheat. Danger could be precious, making the choice for fidelity all the more delicate; the marriage vows could fly off in the face of chaos if a relationship were not carefully nurtured and protected. But no, he thought sadly, Nancy would never stray, couldn't stray on her own. In order for her to cheat, she needed him behind her, gently pushing her to do it, cleverly designing a setup that she wouldn't be able to resist.

Infidelity was a horrible thing, but Michael knew it was the only way in his case. His own father, Howard, had strayed from his wife, Michael's mother, Marilyn, causing a violently emotional scene when she had figured it out. Michael had been eight at the time, and his mother, normally so composed and elegant, had grabbed his arm one day while he was sitting at the table doing his homework and taken him and his sister out to the car. From the backseat, they had stared out at the bright and cheerful day going past them in the car, purple flowers on deep green stalks whizzing by, and sat in the hot car after she slammed the door and marched up to a small house that sat alone off of a little road.

Before his eyes he saw the door open and a stream of yelling with flashes of a woman in a slip and his father in his undershorts, his mother stamping into the house and back onto the porch, yelling as if she had gone mad. His normally dignified father had looked beaten that day, when at some point Michael had looked up and seen him sitting on the porch in a rocking chair beside his mother, who was crying steadily into her hands. The front door to the little gray house was shut, and the woman was not in sight. Michael's father sat beside his mother, stealing worried glances at her profile and at the car in the driveway where the children sat. Michael was careful to look away at those moments, pretending to be admiring the scenery, a gesture of kindness and discretion out of respect for his father.

After that day, his father came home at the same time every day, made more of an effort to comment on his mother's cooking, and took his children out on a Saturday twice a month to a preplanned outing: boating on a lake, a baseball game, the candy store in town. His mother had won after swallowing the heartbreak, and she retained a steady control over him for the rest of his life. His father had admired her after that; it was subtle to see, but it was there. She had not let him get away with his offense, and she had restored him to his proper allegiances. At first the outings had delighted Michael, until he learned that they were staged and planned by his mother. His father was there only part of the time; the rest of the time his mind was elsewhere and his presence was uneasy around his kids. He knew his father had made a mistake by cheating on his mother; everyone knew it.

He and Nancy were not the same as his parents, though. He wasn't sure why, but he knew they weren't. The rules they played by were not the same.

———

Two numbers were listed beside John Randolph's name, one for work and one for home. Upon calling the work number, an answering machine picked up for John Randolph's carpentry and landscaping business: "Hello," the uncertain voice ventured. "You've reached John Randolph and the Randolph Landscaping Company. I'm sorry I missed your phone call, but please leave your name and number and I'll call you right back. Thanks." Michael imagined Nancy with a carpenter. They would sit down together after he came home from work. She would wipe the sweat from his brow, and they would enjoy the meal she had prepared, knowing they would have the comfort of each other's arms later on that night. He was the type of man who would fall asleep with his arms wrapped around his mate and sleep through the night, untroubled by dreams. A simple man, one who worked with his hands—that was what she needed. He would be content with her, incapable of cruelty. He wouldn't have paranoia, anxiety, or insomnia.

He would be a better husband, one who could deliver the vows as promised, and in his simplicity bring peace. John would not question his life, would only feel grateful to have a wife and children and a roof over his head. Such a man would be seriously mourned at his funeral, for he was of the earth, a genuinely physical creature who proved his worth daily in the little things. Michael hungered to have him close to his family, to protect them from something sinister that he felt had a hold on them, or release them from a secret spell they were all living under. There was no other way he could explain it.

———

Two days later, Michael paced around his study and watched from his window as the man named John opened his car door and unceremoniously stood to his full height of at least six feet. He was thin and looked as though he could be anyone living anywhere doing anything. He was of average looks, with scruffy brown hair and unremarkable clothing. He drove a green truck that was neither new nor old. It was the man from the party, all right. It was Saturday, late in the morning, and Michael had instructed John to come by at a time he knew his wife and kids would be out and had given the reason of interest in landscaping and carpentry for their backyard. He wanted to get a feel for what the man was like, and he wanted to do it alone.

Michael opened the door, and when he made eye contact with John, right away he got the impression of timidity, a kind of beaten-down aspect. Nevertheless, he had an appeal.

The dazzling grin from the party was absent from the man's face, but Michael knew he had seen it there and it could be elicited again. John had said over the phone that he was from a less prosperous local county nearby, which could mean only one thing—a small house, a small income. Michael knew immediately that their house must have impressed him the night of the party, and when John walked through their door again, his prediction was realized.

"This is a great house," John said in his simple way. "I can tell a lot of work has already been done on it. It's in great shape."

"Have you lived in the area long?" Michael asked, as they sat on the living room couches.

"All my life." A picture of his trajectory from childhood through high school flashed behind Michael's eyes—cheap secondhand toys, public school, a working-class family.

"Are you married?"

"No. I was, but I got divorced a few years ago."

There's that defeated quality again, as if life has taken a few hard swings at him, Michael thought as he watched John sit, hands folded in his lap.

"I'm sorry."

"Thanks. It was hard at first, but now I've gotten used to it."

Michael observed that John spoke English well, without a local Rhode Island working-class accent polluting his speech, surprisingly. He seemed uncomfortable, and Michael knew he must hate sitting and talking with people, especially people he didn't know, as Michael himself hated doing so. They had that trait in common.

Michael studied John. Was he attractive in a way that would appeal to Nancy? He was thin but strong and had an appealing face and good teeth. Michael decided that he was indeed attractive, in the sort of way one couldn't quite pinpoint. Michael himself fell in with this grouping, so John was more than likely the type of person who could appeal to Nancy. Michael looked closely at John's face. Would a person want to kiss that mouth or look into those eyes over dinner by the ocean? Yes, they would.

"Do you have children?"

"No."

Michael realized that he should perhaps get to the point of why he wanted John there instead of making so much chitchat. He couldn't help himself, though. The man interested him.

"I was hoping you could do some work in our backyard, jazz it up a little. It's so boring, and we'd like to have a koi pond, a gazebo, and a better, more expanded garden. I don't know too much about how much this kind of thing might cost or how long it might take, but I'm prepared to pay you whatever you think is a fair price. Also, if you have any ideas of your own, we'd be totally open to hearing them. Nancy had the idea of putting in a stone walkway leading to the gazebo. Nancy's my wife. I think you met her at the party."

"Oh, the hostess, Nancy, yes, I remember. She was very nice. It was a great party. Let me take a look at your yard, and then I can give you a better idea of how much it'll cost."

"Sounds great. Coffee? Tea?"

"A cup of coffee would be great."

"Cream, sugar?"

"I take it black."

The two of them walked over the three acres of land that stretched behind the house to the edge of the property. Woods started where the yard ended. Masses of wet leaves blanketed the floor of the forest, and the spinelike trunks of several dead trees were interspersed with younger trees that were still growing. Except for a few scattered birds in the higher branches, the woods were empty of animals. It was a bleak place, not at all spooky and vibrant as a forest should be, but hollow, brittle, and swept clean.

"I bet I can finish the work in less than three months. I have a couple of young guys that help me. You'll meet them. They do work for extra money and help me out when they can. Summer's coming, and I know they need the work."

"However long it takes is fine with me."

When they turned back and walked toward the house, Michael saw movement from within. His wife and son were there; he could see them through the glass. Nancy came out onto the grass, her face startled. Max walked beside her with tentative footsteps, and Michael lifted him into his arms.

"John, this is my son, Max, and you remember Nancy from the party."

"Of course." He extended his hand and shook hers as he looked her in the eye. Michael had again the very distinct impression that they were alone together, in a way, even with other people around them. Nancy seemed glad to see him.

"Nancy, this is a surprise for you. I've hired John to spruce up the backyard, make it more like you wanted when we moved in here."

Nancy looked at Michael and then at John, her face glowing. Michael explained to her what they had planned, and she was clearly happy. Her reaction pleased him; it was evidence that this course of action was leading in an exciting direction. This man excited his wife in a way she could not see in herself. Heck, he himself felt excited by him.

"It was a great party you threw. Your friend Mrs. Keller had been concerned about me since my divorce. I guess she was hoping I would meet someone. Thanks for letting her invite me." Mrs. Keller lived in a big house down the street. She was a widow, and was in her early sixties. An aging beauty and former tennis star at the country club, she now had more spare time on her hands after her husband's heart attack and death. John explained he had taken care of the landscaping for her property for years, and in her boredom, she must have taken an interest in his romantic life.

"Oh, I was glad to. It's always nice to meet new people, and Linda says such nice things about you and the work you did on her house. Let me make you guys some sandwiches. You must be hungry. I'll let you finish talking." That was exactly what Michael wanted her to say and do. He looked at John to see if he had noticed what a perfect hostess Nancy could be if she just put her mind to it.

But where was Ryan? Michael wondered.

These days, he rarely got to see his daughter, except to watch her enter and exit their house. She was like a ghost in their home, leaving only traces of her presence behind. How badly he wanted to have the entire family there at once, presented as a unit. The last time he had seen her, he had seen a book he had given her through the mesh of the bag hanging over her shoulder.

She looked to Michael, being the most educated in the family, for direction as to which books to read. A month or two before Christmas, Michael would take particular delight in going to the local bookstore and buying three brand-new copies of some of his favorite books, most of which were classics. Her reverent, almost sacred treatment of the books he gave her touched him profoundly. She read them earnestly, and then the two of them would have a little talk about the book, its themes, and whether or not it had moved her. Michael was careful to avoid getting books her school's English class would cover, such as *Lord of the Flies* or *1984*. That day, it was the cover of *Clock Without Hands* by Carson McCullers that he saw through the mesh bag. That was one of the three books he had given her last Christmas. Although they rarely talked anymore, he was relieved to see that Ryan was still counting on his knowledge of literature to educate her. On some level, he felt, she must still love or respect him.

There was still hope for regaining a connection with his daughter and for Nancy's future happiness. His fear began to evaporate in the bright sunshine, and he wanted to reach out and embrace John as they stood there. He felt lighter, more available to the world. The family had been stagnant too long, he felt. What was needed was a new presence to breathe life back into them. He had arrived.

CHAPTER FIVE

There was something about giving birth to a baby with a disability that changed things. The crippling effect of Max's asthma along with his tiny body and stunted growth always caused Nancy to question whether or not Max was indeed damaged for life. He seemed an ethereal kind of child who was not fully here living a little-kid life. He had his own intangible interests and sat and played on the floor for hours with objects that only he could see.

Nancy and Max had lunch outside at a little glass table as they watched Michael and the new landscaper, John, walk around the yard discussing plans. In a few days it would be June, and the air was brightening up in preparation for summer. John had already removed a dead tree sitting in the far corner of the lawn, and he had readied the ground below him for construction of an ornate gazebo, removing some rocks and making a rudimentary platform. Nancy had grapefruit for Max, which was his favorite, and had sliced around the edges of each tiny section so he would be able to spoon it easily into his mouth. Secretly making tasks easier for her son without his or anyone else knowing took up many hours of Nancy's day. Being a behind-the-scenes person came naturally to her. There were countless things that she did for everyone in her family that no one was aware of or, if they were, they rarely acknowledged.

The summer before Nancy had left her hometown to become a nanny for a professor at Yale University, a woman she knew had given birth to a baby with Down syndrome. Nancy remembered Gwen's initial shock at seeing the misshapen forehead and the pinched eyes of her newborn baby. As a friend, Nancy had gone to visit the family a couple of days after the mother and baby had returned home from the hospital. Having neither money nor a husband of her own, Gwen was living at her parents' house. To see her friend lying in the bed in which she'd slept as a child, her stomach flabby and deflated under her folded arms, and now in such a difficult situation, Nancy had felt a wave of pity.

She watched her friend's face and saw the bitterness etched into every expression her facial muscles made. Seeing this painful conclusion to a sordid situation, Nancy could not help but feel that God was sending a message to her. She felt not only shame for her friend, who was stuck with such a burden, but also relief for herself that she had not gotten into such a mess. Yes, Nancy had had premarital sex with one man, but she had not run wild like Gwen had. Gwen's body had been the source of pleasure for almost every boy in their tiny, miserable town. Gwen would leave a bar with whomever was available and get into his car, her piercing laugh dying off as the car door shut her safely inside. Nancy was drawn to Gwen's fun-loving nature, but she also felt Gwen was dirty, used, and headed for some kind of disaster. Involuntarily, to some degree she felt her friend deserved the negative consequences of such reckless actions.

Now, after giving birth to Max, she wondered whether God was punishing her for thinking such things about Gwen's baby. Maybe the lesson was being presented to her so that she'd learn the compassion she needed. With that suspicion always at the back of her mind,

Nancy tried to convey to Max with every gesture of every day that she accepted him completely and would never avoid him or his needy ways. She didn't refrain from touching him as everyone else in the family did. He was her special assignment from God, and she knew she should not fail Him. She had been given every tool she would need, every resource to tackle the job of being an effective mother, and she really could not complain about the other things. The missing passion would return after Michael went through one of his spells—he needed her most during his recovery, and they were closest when he was the most vulnerable. He waxed and waned and would bloom for her again.

She considered it a hopeful sign that her husband had chosen to build her a majestic garden with a gazebo, a lovely stone walkway, and roses climbing up a trellis in the garden. She had long since resigned herself to the fact that such things were his way of showing affection, through gestures rather than through words.

She knew that as the days passed, her happiness would deepen as she watched new growth become established in the backyard. Years ago, when the kids had been much younger, she had suggested that they expand their backyard. With so much space, why not use it? But he had refused, saying how much he hated those cluttered, fancy yards that were cropping up in suburban homes left and right. And now, after years of battling over it, he was giving her what she wanted.

Max finished slurping down his grapefruit wedges and then scooped up his orange juice glass. A little bit of juice flew over the edge and landed on his shirt. He immediately looked up to see if she had noticed, his face wary with fear. Hadn't it sunk in by now that she never punished him? She smiled at him.

"It's okay, Max."

She studied his features while he drank. He resembled neither her husband nor herself. He had a tiny nose, and his jaw was also shaped more delicately than those of the rest of the family. But, as she had learned with Ryan, he would no doubt change several times in appearance as he formed and reformed himself. Ryan had resembled her father as a baby and then Nancy all through girlhood. Now, with Ryan a teenager, Nancy felt shame to behold how unalike they were. Ryan's good looks were startling, and they constantly highlighted the gap between herself and her daughter. She could not help but feel that her daughter had come out on top, resembling a female version of Michael at a younger age, athletic and sculpted. Still, Ryan also had that personality that was slightly on edge, which could be seen as a handicap.

She could remember many times when she had watched Ryan as a girl. A sudden view of her daughter streaking across the yard would cause her to catch her breath. She remembered one evening in particular sitting on a chair in the yard watching Ryan and her friend Carol play. It was dusk, and Nancy was pregnant with Max. As they had moved to this house only a month before, the excitement of a new place brought out the best in all of them. Michael, up in his study organizing his files and books, would occasionally gaze down and wave from the window. Lights from inside the house shone eerily in odd squares stretched over the grass.

At least he's trying, she thought with relief. To see Michael's hopeful face looking down at her was all she needed. When he took his medication, he was calmer and she could relax. Over the years, she would know when he had not taken it because his hands would shake. She found her own tension easing when she observed him swallow a pill—the night would be calmer, his face would relax, he might smile at her or suggest they watch a movie. She made sure to keep his pills stocked and always on hand. She would be lost without them and did not know what kind of man she would sleep beside if they did not have those pills. They both knew he needed them, and he was fairly regular in taking them. On the rare occasion when he did not, his eyes had a fierce unpredictability that frightened her. Michael's best features by far were his large brown eyes and long eyelashes. They were beautiful, but their gaze was often cold and unemotional on good days, and on bad ones they flickered with secret, unkind thoughts.

When they had moved in, Nancy could not believe that she lived in this house. It was so beautiful—looking up at the large gray face of the back of the house was intimidating. She felt like an imposter claiming to own it, yet they did. Ryan, then ten years old, darted onto a lit square in the grass and halted in a strange pose, standing with her legs stretched apart, her arms out with fingers splayed, frozen in the light. She laughed, the moment was over, and then she sprinted away to the opposite end of the yard, where she tackled her friend Carol.

For that split second Nancy was mesmerized that someone could be that beautiful naturally, that a person's movements could be so effortless and playful. Watching her daughter was painful—to witness such beauty and then to have it retreat from sight.

That night in the yard, Nancy felt deeply honored to have created such a gorgeous child. All those tense and emotional years with Michael at the college had not been a waste after all. Here she was sitting in the yard of her beautiful new house watching her breathtaking daughter enjoy all the fine things that life had to offer. No one in her family could accuse her of not making anything of herself. Look where she was now.

———

Now, years later, it seemed that the atmosphere of excitement and hope that had been present during their first months in the house had returned to restore them to some higher place from which they had slipped. She admired her husband as he stood by a stretch of grass, sweeping his arms in front of him to show where he wanted John to dig the koi pond. He was still handsome, gallant in stature, and a myriad of happy memories suddenly claimed her mind. The way he used to need her had touched her deeply. She remembered the nights before they were married when he couldn't sleep and she had gone over to hold him in his big lonely bed so he wouldn't have to be by himself. When he was relaxed, he could be warm and loving. He would often lie in her arms if his mind was troubling him and talk free-form, and she would listen with alert attention in the darkness. Sometimes they rubbed each other's backs absentmindedly before going to sleep. Back when Michael's sleeping pills had actually worked, he had loved nothing more than to talk to her while he began to drift off, pulled under by the pill, while her hand loosened the muscles in his lower back. It had been a while since they had had those nights of intimacy in bed, bonded as husband and wife.

She looked over and saw the silver-framed wedding photo of the two of them from so many years ago. In it she looked up at Michael with a huge smile, while he looked kindly down upon her. It was a nice moment captured on film. Nancy then thought of their wedding, which had taken place in the largest church in Greenwich, Connecticut, where his parents had lived. The church had been decorated with an elaborate display of white flowers, and each pew had a glass frame around a single lit candle adorning its entry. She had never seen such an awe-inspiring arrangement of light and shadow in all her life. Outside, in the fall air, she could hear the wind gently knocking against the windows as she walked down the aisle. That evening, she was able to forget their differences in class and the disapproval of his family. They seemed to look at her differently as she walked toward the altar and danced at the reception, for she felt she had never looked lovelier. Their glances toward her were reconsidering, innocent, pure, and she felt that the slate had been wiped clean. Ultimately, it had not, but on that night she had felt free of their judgment.

Nancy missed the elation of that evening.

Something had been lost over the years, yet there was hope. Maybe Ryan would remain at home more often now that the yard would be so pretty. She felt helpless at her inability to stop her daughter from spending so many evenings at Carol's house, sensed that something awful would happen if she put her foot down and prevented it. Michael, too, was strangely passive toward Ryan and would not discipline her in an outright way. Nancy knew she would have to stay strong and continue to try to connect with her daughter. Michael had enough on his plate, and it was up to her to try to keep Ryan safe and on track. As Ryan advanced into the teenage realm and showed signs of being a woman, she continually wielded more power. A strong will lurked beneath her surface, one that could exert itself at any moment. She was the kind of girl, Nancy felt, who would run away from home and not be heard from again, living in musky lofts with degenerate rock band boyfriends. But now, with Michael looking so animated, maybe the two would rekindle their earlier bond over books and ideas. Ryan could read in the gazebo and would invite her friends over to their house instead of leaving it to go elsewhere. She made a mental note to encourage Ryan to bring her friends here when she saw her next.

Nancy heard Michael quietly open their bedroom door and tiptoe over to the bed well after eleven. She knew he was most likely drowsy and hoping to fall asleep right away if he lay down before his mind started its turning. She should let him be, but she couldn't help herself. She waited for him to get under the sheets, then turned to face him, grinning into the darkness.

"Can't sleep?"

"No, I can," she responded. "But I wanted to stay up to see you."

They both paused. The large room around them seemed to grow more still with each passing second.

"Your birthday is coming up. Anything special you want to do?" he asked.

"Nope. We can do whatever we feel like, I guess." Nancy secretly had grown to hate the arrival of her birthday every year. Michael always made a fuss over it, several times throughout the day insisting that it was "her day" and asking what "the birthday girl" wanted to do. During the first couple of years of their marriage she had become giddy with the respect she commanded and the attention she received on that day, yet the fifth time around, she had a sinking feeling each time she was complimented or doted upon. To know that this was how she always wanted to feel and that on the day after her birthday it would all disappear was awful. For those twenty-four hours she had the husband she wanted, and then, after the celebration, with several new presents on their bedroom sofa, she would lay her head down and it would all end.

"We can just go to dinner," she suggested.

"Okay, but maybe I can think of something better." He rolled over onto his side, his back facing her.

There was the back she knew so well. She reached out her hand and began rubbing along the creases of his shoulder blades. A bony man, he always ached along his joints and ridges. Little knots of pain would lodge themselves in his back, always at these same places. He said nothing, but she could tell he was relaxing, softening into his pillow. This was her introductory maneuver to foreplay, but she didn't overuse it. Half of the time she would rub the back of his shoulder blades, and then, as he began to fall asleep, she would curl herself around him, and force herself to doze off as well. The other half of the time she would start to play with his hair and see if he would let the cycle begin. Tonight, like many nights, he was unresponsive as she stroked the back of his neck. She found it hard to let it go. She felt bold, excited. He was the sexiest man she had ever met—his coldness, his troubled nature hidden behind a calm exterior elicited a painful desire in her, one that only seemed to grow stronger as the years passed. She loved tall men with deep voices. She loved men who didn't chatter on and on. She secretly knew that Michael was too smart for her, but she wanted to keep learning from him, to analyze the world and see the deeper layers underneath ordinary living. Michael had such depth. He was unlike any other man she had ever met.

"I don't know where you come up with your ideas, but it's so nice to be surprised. Redoing the yard is a great idea. You're so good to me," she said and then immediately regretted it. Both knew it was untrue.

In the darkness, he searched for something to say.

"I know I have been difficult, Nancy—these past years. I know that." That was true, and for a moment her heart felt it would collapse with relief. From those words, a forceful physical drive emerged. She snuggled up against him and began to kiss the side of his neck. She felt she could coil herself around him until she could elicit some kind of response. Maybe tonight he would give himself over. She would settle for pleasuring him, for anything.

"Nancy, come on, you know I'm not up for that." He curled up tighter into his fetal position, hardening into a ball. Were his eyes open or closed? She didn't know. She retracted her arm and rolled her eyes toward the ceiling. The physicality still tingled at the bottom of her belly, but as the minutes ticked by, it dissipated.

There was something about the way Michael slept that unnerved Nancy. He was stiff as a board and silent the whole night through. Because of his insomnia, she was never sure if he was actually asleep.

He usually faced away from her, and when she woke up, she would move very slowly and deliberately so as not to disturb him, in case he was just lying there awake, waiting for sleep to take him.

On nights like this, she missed her former boyfriend, Tim, who, as awkward and wayward as he was, had slept deeply and snored loudly. Back then his snoring had irritated her. But now she longed for it—the reassurance that he was released into the dream world, no longer her responsibility. She could toss and turn, sigh, mutter, and he would sleep through, surrendered, dead to her in a way that she liked, becoming a body with no brain attached. But her husband was like a brittle insect, motionless, silent, tightly wound up, operating on some vague plane between the current moment and a labyrinth in his mind. He was both available and entirely unavailable. His brooding, ever-turning mind frightened her. She could handle his strange mind while awake, but when he tried to sleep, an ominous being seemed to sneak out of his body and into the room, and it sat in the corner watching her. She didn't know what it looked like, that dark mass, but whatever it was, she knew it was sneering at her.

Maybe the landscaping was a sign that things were changing for the better and she should just be patient. That was always the answer. As time went on, he would step back into his role as head of the house and discipline Ryan. She also had faith that, if something changed, Michael would want her again. He might approach her between the sheets, his face relaxed and his mood lighthearted, with a playfulness that rarely came out. The other housewives she knew fantasized about strangers, young studs they invented to spice up routine sex. She fantasized about her husband ablaze with real desire, years into their marriage.

CHAPTER SIX

When Ryan arrived at Jill's house on that early June evening, Jill had not changed out of her work clothes. For almost two years, Jill had been working at a plant nursery. She took care of the register, but when business was slow, she moved plants and big bags of fertilizer. She often came home with dirt smeared on her oversized T-shirt, faintly sweaty and musty, yet smiling nonetheless. She had dirt on the backs of her legs, and, as usual, her yellow T-shirt was damp with perspiration.

She and Ryan began baking a pie in the kitchen, soft jazz music playing in the background. Jill's parents had brought her up in this house, and they had both died before Carol turned ten. After that, Jill became the new owner and permanent resident. She managed to get by largely due to the fact that she had been left the house with no mortgage to pay off.

The house, although in slight disrepair from age, was larger than many in the neighborhood. In Ryan's opinion, the kitchen was by far the best place in the house. Jill had added midnight-blue tiles a few years back, one of her many solo projects, producing a fresh, comfortable space. Large windows lined the two walls and afforded a nice view of the small yard. Jill said she used the extra bedroom as a study, although she didn't have much to do there except pay the bills.

Carol had already gone to bed, tired from a lacrosse game she had played that evening. Right on schedule, she had come down to the kitchen to take her plate of food up to her room. As she hauled it away, she turned and gave the two of them a little salute before going back up to bed. Carol's conduct was getting stranger by the day as she became more stoic, more robotic in her routines; eating and sleeping were carried out on a tight schedule.

Blueberries and raspberries, freshly washed and shining with little beads of water, waited in green baskets next to the piecrust. Ryan's homework was finished, and the next day was a Saturday. Jill rolled out the crusts, swaying her body back and forth to the music. The night seemed endless, free from pressures. Heat seeping from the oven warmed Ryan's feet as she stood by Jill.

"I don't know what to do about Carol. She seems so unhappy, doesn't she?" Jill asked as she pressed her fingers into some of the knots in the dough. She tore off a little edge of the dough and put it into her mouth.

"Yeah."

"She won't talk to me."

"Go to more of her games. That would make her happy." Ryan reached out, separated a corner from the dough, and, like Jill, popped it into her mouth. The flavor, yeast with a sweetness to it, dissolved onto her tongue once it was moistened by the saliva.

"Am I an embarrassing mother, Ryan?" Jill turned to face her.

"You're better than my parents. I wish I lived here with you. Let's swap. We can put Carol at my place, and I can stay here."

"Shhh . . . not so loud, she could hear you," Jill said, attempting sternness, but as she said it she was smiling. It was clear that the thought had crossed her mind. There was something about the way Jill treated her daughter, and she Jill, that gave Ryan the creeps. There was a lack of warmth to their exchanges and an overall coldness in Jill that Ryan found entirely unnatural. Jill seemed to come fully alive only with Ryan, as if she were capable of giving her love to only one person at a time. At times it angered Ryan, the subtle way Jill ignored her daughter.

"Maybe I could move into the third bedroom—you know, the one you use as a study?" She said it in a lighthearted manner but watched Jill for traces of possibility. Jill smiled, and it did seem to Ryan that it might be an idea that could take form.

Lately, at night, it was getting harder and harder to leave Jill's and return home. Ryan now had her own small domain around the large sand-colored basement couch, an area exclusively hers. Carol never came down there, Jill slept on the second floor, and after hours of company, Ryan was allowed to lie down there alone and read or drift into a nap before going home. A white flannel blanket was always folded neatly over the back of the couch, waiting for her. A large glass coffee table sat next to the couch, and gray wall-to-wall carpeting covered the floor. The basement had a bathroom adjacent to the main room, and it was equipped with a clean bathtub. More and more, as she lay on the couch, sinking into the soft cushions, covered by her blanket, leaving seemed inconceivable. Out of the corner of her eye, she would see a full glass of ice water on the coffee table beside her. If she fell asleep and woke up thirsty, it would be there for her.

Ryan went over and took the bottle of vodka from the cabinet next to the refrigerator. She turned to Jill and raised her eyebrows.

Jill sighed and pressed her hands into the counter.

"Just a splash. I don't want to get into trouble with your parents or whatever. Don't get drunk. I drank too much when I was your age, and I don't want you to end up like me."

Ryan mixed the cranberry juice with the vodka and watched as Jill scooped the berries into the piecrust.

Outside it began to rain lightly, drops sticking to the windowpane soundlessly, gusts moving through the branches of the trees in gentle waves. Ryan felt a slight heavy feeling in her bones as the vodka tingled her throat.

Ryan looked over, and for a second she saw the younger face of Jill emerge in her features. Occasionally these flashes of Jill as a young woman appeared over her older and more beaten countenance, and they always excited Ryan, as she was aware that Jill had once been quite wild, quite pretty. She imagined Jill baking a pie in a kitchen twenty years ago, with her wild gang of friends, laughing, drinking, and eyeing one another with desire and playfulness.

"Jill, do you have any old photos I could see?"

"From when I was a girl?"

"No, when you were a teenager. Or any time before you had Carol."

"Yep. Hold on, there's a box of old photos in the living room."

Jill brought back a brown box and opened it. She pulled out one photo and gazed at it for a moment, frowning.

"Here's me with Carol's father." She said it in a flat voice and handed it over.

Ryan gazed at Jill and a young man, who stood side by side, beaming at the camera. Jill had on tight jeans and a white tank top, with her hair pulled back. She was attractive, yet possessed the same gentle kindness Ryan knew so well. Looking at the photo, it was clear who the boss of the relationship was, and it certainly wasn't Jill. The man had wavy brown hair, a strong and sturdy build, a beautiful face, and an air of magnetism, an assurance that he was the center and all else was in orbit. Jill's smile was more calculated, while his was easy, transfixing.

"What was his name again?"

"Oh, that's Dave."

"Were you in love with him?"

Jill sighed, obviously not wanting to talk about it, which sparked Ryan's interest more.

"Well, were you?"

"Of course I was, Ryan. I mean, look at him. It's clear who was in love with who."

This was the first time Jill had ever seemed annoyed with Ryan, which fascinated her.

"What's wrong, Jill?"

"You ask questions when you already know the answer."

"Come on, tell me about it."

"He was funny, unpredictable. I guess you could basically say he was irresistible. Women always loved him. I felt like I was constantly fighting them off. It was horrible, and I guess it also gave me a charge to be with someone like that."

"Where were you guys when this picture was taken?"

Jill squinted at it. "Oh, out by that damn cabin."

Jill explained that Dave was the type of guy who would immerse himself in one project or another and then would drop each one suddenly and with no warning. Building a cabin was one of his projects, and Jill had been another one of his projects. He had picked her out of their town's crop of girls and possessively taken her along on his group's expeditions. She had been with him during the year he tried to form his band, Poor Rayna, and then she had watched it come apart. She had been with him when he bought a piece of property on the edge of town, about two acres, and attempted to build a cabin on it. It was half built when he, exhausted financially and physically, left it.

"When I became pregnant, for the first five months, he bought books on babies and their developmental cycles and played music to my belly. He even took up the project of building the cabin again as a future place for the three of us to live."

Embarrassed by his parents' wealth, Dave had tried to build the structure as primitively as possible, with material he could afford himself. Ultimately, he could not do it; the thing would not come together. Jill had come upon him one day, coffee in her hand, and was alarmed to find him slumped over, sitting on a log next to a mess of beams and boards. What he had built had somehow come down. When she had asked him about it, he refused to tell her what had happened. His friends Rick and Jamie, who helped him build when they had the time, had apparently left for the day. Or maybe his bad temper had driven them off. Jill would never know.

It had begun to drizzle, and Jill told Ryan about how she had looked at his wet, thick brown hair, his perfect face drawn into a tight expression of anger, and had known she was in trouble. His plaid shirt was clinging to his back, and he'd had a cold, distant look in his eyes. She had desired him, sitting there in the rain. It was strange to feel passion for someone so angry and distant. She had felt increasingly panicked as it occurred to her that he was moving on, moving on from *her* this time.

The rent was overdue, and their tiny apartment was cluttered with boxes of his things, useless things he collected, such as vintage magazines and postcards. He refused to throw them away. The place was damp and unclean, and staying there was loathsome to both of them. But she could do it, would do it, for him.

"Why can't you ask your parents for the money?" she'd asked him one night after an argument with their landlord over the rent. "We need to take life more seriously now that we are going to have a baby. Don't let your pride get in the way."

"If I had known that my pleading would drive him over the edge, I would have kept quiet," she told Ryan. "But two days later he left town. I waited for about a month, expecting him to come back, but he didn't. I moved back in with my parents and had the baby."

Ryan was silent after Jill finished speaking. Jill now appeared to her in a new light. It had never occurred to her that Jill had been through such deep suffering or that a beautiful man she really loved had abandoned her. In fact, Ryan had never really thought of Jill as someone who could even have a handsome lover—the idea seemed cartoonish. The boyfriends Jill had had when Ryan was a girl had seemed fake, disposable. But there was the photo, the proof. Jill's connection to such a man was exciting, amazing.

"Well, I can see why you fell for him. I would've too, even if he was a jerk or a coward or whatever."

"I've always been drawn to physical beauty—it's a weakness in me. I guess everyone is like that. If we could, we would have the most perfect expression of beauty around us all the time, to be closer to the source or something. I've always seen it as a flaw in me. I admire people who don't seem to care about things like that."

The two of them stood there in silence. Something had changed. Jill was no longer the same old Jill she had always teased and berated in her mind. She was mammoth, a woman of drama, a woman who had had love and lost it. Ryan hunted around in the box and pulled out several more photographs of Jill at various ages. Tiny baby Jill in the safe arms of relatives; teenage Jill, her smile too big, her legs toned, her face sunburned. And more of her with this man, his piercing blue eyes locked into the camera, his arms protectively around Jill.

"Did you ever see him again?"

"No, but his parents have been very good to me over the years."

She explained that Dave's parents, stunned by his disappearance, had turned to her and her daughter for a connection. They hadn't approved of her as a possible mate for their son, but once he was gone and the two were separated, their attitude toward her had softened into one of compassion and pity. They'd heard from Dave a year after Carol's birth. He was living in Oregon with some woman, and although he occasionally wrote and called, he never contacted Jill or returned to his hometown. Dave's parents took an interest in Carol, and, despite the fact that their son was no longer living in the town or involved in his daughter's life, they decided to send a monthly sum to Jill for Carol's upbringing. They still continued to do so. It was as if they knew that Dave would be lost to them in one way or another, and they wanted to hold on to him in whatever way they could. He had been sinfully handsome, uncontrollable, and self-destructive.

Growing up, Carol had often talked to Ryan about her father, and it was clear that she thought he would return to her one day. She had been taken with an after-school special where a daughter leaves home in search of her father and finds him in a small farming town in Iowa. When she finds him, he clutches her, his face strained with emotion, and vows never to leave her again. He explains that he has had a room ready for her for several years and that he had been ashamed to contact her until he had made something of himself. The room she is shown is painted a cheery pink, and he has begun a doll collection, adding a new doll every couple of months. The whole thing seemed a sappy mess to Ryan, but she knew better than to voice that opinion. She suffered through repeated viewings of the film—Carol had recorded it on a VHS tape and watched it countless times.

"Do you have the day off tomorrow?" Ryan knew that Jill worked only three or four days a week, and she secretly felt that Jill was lazy. Now that she knew Carol's grandparents sent money, she suspected that Jill used some of it for herself. It was just like Jill to work only a few days a week—this laziness seemed to be part of a general infection, a flaw in character that pervaded all aspects of her. The laziness showed in the features and expressions of her face. She smiled in a lazy way, and being around her, Ryan felt the pull of inertia, the pull to be nothing, do nothing.

"Yep, I do." Jill grinned.

"What should we do?"

"I've wanted to take you to an energetic movement class with me for so long. I think you'll love it. I know, you think it's hokey, but just give it a try."

"What in the world is that?"

"It's a Japanese healing art. Very intense."

"I have no idea what a 'healing art' is. Don't expect me to like it. How long is the class?"

"An hour and fifteen minutes. It's a mix of yoga, Reiki, and energetic realignment. If you don't like it, you never have to go again. I just want to share it with you."

While the pie was baking, they went into the living room and sat on the couch. It was almost ten, and the rain had picked up. Ryan could not imagine leaving now.

"I want to settle in for the night and sleep here, okay, Jill?"

"Will you call your parents and let them know?"

"I'll explain tomorrow," she said, yawning. It would be the first time she had not called home, but she had a feeling it would be no big deal. Her parents never called her out on anything. And Jill would let her sign up for a trip to the moon if Ryan asked her.

"Jill, get me something to sleep in, okay?"

Jill rose heavily from the couch, and they went up the stairs slowly, careful not to wake Carol. In Jill's room, Ryan took the oversized T-shirt and shorts offered and pulled off her clothes right there. She felt she had never in all her life been this relaxed. This was why people drank and why people needed other people to live with, no matter how irritating they were—someone to watch you and know you were alive each day.

She stood in her bra and underwear, and Jill looked away. With great satisfaction she unhooked her bra and reached for the T-shirt. She saw Jill stare at her once in the mirror and then look away, picking up some laundry from the corner of the room. Unlike the rooms in her own home, the rooms in Jill's house were cozy and livable. She felt that this was where she was supposed to anchor herself at the end of the day. She would do anything to be able to stay here and claim it for her own.

"Good night, Jill." With the large shorts and shirt hanging over her frame, she went downstairs to the basement to go to sleep. From the couch, she could smell the berry pie that was cooling in the kitchen upstairs.

She wondered what her family would be doing at that moment. Dinner would be finished, and Max would be in the bath or in bed, being read his bedtime story by her mother. Her father would be in his study, and the house would get quieter and quieter. Vacancy would chill the halls. Her mother would be asleep already, and the house would get quieter still, until, at last, nothing. If she were home, she would become more and more aware of the fact that only she and her father were still awake in separate parts of the house. He always had something to occupy himself with at night, a book to read or some work to finish in his study for the next business day.

When she was younger, she and her father would often read together. They had had so many rituals that excluded the rest of the family. Surrounded by books in the study, she used to sit in one of her father's leather chairs, adjacent to him as he sat in the other chair. Her mother had never bothered them while they were in her father's domain.

Now that she no longer joined him for nightly reading, she imagined that he probably left certain work unfinished, work that could easily be completed between the hours of nine and five, solely for the purpose of having it to fill the hours at home. She realized that his days were constructed very carefully, with intense deliberation. If that careful structure were abandoned, she felt certain something would happen—the walls would buckle, or their front door would refuse to close and seal them safely in. Ryan remembered that this was the time of night when he would be having his glass of scotch. To know that they had both been having drinks at the same time soured her experience of it.

Ryan felt a chill pass through her as she suddenly remembered one evening several months ago. Her father had had a little too much to drink and had leaned over and, while hugging her good night, his face in the nape of her neck, had grazed her neck for a moment with his teeth. When the teeth went into the skin, she paused, freezing their embrace. Her arms seemed to lock themselves in place, and when he pulled away, she felt a slight moistness on her neck. Feeling began to return to her body and the nerves attempted to try to realign themselves. He had smiled and walked up the stairs to his bedroom, as if nothing had happened. He was normal Dad in his own mind, she thought, though he was gripping heavily on the banister as he trudged upward. He stumbled once on the stairs. The light from the hallway lit up half of his face and left the rest in darkness. When he had shut the door to his room, she was still standing there, frozen.

It had all happened so quickly. What was a bite, really? This moment was utterly obscure and indescribable to her. But the "bite" had plagued her mind for days, tensing up her body. As the years passed, her father seemed to become more like a clock that was slowly wound tighter and tighter. He had used to be funny and happy when she was very young, smooth in his manners, but now he was just awkward and his mind was elsewhere, his eyes searching for something.

The brief bite must have been an accident, the result of pills and alcohol, but when she thought of the bite at this moment, her body began its tensing, and yet, and yet, the vodka was erasing it. The memory was becoming sloppy now and sliding away. This vault of a room in Jill's basement seemed to crush memories into harmless little jars full of ugly liquids that could be put away.

She went into the bathroom and started a bath. She brought her glass in and sat it on the edge of the tub. The room had the sterile feel of a hotel bathroom—it belonged to nobody, and she loved that about it. She felt there was nothing more wonderful than to be left alone at the end of the day. How grateful she was for this little pink-tiled room, for Jill, going to sleep two floors above, and for Carol, for not interfering with her coming to this place.

As she lay down in the hot water, she rested one of her delicate feet under the spout and mindlessly let the water fall on it. This gentle pounding calmed her, and she closed her eyes. In a state of deep peace, she thought immediately of Max and felt a swell of guilt. She was well aware that Max idolized her and that it pained him to be left in the house without her. Maybe I can bring him here, she thought, where nothing is forbidden.

———

She drifted off to sleep on the couch around eleven thirty and then awoke to noises overhead. The refrigerator door slammed. Ryan wrapped the throw around her shoulders and went to see what

Jill was up to. She found Carol sitting in the kitchen with a plate of food—chicken, beets, and french fries, steaming hot from the microwave. Carol was clearly surprised to see Ryan emerging from the basement. She quickly looked down at her food, embarrassed for eating such a large amount before bed. It could not be passed off as a "snack."

"What are you still doing here?"

"I was too beat to go home, so I'm crashing on the couch—you don't mind, do you?"

"No, I just didn't know you were here." Ryan noticed that Carol didn't take a bite but held on to her fork and stared down at the table. She had noticed Carol's eyes flash with recognition at seeing that Ryan wore one of her mom's old T-shirts, gray and worn down very thin over the years. It was see-through and showed off Ryan's chest, and she knew that Carol was jealous of her figure. No one really stared at Carol's figure.

"Do you want some food?" Carol asked.

"No, thanks. Go ahead."

Miserably, Carol began to eat her chicken. Ryan just stood there with her hands on the counter.

To ease the tension, she said, "I'll make myself a chocolate milk," as she knew Carol would rather she do something than just stand there.

"I don't eat like this every night . . . there are—"

Ryan cut her off: "I understand why, you work out more than most people, you need extra calories . . . I couldn't do all the sports you do . . . I mean, I would probably pass out or break my ankle."

"Yes, you probably could, it's not rocket science," Carol responded. Ryan had always loved the dry style of her friend's humor, and after silly comments like this she yearned for her company again.

"That's a silly thing to say. Not everyone can be an amazing athlete."

"I'm not that amazing," Carol responded.

They both blushed and looked down. "Why won't you just admit it? Not everyone can do as well as you do. Oh, never mind, I'm just rambling."

"You always were the kind who rambled," Carol said, suddenly grinning.

She finished eating and seemed embarrassed to get up from the table in her sheep-patterned pajamas.

"Do you want to watch a video? I can't fall asleep right away at night anyway," Ryan offered as Carol took her dishes to the sink.

"Sure," Carol replied without thinking. "I took my nightly Nyquil before eating to help me sleep and it should kick in soon, but I could put something on until my eyes start to close."

"Oh, yeah, I remember now you take that to help you sleep." Ryan studied her friend as she moved around the kitchen. She had gotten so bulky and boxy over the years, as if she were one big muscle with no bones or angles mixed in.

Carol stopped and turned to Ryan, seeming to know she was being watched and judged. Her little troll face snapped back to defensive anger that burned behind her tired eyes.

"I know that spending time with me is your number-one priority and that it means the world to you, and therefore your invitation is very important to me," Carol said, pursing her lips and frowning dramatically. "But I have to decline—I know you wanted to feel like a good person, a good friend. Sorry. I know your heart is broken." She gave Ryan one last dirty look.

Ryan stood there, shocked, as Carol walked out of the kitchen, and she considered going home. But then she realized that whether or not she left was of no consequence to Carol, as Carol would not notice one way or the other.

"Okay, good for you, back to your chamber of misery, Carol," she called in response. The words lingered after her in the empty hallway. Ryan took her milk down to the basement and clicked on the TV. She was once again alone, but her anger toward Carol evaporated soon enough, squished into a different jar—deep down, it was clear to her which of them was better.

CHAPTER SEVEN

Michael's mother, Marilyn, had visited the Peninsula only once. The drive from his hometown in Greenwich, Connecticut, took her almost three hours. The visit was a painful memory, as everything had been one degree off the mark, and, except for her time with her grandchildren, it was a minor disaster. The weather had been unforgiving, showing her the worst side of the Peninsula. Persistent rain and fog had chilled the house and made traveling anywhere dreary and unpleasant. Nancy had been nervous the whole visit, trying everything to impress her mother-in-law, but it hadn't gone over well. Her opinion of Nancy was fixed and would not be altered by a fancy breakfast or a well-decorated guest room.

Marilyn preferred instead to have Michael come to visit her, and he did so regularly. She was fragile, plagued with severe osteoporosis, and he traveled to take care of her for a weekend every couple of weeks. It was clear she was reaching the end of her life as she was shrouded in a subtle but constant depression due to the death of her beloved sister. When he wasn't there with her, she had a nurse day and night looking after her. She liked them well enough but was weary around them, and had a hard time not snapping at them when they made a mistake. Michael knew all the subtle things she liked, the amount of silence and conversations she required, and the nurses seemed forever to be trying to figure out how to win her approval. She anticipated Michael's visits for days before he arrived.

———

It gave Michael a secret thrill to sleep in the bedroom of his youth, disconnected as it was from his current life. His room had soft red carpeting, which he enjoyed walking on without shoes or slippers. His mother had redecorated all of the rooms, and except for the furniture, lamps, and paintings, everything was different—new wallpaper and a brighter and fresher feeling. The room was therefore unburdened with childhood memories, and the past few years contained restful visits, with reminders of the old in the notches on the staircase and the same chandelier that hung in the entry room.

This time, as he always did when he was going to visit her, Michael left work early on Friday and got on the road. It was mid-June, and the yard was being reconfigured. Things were changing, so there was nothing he had to do. He knew the drive by heart, so he was able to make all the turns without thinking, to daydream about his time at the university or to imagine himself as an aging professor instead of a wealthy, soulless businessman.

As he chugged along the highway, Michael saw the same chain restaurants, the many towns that contained families similar to his own, but the houses lacked character, all lined up in rows, the grass an unnaturally bright green due to the chemicals doused over them once or twice a year. Michael stopped in the small town of Milford, which was his halfway mark, and got himself some coffee, and then drove to Katie's Deli and bought his mother a rotisserie chicken and a container of their famous macaroni and cheese. On his way out of town he made his final stop at the local bakery for a coconut cake. From there, it was only another hour on the road, and the drive was particularly pretty and scenic as it wound through a sequence of small towns in the hilly country. Michael took the road off the highway and enjoyed seeing trees and stone fences, with fewer houses and people in sight.

As he got nearer and nearer to Greenwich, Michael thought about his father, Howard James, the beloved judge of the town. Michael had grown up in a respectable house in Connecticut, and his father had always stayed up late in his room with a glass of scotch and a huge biography or massive book retelling true stories from the World Wars. Howard had been in World War II, and on the ledge behind him, he had photos of himself standing on sunny beaches, looking intense and prideful, with canopy tents in the background of the photos. He had a sharply featured, handsome face with deep, almost black eyes. His expression was often stoic, yet a mildly flirtatious smile usually played about his lips.

When Michael would trudge downstairs for a late-night snack, he would walk past the open door and hear the ice move in the glass and a page turn. His father had been successful as a judge, but reading and painting were his secret passions. He had a little studio attached to his room (Michael's parents had stopped sharing a bed and had separate bedrooms when the kids were young, five and seven). Michael admired him immensely. When he was younger, he was able to sometimes step inside the room where his father sat in a chair with a little table in front of him that held one of his huge books and his glass of scotch. His father seemed pleased to tell him about the book he was reading, about the history of the world, and about what made this particular writer engaging. It was clear to all that Howard had a fine mind.

Michael had been paid exactly one compliment by his father, and he never forgot it: "Your mother showed me your paper on the Great Depression. She and I lived through that time, obviously, so we know how it was and we learned how to save money by living through it. Your paper was very good. Work hard, Michael. You're smarter than your sister, as you know, smarter than most, actually, and you could go far." After that he turned back to his book and began reading, ending the conversation.

Michael's sister, Sarah, was half pretty, and into boys and concerned with fitting in. She had sandy blond hair that she wore in a ponytail with a brightly colored ribbon. Michael's father was affectionate with her and protective of her safety, but he seemed dismissive of the idea that she would ever do anything of import. When Michael had received that compliment from his father, he had taken it inside his heart and nursed it there. Many a time, when he had struggled with his neuroticism, he thought about giving up—school, his career—but the compliment from his father had presented itself several times along his path as a reminder, and that reminder prevented him from failing. As he got older, his father seemed uncomfortable when Michael would enter his room, so he did so less often and then not at all.

———

Michael arrived at dinnertime, starving, and went right to work heating the food. His mother lay in bed, camped as she was in the dining room by the kitchen. She could no longer go up and down the stairs with ease, and the dining room was convenient, as it was between the kitchen and the front hallway. She had the bed raised and her reading glasses on, yet she was asleep. The chandelier, which used to shine onto the polished dining room table, now shone down on the worn oriental rug in the center of the room. Her bed was several feet from the zone of twinkling light. The dining table and chairs had been moved down to storage after his mother had cracked her hip for the second time. Her crossword puzzle lay untouched, a wrinkled mess in her lap. Looking at her sleeping face, Michael saw that it had a dignified, though no longer stunning, kind of beauty to it, and he could still see traces of her younger face in this one.

When she awoke, she glanced at him and then at the clock. She smiled with a deep satisfaction, as one of the qualities she loved most in Michael was his punctuality. It was a sign of intelligence, she felt, when a person's internal clock was wound as it should be and could match the tempo of the external world with its many events.

Her osteoporosis had caused her spine to curve inward to such a degree that it pushed into her lungs, making it difficult for her to breathe or even move around. The constant pain of it caused her hours of silent agony. She had arthritis in her fingers, a condition she was used to after so many years, but on cold mornings, the ache was another strong punishment upon waking. Michael knew she concealed from him just how painful it was all becoming for her, so as not to worry him, and he wondered if her day-to-day existence with her nurses depressed her. It wasn't clear to him how long she had left, and at home he would often worry that she might slip away in the night with him hours away, not there to hold her hand.

Marilyn had never quite gotten over her older sister, Elizabeth's, death. Even though it had happened five years ago, it still affected her strongly, even more profoundly than her husband's passing. Elizabeth had been "a wit" and had had a wild independence that was so much a part of her no one challenged it. She had adored Marilyn, and the two had been close with a feverish kind of possessiveness similar to the bond lovers share. Their affection had not lessened when each had gotten married. Now that Marilyn had so many empty hours, her mind wandered back to Elizabeth easily and the memories caused her much pain.

With Aunt Elizabeth gone, Michael felt he now had a special place in her life; he was her only love left. He knew that she cared for her friends, but she never loved them, for to her, family was the only source of real love and devotion. Marilyn lit up every time upon seeing him, and their already strong bond seemed to deepen as she entered the final phase of her life.

Michael had always been her favorite child, and, although they quarreled, it was clear that each pleased the other in a basic way. His sister, Sarah, lived out in Nevada and kept only the most minimal kind of contact with the two of them. To everyone's astonishment, Sarah had refused to finish college and had become deeply religious. For their intellectual family, this was the worst kind of sin. She called them once every couple of months, and they endured the tense brief conversations as best they could. His mother rarely mentioned her, for there was really nothing to say about her that didn't elicit a baffling kind of shame. Sarah had married a deeply religious Christian. She sent them all pamphlets in attempts to convert her parents and brother to her faith. She had had child after child while living in a tiny house in rural Nevada and sent a photo once to her parents of herself and her husband standing on a dirt "lawn" littered with rusty toys, with the unimpressive house behind them. She had drifted off into her new family and lost touch with Michael and her parents, and it was just as well.

———

Michael brought out her tray and sat down in his chair across from his mother. They ate together, teased each other, and made insignificant remarks.

"You're copying me again," she said with a straight face, as she brought a piece of chicken breast to her mouth. She was referring to his eating the chicken first, a habit they both knew they shared.

"Maybe you're the one copying me, since I'm the one who started eating first," he replied. She gave a short laugh and went back to chewing.

"What's Ryan up to?"

"She's a little full of herself these days," Michael heard himself say, and the ugliness of his response pained him. He felt momentarily paralyzed and then shook it off and his thoughts resumed their regular flow.

"She has every right to be. That is one precious girl. Bring her with you next time." Michael quickly wondered if his presence alone was not enough for her, then dismissed the thought and concentrated on his food. How could he tell her that Ryan despised him and would never agree to spend time with him? He was careful to preserve the atmosphere of peace. They would retire early, and, unlike in his own house, he would sleep well here. He could feel it in his bones.

"How's work been?" she asked between bites, her antique face still beautiful in its own way.

"Just fine," Michael answered. He thought about what would happen were he to get fired. It wouldn't matter, as he had saved up so much money over the years from working there. He wouldn't even need to work anymore, considering the inheritance he would receive when his mother died. Money was not an issue and never would be, but he found none of it enjoyable. He had hundreds of thousands of dollars in the bank. He thought of John, who probably had thirty thousand saved up at most. He wondered what John would do with all of Michael's money were he to possess it.

Michael thought about tomorrow morning, when Marilyn's two closest friends, Betty and Anne, would come by. He would play bridge with them, and the women would have a great time teasing him and beating him out of money. He would make many trips to the kitchen while they played, refilling the ladies' teacups and bringing out cookies and pecans. These simple acts were appreciated by all, and he never felt so useful.

Michael could hear the familiar sound of Betty's deep voice in his head. "Doll, bring me a teaspoon of sugar," she'd say, her eyes on her cards, a smile playing at the corners of her mouth.

After he did the dinner dishes, he and his mother played gin rummy for a while, and then he went upstairs to his room. Once in his room, he checked his mother's answering machine to see if he had received any calls. There were none. He was surprised, as Nancy usually called him on the first night of these visits.

———

The next morning, Michael was up before his mother and, instead of waking her, he made her breakfast, knowing she would eventually awaken from the noise.

He was looking forward to the day ahead. It always unfolded without their noticing the passage of time. After breakfast they read the paper together and did the crossword, and then Michael set up the card table in the living room for the group of ladies. Betty showed up first, a plastic container of Virginia ham in her hand, and helped Marilyn make her way into the living room with her walker. Betty still wore elegant shoes over her swollen feet, even though she would have been more comfortable in orthotic shoes.

"Great to have you here, Michael," Betty called to him as she passed the kitchen, and Michael smiled to himself as he made her usual cup of orange spice tea with a lemon slice. When he set it on the coaster by her place at the card table, Betty looked up at him and remarked, "Still so handsome, isn't he, Marilyn? You always were a real doll, Michael. Such a well-formed face."

"Well, I had a good gene pool to work with, didn't I?" Michael said and gave his mother a playful smile.

Anne showed up fifteen minutes later, as she always did. Older people had such lovely, predictable routines—the same schedule, the same beverages, and similar conversation. Everyone knew his or her place—all was in order.

As they sipped their tea, they set out the cards and began their game. Michael preferred it when his mother or one of the other ladies won. For when he won, as he often did, he became embarrassed and quickly gathered the old, brittle cards together to start a new game. After an hour or two, when his mother started to tire, Michael escorted her back to bed to lie down for a little while and then made lunch for the group. After a meal of sandwiches with a few potato chips, Marilyn once again made her way back into the living room for another hour of cards. Then Betty and Anne left, kissing Michael and fussing over him before he closed the door.

Next Michael faced the only awkward part of the day, the span of time after his mother's friends left and before dinner. There was nothing to do. This block of time was troubling, as both of them were moody at the hour of four p.m., their personalities tired and soured, struck with a certain rush of melancholy that colored the progression to dusk. She chose this time to clean her dentures, which were her principal source of anguish. Throughout her life, she had flossed and brushed her teeth after every meal to preserve them for as long as was humanly possible. The method had worked until she was seventy-five, by which time her teeth were in such bad shape that she'd had to get the dentures. She called them "a disgrace" and fussed over them in private and in his company only.

When she was irritable, her normally saucy comments had a biting edge, and this mean-spiritedness was something Michael respected in her, even though he hated to be on the receiving end of such sharp-tongued commentary: "Don't stare at me with that gaping stare, it's not attractive. You shouldn't tease Betty so much—she can't handle it. She's not the kind of person who can handle that way of teasing. I'm sure she's at home right now, thinking of all the things you said to her. Don't drop that with your fumbly fingers." Though they had both been mean, Michael mused that he had turned out so differently from his parents. Neither of them had had mental troubles that he could detect. Where had his twisted mind come from? They were both bizarre in their own ways, but neither of them was a "disturbed person."

When he pushed her into the corner of the kitchen in her wheelchair and they began cooking dinner together around five, they would both become lively, almost giddy, as food was in sight, and the rest of the evening was a breeze ahead of them. Michael placed a cutting board on her wheelchair tray. She liked to have something to do with her hands, and she would slice up a tomato with her knotty arthritic fingers. Then they would finish the crossword begun earlier, mulling over meaningless conversations, retelling old jokes such as the anecdote of his father putting the cork in his ear at The Old Inn, or the day he'd appeared at the pool in his army-green swimming trunks and done a cannonball into the pool. His father had rarely acted out or shown emotion of any kind, so that the times he had were unforgettable for the family.

"The house is nice with you here, Michael," she said as she sliced the tomatoes. He turned to her, and she quickly said, "No, no, don't worry about not being here all the time. I'm like you—I like being alone. I always have. I have my friends and nurses for company. They drive me crazy sometimes, though, so clumsy! They seem to take up the whole room. I liked one girl a lot, Cora, but she had to move back to Trinidad to be with her husband. Sad to see her go . . ."

His mother had become more solemn after his father's passing, but it also seemed as if a burden had been shed. The vigilance over him and his activities, which had lasted for almost fifty years, had been released upon his death. Though he had never strayed from her again after the incident when Michael was eight, a minor, ever-present wariness hung about her previously carefree self, as if she had known she was now in charge of this man who had almost ruined them. She had had so many suitors before she had agreed to marry his father that Michael wondered if she regretted her choice. She had been beautiful, a tall Greta Garbo type, and could have had her pick of men.

Michael's father had loved that his wife was a great reader, like himself, though her focus was literature. At cocktail parties, her long lean figure perfectly displayed in a tasteful black dress, she would often surprise the men with a witty comment about a new book or about political developments from reading the paper, and he saw his father's face soften and shine with admiration as he watched her, his cultured and intelligent wife who knew when to stay quiet and when to dazzle all around her with a quick, clever remark.

Even though he loved and admired his wife, Michael's father had always eyed his friend's wife Sally, who was blond, unlike his wife Marilyn, and who had an hourglass figure. Sally was a bit of a flirt, and it was clear from her presence that she was not intelligent. That somehow appealed to his father's lust, and he flirted with her at dinner parties. Michael would park himself on the landing and listen to the commotion of their parties below, his father's deep laugh, the records playing horns and trumpets, and the velvety female voices of the singers floating up the stairs. His father had come up the steps once when Michael was twelve in the middle of the party to get something from his room and seen Michael sitting there. His father had had a few drinks and his expression was more relaxed than usual.

"Did you see Sally in that green dress?" he asked Michael and grinned conspiratorially. "I'm not sure it is legal for a dress to be that low cut, I mean, if she's not looking for paying customers, that is. Could see those tits from a mile away." He looked again at Michael and laughed. Michael tried to grin back, but it took a bit of effort, and his father became uneasy at his lack of response and stood there, shifting from foot to foot. He sighed, trudging past Michael and into his room. Michael was ashamed then—he had not given the proper response. But he didn't know why he was ashamed or how to act like his father wanted. Now he was here in the same house, the memories were as fresh as ever, but the figure attached to them was now in a box in the earth. Funny how the mind floats down the same corridors over and over, Michael mused.

———

After he turned out the light in his mother's room and went upstairs to his own room, Michael felt the anxiety return. These visits were so short—he barely had time to get settled in, and then he had to leave. All of the tasks that he would have to do tomorrow before leaving lingered in his mind. He would have to check the oil in the tank and fill up the car with gas. He cursed himself for not filling it up on the way there. His laziness was now crippling his good time. He had a work meeting Monday with Henry, one of the senior managers, whom he knew felt Michael was too uptight. But Henry couldn't touch him because he was so smart about staying on top of the numbers.

Without his superior intellect, Michael knew he was nothing. His mind was beginning to race. He sat on the carpet and then lay down in a ball and tightened up hard, closing his eyes. He wasn't sure if he could go back. Being in the house with his mother just worked. The two knew how to live together, and it felt as if he might indeed still be a younger man when he was here with her, one who had not chosen incorrectly but who would take the right path this time.

He opened his bottle and shook a pill loose, then crawled over to his glass of water to wash it down. Henry judged him for being so uptight, and there was not a damn thing Michael could do about it. Yes, he was not easygoing in the least, he ruined things with his uptight nature, but if they only knew how much effort it required for him to appear normal, they would forgive him his strained and stern countenance. Every second of every day was a wrestling match between him and his nerves. And it was all because he had faulty wiring.

Panic seized his heart, the whole chest constricted, as he imagined going into the office on Monday and seeing Henry's face that never quite smiled big enough for Michael; the disapproving look on his daughter's face; climbing into bed beside Nancy and switching off the lamp, feeling the mild hope for sex that drifted from her side of the bed. He could feel her expectant emotions all day, every day. They never seemed to go away.

As the minutes passed, the pill kicked in to a degree and dulled down his racing thoughts. He got up from the floor and quietly exited his room to roam the house.

The house had a smell of old wood to it, and Michael walked around the upstairs after his mother was asleep. The floor beneath him creaked, but he knew that nothing except the banging of pots and pans would wake his mother. She slept like the dead now, her bones heavy on the hospital bed that had been moved into the house. The nurses usually bathed her before he arrived, as she liked to preserve her modesty. Once, while she was napping, he had pulled back the cover to find her TV remote and been frightened by the gauntness of her frame. There was elegance to the complete lack of fat, but her bare legs still startled him and he felt he had committed some form of treason to see below her sheet.

As Michael walked around, looking at his father's paintings through the dim glow of the antique heavy-lidded lamps in the hallway, he questioned what he would do when his mother passed away and he no longer had the delight of these simple excursions.

He got to the door of his father's old room. His father had been a stoic man, with distinctive features, and even in his last years, when his face had been rumpled with lines, he had had features that were unique and dignified. In his final years, Howard would still receive phone calls from friends and relatives asking his advice on various matters. He was thoughtful and didn't rush into speech, and when he did speak, he spoke the truth. When Michael had seen him in court, he had sat above the others in his black robe, considering the truth as he studied the men and women placed in front of him. He had listened to the lawyers prattle on, unmoved like a boulder, and when he had spoken, the room seemed to tremble. What would it be like to be that confident?

Michael occasionally felt a tinge of gratitude that his father was dead, for his life had been spent battling with the man in the subtlest of ways. Growing up, he had felt his father was constantly watching him, as if he were a criminal in his father's courthouse, as if convinced that something was wrong with him. Then, when Michael had had his breakdown at the end of the first year of university, the worst year of his life in many ways, his father had seemed frightened of him. The breakdown had managed to confirm the suspicion that had always haunted their relationship—that Michael was indeed damaged in some unalterable way.

———

It was his mother who had driven him for a trial stay at Chestnut Hill at the start of summer break after his freshman year. It was she who had called him every day and showed no embarrassment for him, at least none that was visible. When they gave him a temporary diagnosis of schizophrenia, one that was eventually changed to neurotic paranoia, an ugly term but still a better one than the first, she had been at his side and had not broken down into weak tears or turned her head away. She had known all along that he was capable of greatness and had not been daunted by this awful test. Like Nancy, she had nurtured his troubled mind with unconditional love and kindness.

The nervous breakdown had come two weeks after a night of drinking. Michael had gone to a party where he hadn't known anyone. He had drunk too much and remembered standing in a corner by himself most of the night, listening to others' conversations. Then the night had turned and he could remember only flashes of it. He had his arms wrapped around someone's chest, and there was laughing around him. He could not remember who it was.

The next day, he had awakened alone on the lawn, and the hangover itself was enough to induce a state of misery. But when he walked around campus, he could feel eyes on him. He had done something wrong, but he could not remember what it was. He didn't know who else had been there. He could not remember how he had gotten home. That seemed a paltry reason to break down, but he felt a strong desire to take a whole bottle of pills, and he found his hands were shaking. He could not even explain it to his one close friend, Alex, who hadn't attended the party. Losing all control in front of a group of strangers had brought him to his knees somehow, emotionally. He could not remember what had happened.

When Michael was released from Chestnut Hill, he had gone back to live with his parents for the summer, and the long, empty days had been excruciating. He had insisted on sleeping on the third floor, and when the heat became unbearable, he had felt too embarrassed to complain since he had chosen it in the first place. When his father returned in the middle of the afternoon from the court house, Michael would invariably be up on the third floor with his nose buried in either a novel or a book that he was reading for his second-year philosophy class that fall.

When Michael passed his father's study to go down to the kitchen, he would often listen outside the door to see if his father mentioned his name while he talked on the phone. He was sure one time he heard his father say "living with a lunatic," but he had no proof, as the conversation wasn't even about him. His father had been speaking with an old friend who was a doctor, and they were discussing playing golf that weekend. The comment would have been completely out of context, but it was possible he had said it. Michael then began listening to every comment his father uttered. From upstairs, he would lean over the banister whenever his father spoke to hear if his name was mentioned. His father's tendency to mumble only added to the problem.

Once, during Christmas that year, his father had left the group assembled by the tree to make himself another scotch and water. Michael had been telling the family a story from school, and his father had left in the middle of it. He could have sworn he said "Fuck you" from the other room under his breath. But he had no proof. If asked, his father would only deny it.

Michael stayed at Chestnut Hill for exactly six weeks, while they tried different medications on him and a lot of talk therapy. He spoke of worrying about what other people thought of him and how, when he was drunk, those worries intensified. By the end of the six weeks, they seemed to believe he was stabilized and released him. While he was home, for the rest of that miserable summer, Michael had made a decision—to overprepare for the coming year and to make it the best academic year of his life. He read every single book on the syllabus before classes started, so that he could use the actual semester to do outside reading and research on the topics presented. His professors were amazed at his performance. He started a habit of advanced and thorough preparation for himself, a trend that continued through the rest of his four years.

His mother visited the school frequently, and when Michael received his academic awards at the end of the year, she stood in the back of the room in an elegant black dress. She helped him keep track of his prescriptions for Valium, and they tried it in combination with Thorazine to see if it would relieve his anxiety. She adored him and doted on him. Often, in their all-night study sessions, Alex and Michael would eat the snacks of crackers and cookies she sent in care packages. She had been so lovely, with her pretty face, nice teeth, stylish clothes and jewelry, and long legs. She pinned a diamond brooch on her black dress, simply because he loved the brooch and loved her style. But beyond the beautiful exterior, there was something even better: an authentic, loving spirit, proud of him always, the best of feminine grace that came from mothers.

———

Michael imagined the house being packed up and sold once his mother died and all the boxes and old paintings in the attic being carted off. The tranquility of the house would be disrupted, as new owners would move in and tear into it, updating it, pounding into its flooring, and removing the older kitchen appliances such as the oven and stove, which worked just fine and which he had grown to love.

Soon enough it would happen, though, and there wasn't much he could do to stop it. Michael was stuck on the Peninsula with his family—he had been the one who had demanded they move and stay there, despite the unfavorable climate for his son's asthma, and he could hardly now abandon it to come and live in his mother's house after she passed away. The house would have to be sold; the perfection of the place would have to be sacrificed. The elegant and tasteful family of possessions that decorated the shelves and tables would be removed and dispersed. The jewelry would be given to the female descendants, and they would wear it cautiously, unable to shake the associations each piece had with death and passing. It was an impossible thought. For now, though, he had this place, his mother's house, away from his own home and family. It was an uncomplicated space, and he could lie in the grand room almost as if he were back in college on one of the holiday breaks, his life unwritten, no ties to anyone. It felt that way with his mother sleeping in another room. Michael shut the door to his room and stretched out on the big bed, the silence in the house all-encompassing.

He remembered all the weekends he and Alex had come here to stay with his parents. His mom had fussed over the two young men, and they had slept on the third floor after watching shows on the TV set in the den. His father had been away fishing, so it was just the three of them in the house. His mother had brought them powdered doughnuts in the den as they watched TV, and she had washed all their clothes and made them breakfast. At dinner, she had listened to them talk about what they were learning in their classes, how they had impressed this professor or that with a well-thought-out comment during class, and she beamed at them both. Michael would have done anything for his mother, so proud was he of her beautiful face and smart dresses and pearl earrings.

Recalling those happy days, he fell asleep easily.

———

The next morning was a Sunday, and Michael knew that John would be beginning work on the gazebo that day. He decided to drive back home from his mother's house a couple hours earlier than planned so he could join John. The thought had occurred to him in the middle of the night when he woke up in his nest of covers. He hoped he might see some trace of the joy John felt being around his wife. It pained him to leave his mother, but he would have to go at some point that day, and he wanted to be around John. He could help out and be part of it all somehow. He wasn't that good with tools, but he could certainly follow orders. He could saw planks. He could pound nails if he were told where to place them. The trees and sleeping houses whizzed past him in the early-morning light, soft jazz music coming from the radio. It would be nice to be part of building something real and lasting for his family. Maybe he would elicit Max's help. This could be a way for Max to learn to be more manly, less of a spectator, and more in the action of life. These were the types of projects a father was supposed to do with his son.

He arrived home a little after ten, and Nancy was in the kitchen with Max. He told his son about his idea, and Max got up, looking confused. Nancy beamed at Michael as he took the boy out to the yard. John had papers spread out on the ground with rocks holding down the corners. Ten feet over, boards and beams lay in a rudimentary configuration. He turned, smiling with surprise, when he saw Michael and Max.

"Want some helpers?" Michael asked, feeling easygoing. Max looked to Michael and John again, a bewildered look on his face.

"Hey, little guy," John said to Max, getting down on one knee. A wide smile illuminated Max's face, and Michael suddenly felt very proud of his son. It was nice to have a quiet little son who didn't terrorize the house or make a fuss. With his little baseball cap on, Max was quite handsome. John would have liked a son like this, Michael thought.

"You ready to do some guy stuff, buddy?" Michael said down to Max, who looked up expectantly and didn't answer. It occurred to Michael that Max had no idea what "guy stuff" was. Who better to teach them than John? John was not macho, but he was a guy's guy and could probably throw a football very well and understood all the intricacies of pipes that ran below a house—two things that Michael could not do well.

Michael held the boards in place and John gently hammered in the first nail so it pierced the wood in a tiny stab; the wood held it, and there were several bangs needed to drive it all the way in. Max held the hammer as it wavered over the nail. He looked up at Michael, who nodded with encouragement. Max brought it down, and the small thud sent the nail in deeper. He blushed with astonishment and looked up again at John and Michael.

"Great job! Let's do another!" John said. He was very good at this dad stuff. Michael suddenly wished that John had been his own father—he would have turned out all right then, with no faulty wiring. Though his father had not been mentally ill, he had not been a normal father by any means. His silence had been laced with disapproval of his children, and he had kept himself at a distance from Michael. How he had loved to look through the glass door and see his father standing before a canvas of a still life of flowers, paused, with a paintbrush in hand, considering his next stroke. How he would have loved to learn to paint alongside his father, but he would never have dared to disturb his father's painting; it was his sacred time to himself. He remembered that in later years he had asked his mother if she and his father had ever been in love. Without hesitation she had replied, "No, we were not in love, we were obsessed with each other." And Michael could see the fascinated looks they sometimes gave each other, which indeed hinted at obsession or some sort of watchful compulsion. His father was fascinated with his paintings in the same way; he would study them as he painted them, with a cunning eye to detail.

———

The hammer was lifted by the small hands and then brought down again and again throughout the day. At one point Michael helped with a bang to get the nail back to straight stature, but Max seemed to enjoy that part too. Nancy brought them iced teas, refreshment they needed, but when Michael saw her in the yard, his face and mind darkened. He had forgotten about her for a moment, and there she was, never far away. Once he took the iced tea with a lemon wedge clinging to its side and drank down the sparkling golden liquid, Nancy said, "Wow, great job, guys! I'll let you get back to it," and she collected their glasses back on a tray and walked away. Michael's heart warmed toward her more with each retreating step.

John used his electric saw to split the wood into the exact size needed, and Michael and Max continued with little nail projects. They gave Max the project of collecting the extra sawed-off wood bits and placing them in the shiny black trash bag on the lawn. It was a mild afternoon, breezy and warm, and the flowers John had planted at the edges of the yard bloomed white, fuschia, bright yellow, and violet. More insects were interested in their yard due to the flowers—they zoomed from flower to flower, something Michael would never have noticed if he had not come out on this Sunday. Something that would never have happened if Michael had not brought John into their world. The edges of their world were flowering, structures were being built. An injection of goodness was filtering in. His mind was cooperating with him that day. It was still; no tremors of paranoia were filling in at the edges. He forgot about his pills, and they seemed to sleep in his pocket, unaware of their duty. Normally his soft hands caressed the sides of the brown plastic container when he stood among people.

———

Two hours in, Max sat down near them and twirled a leaf in his hand, then began to move the dirt with the edges of a sharp rock. He was content there, so Michael helped John with the measuring and sawing, and pretty soon, the foundational boards of the gazebo were intact. The gazebo would be a place to sit and look at the flowers, a place for people to sit and whisper secrets in the shade. It would be here soon. Maybe he could come out here when he couldn't sleep in the fall with a blanket wrapped around him and a cup of hot tea in the moonlight, while the world slept around him. At the end of the summer, he and John could sit out here with a six-pack and admire their work . . . it would be late evening. John would have no one to go home to, he could stay for dinner, heck, he could stay over. They had a guest room. Maybe he'd want his own room?

Nancy brought them out ham sandwiches, and they ate sitting on the grass. Michael saw a bush rustle in the corner of the lawn and looked for the fox, for his sparkling, mysterious eyes, but he did not emerge.

"Thanks for the help . . . nice of you—" John said to Michael in between bites.

Nancy had taken Max in to wash his hands before he ate his sandwich.

"I was glad to . . . hope we didn't slow you down, me and my team," Michael said, and his body tensed. Anxiety flushed through him again, through the wires, and then vanished, leaving him a little more tired than before.

"No, not at all. Tomorrow I'll have my guys with me, but you two are welcome out here anytime. It's hard to do it alone—no conversation. You know?"

Michael did know how hard it was to do it alone. He certainly did know that.

CHAPTER EIGHT

The morning seemed to burst down upon the earth instead of revealing its hues gradually. It was uncommonly hot, and the world appeared prepped for the odd and the absurd. As Ryan rode to the class with Jill in the morning, she noticed a man walking at the side of the road in black pants and a black shirt, who, as the car approached him, jumped and tapped his heels together. Jill was overexcited by the anticipation of the energetic movement class, and she sipped from her travel mug of tea and hummed to herself. She was unusually quiet, and a sly smile kept creeping onto her lips, but she said nothing.

"Why are you smiling like that?"

"I just think you are going to really like this. I do. I know you'll have a strong reaction to it, like I did when I was young," Jill answered.

"I don't know what you're talking about, but you're creeping me out. You can't bring me back to your hippy-dippy days, Jill, much as you'd like to," Ryan responded.

Jill winced once but then kept smiling to herself. She flipped on the radio and began humming along to the Cars.

"We're almost there," she said and banged the flat of her hand against the wheel to punctuate her statement.

———

The energetic movement class was surprisingly crowded with middle-aged women and men, and the room was decked out in garnet-colored curtains that almost matched the rust-colored carpet. The first half of the class consisted of flowing movements of squatting and reaching, with audible deep breathing. Next, everyone lay down in rows and the teacher, a young, petite woman named Dari, came around and gently put her hands on each person for several minutes. Ryan had to wait twenty minutes before her turn came, and the absurdity of lying on her back for no reason in particular began to make her angry. The room seemed shrouded in mist, which alternated from hot to cold as it grazed over her skin. The lights were dimmed, and the entire experience had the reverence of a sacred ceremony. She imagined how she would laugh in Jill's face once it was all over. Then she felt Dari kneel down next to her, and two small warm hands pressed down on her, one hand on her thigh and one below her heart.

She opened her eyes and looked up at Dari, who was staring down at her, clear-eyed and smiling. Ryan snapped her eyes back shut.

"Try to relax your head. Here, I'll cradle your head in my hands. Try to soften your neck." With surprising skill, the tiny hands scooped under her neck and held it. Ryan's head began to spin, and her legs went numb. She wanted to slip into sleep but firmly jerked herself back from the edge each time she began to drift off. Dari released one hand, and she heard a gently spraying sound above her head as she released aromatherapy into the air. An earthy smell tinged with sweetness wafted down. Quickly, both hands were moving under her neck, rubbing, pulling, and she felt suddenly delirious. Exploding images accelerated through her mind, and she tingled all over. Then her head was placed back down with tenderness, and Dari had gone on to someone else.

———

After the class, Ryan did feel energized, but she did not admit it to Jill. Instead she shrugged her shoulders and gave a little yawn; she couldn't bring herself to tell Jill she had actually liked the class. She didn't feel like returning home, so she suggested to Jill that they surprise Carol by attending one of her games. While they were cruising the streets in Jill's beat-up Toyota, Ryan felt the sudden urge to stop by, pick up Max, and bring him out into the sunshine. When they pulled up to Ryan's house and went inside, Max was playing on the living room rug with his giant plastic insect toys—a bee, an ant, a caterpillar, and a fly. The toys could be disassembled and reassembled to make stranger and stranger insect hybrids. Max ran to her carrying a giant ant with glittery wings and threw his arms around her waist.

Her mom came into the living room from the kitchen after hearing them come in. Ryan had noticed that Jill always nodded excessively whenever she was around Ryan's parents. She looked around a lot and nodded her head as if approving of all she saw.

Max stayed close to Ryan's side, watching her every move. Boredom hung thickly in the air, and it was clear he was relieved to be getting out of there. He had on one of Ryan's favorite outfits of his, green corduroys and a red-and-black-striped shirt, with tiny brown shoes that complemented the pants nicely. He seemed hungry for her attention. In the car, whenever she looked into the backseat, he was staring at her. Only when she would beam at him would he mimic the full, unbridled expression he saw on her lips and grin in response. Often, even as a toddler, he had looked to her, watched her to see how to act, what to do. He would follow her around and see where she decided to sit and how she held her body. Then he would tentatively come around to where she was and sit in the same position next to her.

At the game he sat on the bleachers and seemed stunned. It was a sunny day, with a brisk wind, and the sun reflected harshly off the silver bleachers. Carol didn't yet know they were there to see her. She charged forward and blasted toward her destination goal, time after time. When the crowd roared for the team, Max looked up at Ryan quizzically and then, after a delay, would raise his two fists and twist up his face and say "*Ahhh . . . rrrr.*"

Sitting there, Ryan felt that they were a family, had always been one. Carol was also a member of the family, for there is always a downer member of a group, a reminder of how not to be, and Carol was it for them. For better or for worse, they were linked. Ryan scooped Max up onto her lap, and he lay back. She had the distinct impression that he was trying to melt into her, merge with her, and, out in the sunshine, this didn't bother her.

When the three of them approached Carol after the game, she seemed pleased, especially since Max was there. Carol had seen him grow up, had even been there the day he had been brought back from the hospital—that was how inseparable the girls used to be. The four of them headed for the parking lot and decided to stop by the ice-cream stand on their way back to Jill's. Carol, in her gray station wagon, followed Jill's car, and they returned to the house with cones.

They all sat in the living room and played Parcheesi. The presence of Max united them all. Max was more animated than usual, and Ryan felt confirmed that it was good to get him out of the dreary energy of their house and into the normality of Jill's. Jill fried up some burgers, and they ate an early supper. As dusk was approaching, they put in one of Carol's old movies, about a pack of wolves that raise a little boy, and they all settled comfortably around the TV. Carol lay on the rug with some pillows, while Ryan and Max lay on the couch. Jill sat in an armchair beside them. Midway through the movie, as both Carol and Max were dozing, the phone rang. Ryan sauntered over and picked up the receiver.

"Ryan, why didn't you call? I was getting worried."

"I'm sorry, Mom, I totally forgot. Max is asleep. Can I bring him back in the morning? He seems happier than he's been in months."

"We shouldn't put such a burden on Jill. You're over there so much anyway. Why don't you two come home?"

"It's no big deal. Jill doesn't care. She likes having us here."

"Okay, fine. Come back in the morning. But Ryan, we are having a talk tomorrow."

———

Nancy felt a tremor of anger when it occurred to her that neither Jill nor her daughter had thought to invite her along to the game that day. The thought had never entered their minds because *she* never entered their minds, except as a means to an end. A small pebble of sadness plunked down into her belly. Every time she was not included, welcomed in, every time other people's eyes passed over her in search of someone else, someone better, it registered in her, a little check mark next to some truth.

She thought back to earlier in the day, when Ryan and Jill had come by for Max. They had seemed like a guilty pair, guilty of something. Nancy had tried to make conversation with Jill, as she always did.

"Great to see you, Jill. It's been a while—almost a year," Nancy had said, trying to make eye contact with her.

"Yep, it has," Jill had said and nodded as she scanned the living room and then rested her eyes on Max.

"Mom, can we take Max to see Carol's lacrosse game? I'll take his inhalers and everything. He never gets out much. Let me take him."

"Mom, I want to go!" He had looked into his mother's eyes, pleadingly. It always bothered Nancy that Max expected her to say no to things, or to be unreasonable, when she never was. As if she would withhold the thing that he wanted. She always let him do whatever he wanted. And he always expected her to punish him when he made a mistake, and she never did. Where had this come from? To flinch when there was no danger present—none of it made any sense.

"Sure, you can take him." She had packed a small backpack for Max, some juice, a snack, and a coloring book and markers in case he needed a way to occupy himself. Jill stood by the couch in her baggy linen pants and tank top, and Nancy noticed the sweat-stained circles under her armpits. She never would have noticed these kinds of things in the past, but being married to Michael had trained her to look for imperfections. Over the years, his gaze had landed heavily upon her, day after day, and the comments on her choice of clothes or choice of decorations in the house had trained her to look for what was right and best and to abhor things that fell short. She began to wear more expensive sweaters and decorated their home based on ideas from the magazines they received in the mail in the hope that that heavy gaze would look elsewhere or soften into appreciation. Now she realized she had caught the bug herself, pitying those in her view who were less than perfect.

"Would you like to sit down, Jill, and have some lemonade or water?"

"Oh, no, but thanks all the same." Jill had never accepted her offers of beverages on the rare occasions she had been to the house. It was rude to say no every time something was offered. It showed bad character, Nancy thought. Jill looked like an oversized teenager, big boned and clueless about fashion. Nancy didn't know what her daughter saw in this woman—why she was more preferable company than herself.

———

Nancy had had the entire day free after Max left. Book club was that afternoon, but thinking about it gave her no pleasure and she decided to skip it. That month's book was Miranda's pick, and hers were always painfully weird and experimental, almost incomprehensible. Nancy always dreaded the month when Miranda selected the book and led the discussion. She felt Miranda was showing off her graduate degree by choosing books that no one but she understood or enjoyed. The other three women in the group were appeasing, tried hard to show that the themes were things they could grapple with, but they never convinced Nancy. She had joined the group three years ago because Michael's friends' wives were in book clubs, and Nancy, after all, had always enjoyed a good story.

That week they were reading something called *Fall the Tower* by a Chinese author, and Nancy was agitated by each and every word of it. The main character, a man named Scrub, was obsessed with a tower he had once seen on a trip with his parents when he was six. There were twenty-nine pages where he discussed this tower in bed with a woman named Gigi after they finished having sex. She kept asking him questions about it, entranced by his reveries and excited by his tales of the secret rooms in the tower, tales he had concocted entirely in his own mind. They took breaks from the discussion to resume fornication, both incredibly aroused by the tower. It was absolute nonsense.

Nancy knew that Miranda would say something like "The tower is the symbolic thrust of this intellectual exploration." Her statements were growing more and more tiresome. It was just a chance for the "ladies" to show off their "college" talk. Nancy was embarrassed by never having attended college, but with each passing book session, she detested more and more the high opinions of the educated. She wanted a good old-fashioned story, clearly laid out, with a hero and a heroine, a villain, and a clear plot. Why did modern plots seem to stray so far from that time-tested formula?

She had loved reading fairy tales to Ryan and Max every night. Michael had hated reading simplistic children's stories—it was as if he couldn't wait until the kids were older and he could begin his tutorial on literature. It was a tough year when Ryan had stopped wanting Nancy to read to her at night, when she was around seven years old. She could remember clearly a series of yawns, and even some mean-spirited giggling, as Ryan had grown bored with her story.

Ryan had gotten up from the bed and said, "I'm going to go downstairs to get some milk."

After fifteen minutes, she hadn't come back, and when Nancy went downstairs, the kitchen was empty. Michael's study door was closed, but she could hear through it the murmuring of voices. When she'd opened the door, Ryan was on Michael's lap and he was reading to her from *Treasure Island*. She had her eyes closed, imagining each scene. They both had looked up at her, and she could sense the guilty pleasure they took in each other's company. Nancy had pretended to blow the whole thing off—who was she to care who her child picked to read to her? But really she was crushed. That evening, in her mind, had been the beginning of a separation, a gap between herself and her husband, as well as one between herself and her daughter, one that had never been repaired.

Even though Ryan and Michael were no longer close to each other, she felt she had permanently lost her connection to each of them. It was subtle, but the roots of disconnection grew deeper and deeper. Who would have thought that something so innocent as books and education could cause her to feel isolated from her own family?

Maybe when Max reached high school, he would turn on her also. Once he began to intellectualize, he would see her differently. The objective facts of her status and background would dwarf her motherly charms. Max would become more and more of a bookworm. If he had problems, he would go to Michael for help, Michael who had been so cold to him all these years. The coldness would be forgotten as the first six years of his life became submerged in the realm of the unconscious.

She picked up *Fall the Tower* and wondered whether she could bring herself to go to the meeting. The book had had to be specially ordered and picked up at a tiny local bookstore, because an independent press had published it. Nancy felt suspicious when she went to buy it, as people are when they purchase something that isn't of their own taste.

She hadn't finished it and couldn't bear the thought of the two-hour discussion with Miranda. She wouldn't go; she resigned herself to it. The day would be empty otherwise, but she would fill it somehow.

She finished washing the dishes in the sink and then went up to her bedroom and put two of Michael's shirts in the laundry. She thought about her parents and what they'd used to do on Saturdays when she was younger. Saturday had been treated in a similar manner to the other days of the week. The children's chores were expected to be completed before lunch. Nancy had had to share a bedroom with two of her sisters, both older, so she had never had any privacy. The house had one bathroom, its lock eternally broken. Sitting on the toilet was an anxiety-ridden experience, both eyes on the knob so that in case it turned, she could jump and slam it shut before anyone walked in. There were usually voices in the hallways of their small house, and one of her brothers and sisters was always caught up in some drama, which would be announced to whoever would listen in the kitchen.

She had looked up to her brother Dale, with his glittering blue eyes, who was the most charming and handsome one in their family. Dale was softer and kinder than the rest of them, and when he had moved to Richmond upon turning eighteen, she had thrown a fit. It had taken her years to get over his leaving, as she had taken it as a personal slight. The house seemed smaller without him there, and her family members irritated her more than ever. Suddenly all their loud voices and rude manners seemed horrific, and she became withdrawn and moody until high school, when she was finally allowed to stay out later.

Now she had space and silence, endless amounts inside and outside. The house had a voluminous sequence of rooms, many of which were uncomfortable and stiff, and the temperature was forever a degree or two too cold. The woods beyond the yard had a haunted quality, an unidentifiable angst or shiftiness. One tree sat in the far-right section of the yard, and its isolated position made it seem like a statue of sorts, watching over the solemnity, a guardian of absence.

There were days when she wanted to weep with gratitude for her good fortune and days when she missed the busy atmosphere of her childhood home. She would have given anything to have the vacuum filled with messy and straightforward people who came and went with ease. Their current house was decorated like a museum, cold and unsettling, and she longed for one room that was completely hers that she could break in to her liking, one that would be soft and comfortable, with bright, cheery colors.

Michael's upbringing had been quite different from her own, so he was used to all the empty rooms and cool beauty. Brought up in a large home in Connecticut where his mother still lived, it had been just Michael and his sister, each with his and her own areas of the house, and a maid who came in and put all in order twice a week.

Nancy's guilty pleasure had been reading V. C. Andrews books. With all their grandeur, they told tales of huge lonely mansions and high-society, pampered individuals, each with a crippling private loneliness no one but the reader could understand. When she had first met Michael, he had reminded her of some of the characters from the books. She liked to place him in the settings of the novels she had read. When she had finally seen his parents' home, she had to admit that some part of her was disappointed. Yes, it was grand and beautifully furnished and quite large, but their home was no mansion and was diminished in her mind by the gothic halls of V. C. Andrews.

Michael had used to tease her about those kinds of books when they were first married. She had read a passage aloud to him in bed one night, and they had both had a good laugh. But secretly, as she read it, the words had seemed powerful to her and commanded her attention. She vaguely remembered the passage—it involved one of her favorite characters, Anne, a stepchild of the family, who was praised for her beauty. She was descending the staircase into one of the long halls at night and looked through the huge windowpane at the moonlight. She was alone and in the process of contemplating the events of the last night. Her virginity had been coaxed from her, and she began to know that the man who had taken it would no longer want her. She remembered a specific line that Michael had repeated and laughed over: "She was no longer the keeper of the treasure in the eyes of men." It had struck her as sad, and as overly sentimental as it was, she had loved it.

How different her life would have been if she had married her former boyfriend, Tim. She would still be living in West Virginia and would be around many of her high school friends and their husbands. She would know the business of everyone in town and would have a smaller house and a mortgage to pay off and would be working, most likely as a teacher for the elementary school or in a day-care center. Tim would have made a good husband, although she would have become bored with him. She would have been queen bee, the beloved rather than the lover. But she would have always wondered what would have happened if she hadn't left and gone to live near the university. She had gone looking for something better. If she had stayed with Tim, she would have always wondered if she could have done better.

———

She heard a knocking at the door, and then she heard it open. She came down the stairs and saw John standing in the doorway.

"I'm so sorry. I didn't think anyone was home, so I used my key."

"It's no problem, I'm glad you're here." The statement seemed too intimate or revealing, and she instantly regretted it. "Would you like something to eat or drink?"

They made their way into the kitchen, and she heated a cup of coffee in the microwave.

The silence was awkward, and she was eager to get out of doors. She felt ambivalent toward John—he was easy to be around and required little formality, but she secretly felt he must find her to be a poor match for Michael, and she distrusted his presence. People from her own background could surely see through the ruse of her being in such a privileged position.

"I'm not up to much. I can come outside and see what you're working on."

The two stepped out, and the air was clean and warm around them. John began his work, clearing out rocks from the square of dirt that would be the site of the gazebo. It was particularly quiet in the yard, and their chitchat hung in the air without reverberation. She found she was able to relax around John. She was used to the constant tension that clung to Michael that always kept her on edge, and in its absence she felt her mind and body relax.

She sat in a chair and watched John work. He had nice lean muscles, similar to Michael's physique. Leaning forward, he dug awkwardly, putting his full weight on his shovel to force it to pierce the soil.

He smiled at her. "I'm not used to being watched."

"Oh, I'm sorry, I'm making you nervous. How stupid of me. Let me help."

"No, no, I didn't mean it that way. I meant that I must seem like I don't know what I'm doing. Please stay and relax—it's nice to have the company."

"Normally I would be going to book club now, but I skipped out on it today."

"Why's that? Bad book?"

"In my opinion, yes. Although I'm sure everyone else is raving about it." She paused.

John spoke up. "My wife never joined a book club, but she did read. She read a lot of mysteries and sometimes horror books. She would read them at night while I slept. She was a night owl. Always thinking. I was a morning person. I mean, I am a morning person."

Nancy tried to picture his wife and imagined a slimmer, wiry version of herself, only tougher and more blunt. The more she thought of the woman, the less her persona resembled Nancy in her mind, although they would always have one thing in common—their roots. This woman, unlike Nancy, had probably been mean and a little intimidating, but they both had come from the same background—as much as she read, his wife probably had the trash in her. She probably had the local county accent, so similar to the way people talked from her own hometown. Yep, a trailer girl was what John's wife was; there was no getting around that. A spasm of hatred passed through Nancy as she stood out on the lawn, and then it retreated.

She found it harder and harder to stand outside with John as the minutes passed. She became very conscious of how unattractive she had become and how unappealing she was to men. She'd used to feel reasonably attractive, but then the photos would come in from weddings and birthdays and she would gasp when she saw herself. She was lost in her own body, solid and round, and she was stunned that she had not noticed. Enough of the photos had shown the same image to convince her that she no longer had traces of loveliness, so it pained her to be around men, especially one on one.

She had talked with John at the party. She could hardly remember the conversation, only that she had felt wild from too many drinks and her old self, the part of her that could charm, had made an appearance. Without alcohol it vanished, and as hard as she tried to find it, it was too stubbornly slippery to stay put for long.

As she sipped her water, she thought about the groundwater problem on the Peninsula—she wondered what John thought of it.

"I never know whether to listen to people when they say that the groundwater's polluted. What do you think? Do you drink it when you're at home?"

"I don't have to worry about that. I live on the mainland." He thought for a minute. "But if I did live here, I would probably drink it—I don't like to listen to rumors. Who ever knows if they're really true."

"I buy bottled water, but it's such an effort to always remember to use it and so much easier to just take water from the faucet. Still, there are so many cases of cancer on the Peninsula—it does make you wonder. People seem to get cancer here pretty young, and there's a lot of breast cancer. They think it has to do with drinking the tap water your whole life. If it's true, it's a very sad thing."

"I agree with you. How did the water get polluted in the first place? What do they say?"

"I don't know. I never quite got it. Something about minerals . . ." John kept working, and Nancy glanced around the yard and then at the house. It irritated her that her husband was not there.

"I should go back in and occupy myself somehow," she said. The shame was overwhelming, all from just standing alone with a man in her yard. She felt this shame around Michael's Yale friends, whom she knew pitied her, but she had thought she would be safe with someone like John. Apparently there was no one who was safe for her to be around.

———

She went inside to shower, then dressed up in her cream pants suit and drove to Orin. She parked, went into an expensive boutique, Gina Hurley, and moved around the small store with attempted confidence. The two women who worked there took notice of her and brought her the only dresses and tops they had in her size. They didn't say so, but it was clear that the selection for the unthin was limited. She tried on the five items, all of which looked horrible. She bought two of them, just because not to buy them would somehow be more humiliating than to leave with nothing.

Then she went to a movie by herself in the late afternoon, got the popcorn, soda, candy combo that was advertised, and enjoyed herself immensely. Two high schoolers were kissing in the back row, and an elderly man sat unmoving across the aisle from her. The film was a romantic comedy, whose every turn was predictable, and Nancy felt a joy she hadn't experienced in years as she slouched in the purple velvet chair and sipped her Coke. After it was over, she paid for another movie and went in, but twenty minutes into it, the moment had lost its thrill, and she walked out into the warm dusky air to look for her car.

When she returned home, John was still out working where she had left him. She remembered that he did not have a family of his own to return to, but still, the image was pathetic. The two kids who usually helped him had another job they were working on, so John was stuck doing all of the work himself.

Giving in to the fact that she was stuck with him, she leaned her head out the door and called, "John, have you had dinner?"

"I brought along some chips with me and have been snacking on those," he called back, his voice echoing across the empty yard.

"Come on in, and I'll heat you up something," she called and let the door slam before he could reply.

John walked into the kitchen and went to wash his hands in the bathroom. It was clear that he felt awkward, and, before he could say something about it, Nancy asked, "Do you like spaghetti with meat sauce?"

"Yes, I love it, but—"

"It's no problem. I can reheat leftovers, no big deal. Have a seat and have a glass of wine with me." As soon as she said it, she realized what a relief it was to have someone to talk and share wine with. When they were first married, Michael had taught her a lot about wine, and they had gone on several wine-tasting trips. It had been so long since the two of them had sat out in the evening, sipped wine, and talked about the day.

"I've been meaning to try this bottle. Someone gave it to us at our party, and we haven't opened it yet. It's supposed to have a gorgeous taste." She brought out two glasses, poured a generous amount in each, and set John's down in front of him.

"Where's Michael?" he asked.

"I don't know, probably at work. He works on Saturdays from time to time." Nancy did little to disguise the bitterness in her voice.

John didn't reply. He drank some of the wine. "Mmm, this *is* good. I don't know much about wine, but I do know what tastes good."

"Let me try mine. Yes, it is delicious." She put the spaghetti into the microwave. "Thank God for wine. It's perfect at the end of the day."

"You got that right. I should get into the stuff. Replace my beer with this. It tastes healthier than beer."

"It's not as fattening. Not that you need to worry about that," she said, glancing at his slim frame.

"Neither do you."

"Well, that's debatable." Both were silent. Nancy appreciated the comment but had no response. She would take it—maybe her appearance wasn't as bad as she thought. It was amusing that all the men in her life were very thin, to the point of being waiflike, while she had never had the luxury of being skinny.

She set the plate of spaghetti down on the placemat in front of him and sprinkled Parmesan cheese over it.

"Aren't you eating?"

"I ate already," she lied. She hadn't had dinner, although she had stuffed herself with popcorn earlier. Besides, she didn't like to have people watch her eat, especially people who weren't her family. Michael's mother had once remarked to him about the way she ate, and she had never forgotten it. She had not been meant to hear it—the remark had been made in stealth and in low tones, and Michael had been offended and stood up for her, but she had still heard. "Noisy eaters" is what she had said, referring to both Max and Nancy.

John was a tidy, efficient eater, never getting sauce around his mouth. The wine relaxed him, and she noticed that he was not a bad-looking man.

She poured him another glass while he ate, as well as a glass of water.

"I'm glad I didn't go to book club. Maybe I'll drop out. I don't see why I need to discuss the books with everyone. It's not really my thing, anyway. Since you're done, let's sit out on the patio and drink our wine. Oh, I have pie—do you want a piece? It's apple."

"Oh, yes, please. That sounds perfect. Let me wash the dishes."

"Okay, since it's only one dish I'll let you."

They cleaned up the kitchen, and then Nancy flicked the switch for the low-level lighting that decorated the back patio.

"These lights are probably my favorite feature in this entire house. Does that sound silly?" She felt extreme pleasure in turning on these little lights that, by day, were camouflaged into the wood of the patio. At night the little bulbs, twelve in total, cast a ring of pale light over the floorboards, reminding Nancy of a fairy village on a hillside.

She and John sat in adjacent chairs at the edge of the patio looking over the expanse of the darkening yard.

"This is nice, isn't it?" Nancy murmured once she was seated. There were fireflies hovering over the garden and up into the trees.

"That's the only bug I know of that I like," John said.

"Fireflies?"

"Yeah. The only beautiful bug around, unless we were in the Amazon. I'm sure there are pretty bugs there."

"You ever traveled overseas?"

"Me? Naw. You?"

"Michael took me to England and Ireland. It was amazing."

"Did you stay in a castle?"

"Actually, we did. But only for two nights. It was very romantic. They had candelabras on the hallway walls and electric candles in the hotel rooms. I think the style was gothic."

"Gothic like Dracula?"

"High ceilings and long velvet curtains—dark lighting."

"Spooky. But it sounds like a lot of fun."

A fox walked lazily across the yard, and its presence disturbed a rabbit chewing on some grass twenty feet away. The rabbit jerked its head up, listening, its eyes wide with terror, then turned and scampered away from the fox into the dense bushes.

"My shoulders are cold. I'm going to go inside for a throw—do you need one?"

"No, I'm okay. Oh what the hell, bring me one."

"I'll grab the bottle while I'm at it too."

She came back out and gave John the white throw, which was softer than the pink one that she kept for herself.

"This is a little slice of heaven here, this property. You sure I'm not bothering you by being here?"

"Not at all—I need the company. It's been a long day, and, as you can see, my husband is not around." The bluntness of her statement silenced the two of them for a minute.

Nancy was aware that in the darkness she probably appeared quite pretty to John, and she basked in the knowledge.

"I'll open another bottle," she said and went into the kitchen.

When she returned, she poured John another glass and then sat down again next to him.

"What do you think is your best feature?" she asked.

"Physical feature?"

"Yeah."

He laughed and covered his mouth with his hand. "I've never been asked that before. I don't know, let me think about it. What's yours?"

"I have excellent hands and feet. I always have. Beautiful, dainty hands and nice nails and lovely-colored skin. My feet haven't aged a day since I was a girl. And they never smell."

"I guess mine would be my back. I don't have back hair, and I have strong back muscles. My wife also said I have a nice mouth." He blushed and was silent. "You have other nice features, though. Hands and feet are great, but you have other, more obvious good traits."

"Like what?"

"Nice eyes and hair. I'll stop there before I say something out of line."

"Come on. No one needs a compliment more than me. Who cares if it sounds out of line?" The truth was, she was desperate for the compliment.

"You promise you won't get offended?"

"Yes."

"You have nice breasts."

Nancy began giggling and looked away quickly. "That was out of line! But I can't say I'm not flattered. I've been told that before." She threw her head back and laughed. "Oh God, we should stop. This conversation is getting to be too much. Where the hell is my family?" she asked, and the two of them laughed.

"We've been deserted," John replied and searched her face. "Should I leave?"

"You probably should, although I've been having so much fun. I haven't had a belly laugh like that in ages. Thank you for that."

"No, thank you. You've been quite the hostess. The meal was excellent."

"I can't really take credit for that—it's from a jar." Even as she said it, she noticed that she felt a satisfaction that had been missing for years. John was easy to please and take care of. He operated from the code of regular men.

"Yeah, but why does leftover spaghetti always taste so much better than when it's fresh?" he asked.

"It does, doesn't it? Are you okay to drive?" She suddenly wished she had not cut the evening short. She did not want him to leave, but there was no way she could ask him to stay at this point.

"Yes, definitely."

They walked toward the front door, and he stood there for a moment with his keys in his hand. "Well, see you Monday bright and early."

"Yeah, have a good rest of the weekend, John."

After he left, the silence in the house took on a new texture, and for a moment she felt inexplicably frightened of the dark. As she stood there alone in the downstairs kitchen, she realized why. It was happening again. Michael was headed toward one of his breakdowns. Could they survive another one? The thought was unbearable, and she tried to dismiss it. Maybe after all these years she was becoming paranoid for no reason. She took a deep breath and went to lock the patio door.

CHAPTER NINE

John was becoming a permanent part of their lives, or so it seemed to Michael. He had been working in the backyard for a couple weeks now, and having him around eased Michael's mind in an inexplicable and yet fundamental way. John was always cheerful in a quiet manner and seemed to admire Michael, how he had a large house, a successful career, and children. He smiled at an offered glass of iced tea with sincere gratitude. Why couldn't Michael appreciate the little things like that? Perhaps it was his wealthy upbringing; perhaps he had been spoiled, always wanting more, more, more. Now he saw John's face in his mind's eye, handsome in a subdued way—there to restore order should a family emergency rise.

Michael had gone to bed that night at eight, while it was still partly light. He lay down just to rest for a minute, and the warm breeze and the smell of the hydrangeas through the window, the sky all lit up with pink, bewitched him. He found himself heavy, a delirious form of slowness, and the sheets felt better against his skin than they ever had as he lay in them, and he could not bring himself to get up but felt he would sleep forever.

Michael drifted off holding that stoic and trustworthy face of John's in his mind. John wouldn't let them down. He had stayed for dinner with Nancy the other night, and imagining the two of them alone, eating and talking, gave Michael pleasure. Nancy should be able to enjoy a nice meal with a grounded, normal, single man.

———

Michael awoke at five in the morning with clarity of mind and did not feel like sleeping a second longer. He went down to the kitchen to make breakfast for his family. He was ashamed when he realized how rare it was for him to pamper his family, and he was especially vigilant with carrying out his tasks.

Looking out into the dimly lit yard, he saw John's partially constructed porch extension and gazebo and felt genuine happiness that John would be here in a little over an hour to work. He wished he could skip work himself and stay to help him out in the yard. Michael's fondness for John was growing.

He felt he should have made more of an effort to introduce John to the others the night of the party. Trying to imagine John as a student at his old university, his mind produced no image. He would probably consider the classes to be a waste of time, with all their abstractions and intangibles.

He loves what's practical, not what's abstract, Michael thought. Why can't I have more of that? I wonder if practical men are better in bed? Are they more vigorous lovers because their minds are turned off? He felt that John would commit himself to the task of lovemaking with the same diligence he would bestow upon removing the weeds from Michael's garden, completing a task without distraction. It was possible to imagine the type of lover John might be, eager to please, kind, and surprisingly long lasting. His unassuming nature would create a better lover. Michael himself had never been able to commit himself to the task in the right way, except for a few times when drunk. He always wanted to get it over with at a certain point, and rhythmic movements could be maddening. A man like John would get the job done and done well. Michael would give credit where credit was due. When he picked, he picked well. Good for Nancy, he thought, only the best for her.

Looking through the fridge, he found a bag of oranges in one of the bins. He began squeezing them with energy and pouring the juice into cups. With bacon frying in the microwave, he began to make fruit cups. There were enough berries in the fridge to make a nice assortment of colorful cups for everyone. Michael imagined the pleased expressions on their faces when they came down the stairs, and he relished his own happy feelings that morning.

Maybe he could create something beautiful to leave behind for his daughter. If his novel was a success, he could redeem himself in her eyes. She loved books, loved to lose herself in a good story, just as he did. Perhaps she would see that he could indeed brighten the world with some beauty instead of always bringing darkness. He placed a fruit cup in front of Ryan's plate—the most colorful one.

Michael had used to think a lot about how he first met Nancy. He had stopped thinking about it because it became far too disturbing to remember those days. He felt that there had been a real succulent innocence to their involvement, actually, and it startled him to remember it. It was too painful to recall how they had been then, knowing what they had become now.

He knew he was indebted to Nancy for her loyalty through the series of events that had taken place when they were in their early twenties. He had acted out his rage several times in front of her, and she had still stayed up all night to sit beside him while he finished an important essay. She was the only person who had seen him turn into a monster, and she had loved him through it all. He used to consider her a saint; the depth of her kindness was immeasurable. Despite all his academic achievements, Michael felt he was nothing next to her in those moments. They were two ends of the spectrum colliding at the center and resting there. She didn't judge him, and she was the only one who knew how far his mind could stretch toward the unsavory, as well as the unreal.

He knew he would have been happiest had he stayed in the academic world; he knew he was nothing without his intellectual prowess being carefully cradled and nursed. It would have been so easy for him to have become a professor, so natural, that it was horrifying that he had given it up. His mental problems would have been overlooked there, as all professors are seen as slightly crazy; it even added to their charm.

And my family, he thought in the empty kitchen. They would have been a hell of a lot happier if I were happy. A miserable father brings down the whole crew.

It was almost eight. Where was everyone? He crept up the stairs and into his bedroom. Nancy's robe was draped on a chair outside their bathroom door—she was in the shower. He went back out and into Max's room, which was shockingly cold. Max was still nestled under the covers, his face not visible, his raspy breath audible. Nancy usually woke Max before her shower. Today she had not. The door's hinges squeaked as he opened it. Max's body did not move, but his breath continued—slow inhales and rough, fast exhales.

Michael felt odd standing there, so he laid a hand on his boy and roused him. Disorientation colored Max's face as he looked up. After his son was born, Michael had known there would be no more children. His physical condition seemed to be some sign that what they were doing was wrong in some way and that they should not continue.

"Time to get up," he said awkwardly, his hand still on Max. Max got out of bed so quickly that it occurred to Michael that maybe his son was afraid of him. Heading straight to the neat pile of clothes Nancy had laid out for him the night before, Max wouldn't look at him.

"Do you need any help?"

"No, Dad."

Michael wanted to go into Ryan's room but thought better of it. She had been up late the night before talking on the phone. He couldn't hear what she was saying but was sure she was talking to a new boyfriend of some kind because of the incessant loverlike murmuring sounds. He could scarcely picture who the boy would be, but it was undoubtedly some horny pimply type of kid. He wondered if she'd bring him back to the house. No doubt he'd been briefed on dear old Dad. Michael was sure that the boy had to know he was strange; Ryan would have told him.

Back in his own bedroom, Michael sat on the stool in front of Nancy's vanity table and looked at all of her cheap cosmetics. He wondered why, after all these years, she still insisted on buying drugstore makeup. They could afford department store brands.

Michael remembered how his parents had had a good laugh at her expense when Nancy had thrown her first dinner, celebrating their engagement. The event had taken place at Nancy's small apartment, and she had cooked the dishes she felt were appropriate. God only knew how it had ended up looking like a smorgasbord of cafeteria food: macaroni and cheese, peas and carrots, even a basket of potato chips on the corner of the table. The effect of the evening had been that his parents thought he had lost his mind to marry her—someone so common, so unrefined. Although he would have been just as ashamed to present a woman like Alex's Meg to his parents, whose imitation of elegance would have been immediately clear to them. She was a bauble next to a gem like Michael's mother.

———

Michael went back to the kitchen and poured the pancake batter into the frying pan. A stack of three or four pancakes had accumulated before he noticed Max sitting at his seat at the table. He had his head bowed and was swinging his legs back and forth.

"Hungry, son?"

"Mom usually cooks."

"She'll be down soon. Doesn't Mom deserve a break?"

Michael went to the stairs. "Nancy!"

Upon seeing Nancy's smiling face, Michael became excited, ushering her to her chair and placing two pancakes on her plate.

"Tea, Nancy? I know you love tea. Well, guys, I am not even half as good a cook as your mother," he said in Nancy's direction, and she smiled, "but I am trying. Hopefully, it will be edible."

"Michael, this looks great!" Nancy said in her cheerful way, and he smiled to himself. She loved him, and he wanted to give something back to her.

He brought her a cup of herbal tea and gazed out impatiently into the yard.

"John should be here soon. He doesn't have the day off, does he?"

"No, as far as I know, he'll be working here. Thank you for this. This is such a rare treat, Michael." She looked up at him, and again it struck him that although she spoke with sincerity, she also appeared mildly frightened of him as well. Was she? He wasn't sure.

Am I such a monster that my family is afraid to make a move or ruffle my feathers? he wondered.

Ryan came down and gave him a nasty look, making no effort to appear happily surprised.

"Please have some food, Ryan."

"I'm not really hungry. I'm just going to head out."

"Please." It came out a little more forcefully than Michael had intended. Desperation was evident on his face. She stood looking at them, her hand resting on a banana. Michael wondered why everyone was being so silent.

"Ryan, your father would appreciate your sitting down," Nancy interjected. "He's treating us to a meal—let's enjoy it. Look at all this food." Nancy had had a talk with him earlier that week and let him know they both had to really work on being harder on Ryan. She had been acting lately as if there were no boundaries, and they needed to get on her case about it. He admired the way Nancy was taking control; he admired the strength in his wife.

But now Michael could feel the joy draining out of the situation; his attempt at parenting was falling flat. Ryan looked at him as if she were studying him for a moment, wondering whether or not she should show him mercy. She looked calmer and happier than he had seen her in years. She picked up the banana and said, heading out the door, "Sorry, I'm going to be late. You guys enjoy."

Michael could not get the look on Ryan's face out of his head. She was too young to be doing stuff like sneaking around with boys. He had prayed that this sort of thing wouldn't happen until college—that she would save herself until then. But kids were doing that less and less. High school was the time for it these days. Michael reassured himself by remembering that this was most likely the hardest part of his life. Having a teenage daughter who hated him and was having sex was the toughest thing he would ever face. That and his faulty career choice—there would be no bigger struggle.

CHAPTER TEN

A few days after the first class, Ryan had woken up early and felt pulled to go to the energetics class secretly, without Jill. She left the house undetected a little after six thirty, a mug of coffee in her hand, and she felt very adult drinking it in the car in the early morning by herself. During the class, she could feel Dari's eyes on her. They all stretched in the darkness, and she lay limp while Dari realigned her legs and arms in relation to her spine. Lying there like a rag doll in confident hands, she went into a kind of half sleep while she was moved into and out of positions. After class, the two girls stood in the sunshine as the day awakened. Ryan clung to her mug of coffee from earlier, taking sips. Dari talked about backpacking out west, about camping in the desert.

"You want to hang out sometime?" Dari had asked her, for the first time her voice losing its casual nature.

"Yes, I would," Ryan responded, and they both looked out at the rocky beach spreading ahead of them behind the little rickety studio. The sea was alive that day, jumpy at the surface due to the wind. Sailboats were out, as well as the many fishing boats that always chugged out from the shore to sea and back again, unloading lobsters, bluefish, cod, and striped bass from black mesh nets on a mechanized belt that brought them up to ground level for visitors to see. Gulls hovered around the port to the girls' left, screeching with delight and taking little airborne dives to try to get at the fresh fish. Both girls watched the vibrant ocean and the busy boats and quietly sipped their coffee, savoring the new friendship and stealing smiles at each other.

Ryan returned to the class often and a few times she was late for school because of it, but when she walked through the front doors, the hallways were empty. And when she slipped into her classroom, no one paid any attention, not even the teacher. It was odd, this looseness and this tolerance. She felt it from all the adults she knew. The doors at the end of each hallway were propped open, fresh air pouring in, and the brightness of the sun outside glittered on the windows that lined the shadowy hallways. Everything was emptied out—it was the end of the school year, and everyone had their minds focused elsewhere.

She quickly retreated to her own mind and thought of Dari, petite little Dari with her easy smile and her bony body. That morning the two of them had sat outside drinking coffee together from a thermos Ryan had brought. Dari was a couple of years older, yet she had that ageless creature appeal, an almost elfin look to her that made her seem childlike or androgynous. She asked none of the typical questions, demanded no formalities or pep. The two of them had an unspoken agreement that they would see each other often, as often as was possible. It felt as if no matter what they ended up doing, they would somehow find their way back to each other. They spoke on the phone at night, right before bed. Ryan found it the perfect way to be sent into sleep, curled up in her bed in the dark, their voices low, saying whatever came to mind. Life itself seemed to have changed over the past couple of weeks—never had she known such peace. She felt tolerance toward her mother for the first time in years. When it came down to it, her mother was harmless, after all, and there was no use in harboring anger toward a harmless person.

Dari had graduated a year before from the same school, and had been a universally liked person. So when she showed up at the end of the school day to spend time with Ryan, Ryan felt a surge of pride to be connected with such an easygoing, pretty, and likable sort of person. Dari always wore her brother's bomber jacket, half hanging off her tiny frame, and her hair was disheveled in an attractive kind of way. The girls stared at her with a mix of puzzlement and envy—she was thin, and there was something lovely about her.

Ten minutes before her last class got out, Ryan would sit, excitement growing inside, and feel as if she might explode out of her seat. At the end of class, she would seek out her friend loitering in the halls, and they would leave the school together. The weather was balmy and windy as they drove through Orin and stopped for fries and a Coke at Sammy's on their way out of town to sit by the water. The owner, Rick, tall and ruddy-faced, still came over to talk to Ryan because he had seen her grow up over the years. He brought their food over himself and beamed at the two pretty girls. It was getting close to summertime, and they anxiously discussed options for spending the upcoming days well. Sometimes Dari would sit behind her on the rocks and would place one hand on Ryan's forehead and one at the base of her throat. They would sit that way as Dari balanced out her energy, and although Ryan often felt skeptical that anything was happening, she knew only that the touch felt right on her skin.

It seemed that Dari produced delight after delight, for not only was she wonderful company, but her family, whom Ryan had come to know shortly after they met, was the shining example of what a family should be. The Winstons possessed that magic of easy living that was so enviable to those who don't have it and so natural to those who do. They were unlike any other family she had ever encountered. They lived up Route 38 several miles in a wilder part of the Peninsula's forest. Dari's father and mother had designed the house themselves, a massive wooden structure with an intricate system of wooden beams, supporting many staircases, levels, floors, and half-floors. The tiny kitchen had low ceilings and a slate counter at its center, around which the entire family sat on stools upon coming home, eating whatever was around and chatting about whatever they felt like. Dari's mother, Lydia, owned an antique store down the road that rarely got customers, and her father was often out of town derigging bombs in the Middle East. Quite an unusual job, but no one discussed it as if it were anything out of the ordinary.

Seven in total, they seemed to thrive as a group, feeding off each other's vitality. Dari had two brothers and two sisters. There were several family photos showing them all perched on some mountaintop, grinning into the sunlight, healthy and strong. All of the children were remarkably beautiful. The eldest brother, Tanner, lived in another town and hadn't yet been to visit while Ryan was there. Yet there he was in the photographs, with striking blue eyes and tan, muscular arms.

Dari had learned yoga from her mother, who had taught it in the 1970s, when she was still living in California. Lydia had once been beautiful before her body gave in to the arduous task of bearing five children. Ryan could see her, slim, smiling with Mr. Winston in the backyard of their house in California when they had first been married. Her firm flesh had become like dough over the years, tired from all the endless creating of life. It must have been incredible to have made other people who now existed in the world, who then felt like separate, individual beings. You create and then suffer, while your creations forget where they came from. You had to have a bottomless kind of tolerance to forgive that kind of neglect.

The magic increased each day that Ryan spent with the family. This kind of productive contentment had always been absent from her own family, and here was the proof that a family unit could work, that things did not have to be bleak and muted as they were in her own household. Ryan was careful never to take Dari back to her own house, because of some vague fear that if Dari were exposed to her demented family, the wonder of their relationship would dissolve under the weight of her own home's malcontent. Her father would find a way to ruin their intimacy just as he did everything else, if only by existing near it, and that idea was unbearable to her.

Ryan luxuriated in the bizarre little space that was Dari's room, up two and a half flights of stairs on a little platform area at the back of the house. Different-colored scarves hung from the rafters, and her bed had a red velvet bedspread and numerous soft pillows decorating its plush surface. A large wooden bookcase in the corner of the room was filled with books of every kind. Ryan often found several lying open on Dari's bed. They were a mixture of fiction and spirituality books, and books of love poetry as well.

Ryan loved the solemn way Dari would pick up a book, her tiny hands clasped around the spine, staring at it, delicately holding it, sweeping her eyes lovingly over the words. Dari had just turned nineteen and was still living at home because she had little interest in college and was unsure what to do now that she was out of high school. She didn't seem to mind that she was three years older than Ryan, and the two girls seemed to grow closer as each day passed.

Two nights ago, Ryan had picked up Dari's journal to read its contents. Dari always left it open, not caring who read it. The average person might jot down some notes about a dream and then proceed with her day, but for Dari that was only the jumping-off point. She would write notes and then create a story from the notes, philosophizing throughout the day about the dream. Ryan began to read the new entry: "the moving statue in bed . . . on a bunk bed . . . white marble . . . muscle . . . ropy hair . . . Greek . . . face moving with anger." Below these notes was written, "I have a metal spear and it appears for a moment that I am triumphant as I smash it into him chipping off part of his marble. Some light blood comes out. I sleep with my spear by me on the wall. He sleeps outside but keeps hovering up to the window. He is strangely able to float. He was a lover of mine? Dad walks up, proud and slow. Dad shoots big slow glass bullets at the light. He is unaware of the danger of him (statue companion). Cannot communicate with Dad."

Ryan set down the journal. Tingling warmth was creeping through her, pausing in between her legs and gathering force there. These days, she couldn't look at Dari in the same way as she had before. Dari was always surprising her with her unique ways, waking up to scribble down dreams, shifting Ryan's bad moods with her energetic work, her small hands working along Ryan's spine. When Ryan stayed over, she watched as Dari slept and to Ryan she resembled a little rabbit, her lips sometimes mumbling nonsense. She was tiny and warm, and she held on to her pillow with a silly ferocity during the night.

That night Ryan was careful not to touch her, but she found it difficult to sleep. She felt slightly delirious, lying inches away from this breathing body, wrapped up in the same comforter, looking at her face in the semi-darkness. She held back from Dari because she seemed asexual. Ryan had never heard mention of a boyfriend, and Dari never spoke of sex or romance, except for slight mentions of them in her dreams. Ryan was partially ashamed of the lust that grew inside her. She felt so exaggerated next to Dari. Full lips, big breasts, hips, hair, everything seemed so huge next to Dari's slight frame and androgynous look. And now with these raging feelings and lustful thoughts she felt even more estranged from her slender friend.

———

One evening, Ryan sat on a barstool in the Winstons' kitchen, talking to Dari's mother, Lydia, and drinking a cup of tea. Dari was out picking up her brothers from school, and Ryan was happily waiting for her. Her body felt limber from the yoga they had done together earlier that day, and it was a Friday, so they had the whole night free and could do whatever they wanted. She had the blissful security of knowing that time was no factor; she could sleep over and need not return home anytime soon.

Ryan felt a moment of guilt when she thought of her brother stuck in the house without her. She had been away as much as possible recently, and the last time she had returned home, she'd seen how lonely her brother had become. He had been sitting at the kitchen table, coloring books spread out before him, his face huddled over the paper in intense concentration. He'd exhaled forcefully as he bore down onto the crayon with his little hand. When he'd seen Ryan come through the door, the level of excitement on his face was evidence of the emptiness of his hours.

"Hey there, Max!" Ryan had scooped her arms around his neck. He'd closed his eyes, relieved at her touch. He had turned around in his chair and clung to her in a way that made her uncomfortable; he was desperate to be in her arms.

"Okay, okay," she had said as she lifted him up, trying to ignore the fervor of his grip. They went out into the yard, and watched her mother and John Randolph deciding on the placement of a walkway of stones through the garden. It was dusk, and her mother had obviously been out in the garden for some time. Ryan saw that her mother had been weeding and planting in one of the flower beds in the yard because her gloves and gardening tools were still lying in the grass by the newly manicured plot of dirt.

Her mother's hair was pulled up from her neck, and her face was flushed from the day's exposure to the sun. She and John were chatting and occasionally laughing as they mapped and remapped the placement of the stones. She thought how nice it was to see her mother fully occupied by something. And how nice not to have her father around, glowering in the corner. She felt she should get a move on to prevent being there for his return from work.

Ryan went up into her room, allowing Max to follow her around. She even let him sit on the bath mat and color while she took a shower because she felt such guilt at being home so infrequently. She remembered the sight of him as she left. He stood there in the kitchen with a quizzical look on his face, watching her go.

She thought of all this as she sat on the stool waiting for Dari.

"What are you thinking about, dear?" Lydia asked her.

"My little brother. I hate leaving him over there. Something seems pathetic about it."

She described to Lydia the way her father completely ignored her brother, the way Max was his mother's creature and would cling to her when he wasn't staring around numbly. She described how painful it was to hear him try to breathe and to witness his constant state of vulnerability. He could never feel confident because he was never comfortable and was forever at the mercy of others' aid or pity. She expected some reaction of astonishment from Lydia after hearing this sad story.

"Who really knows what he's feeling? He's a little boy," she replied. The response struck Ryan as peculiar, especially since she sighed after she said it and looked away. She guessed she had hit some nerve in the woman. She quickly scanned everything she had said in the hopes of finding the error in communication.

"Am I bothering you? Did I say something wrong?" Ryan asked, and the question seemed to hang there awkwardly.

"What do you mean by bother? I just hate pity. It is so ugly to pity another person."

"Well, I don't think you can really understand," Ryan replied, trying to control her shaking voice. "But I can see what a hard time he'll have throughout his whole life, how much social torture. It's easy for you to be abstract because you've never met him. Your family is as close to perfect as is humanly possible."

Lydia laughed. "My dear, you think we're perfect? You have no idea the things Mr. Winston and I have been through—the betrayals, the heartache, and how my children have suffered."

The conversation was quickly taking a dive into the strange. Ryan fumbled to recover it.

"I'm sorry I offended you. I had no idea stuff went wrong for you."

"It's okay, honey, don't worry so much," Lydia reached out and stroked the side of Ryan's face. "Such a pretty face, and always so stern and preoccupied. You could never offend me if you tried. For all we know, Max could be just fine. He could turn out very well. You never know which child is going to head off into the land of broken dreams and which one is going to rocket off into the best expression of him or herself. You just never know. If someone were to look at you, they'd think your life was perfect, right? You have it all—brains, beauty, et cetera. But look how much you suffer, look how much you worry about everything and struggle just to feel good. Don't pity your brother—he may end up just fine. Look at our daughter Kumiko—rescued from a slum in Japan, abused, neglected. It would seem her life would follow suit into disorder, but, no, she is our shining star. She could be preoccupied with the fact that she is the only one who isn't *of us*, but she isn't. She is the most integrated and healthy one of us all. Oh, I'm so excited. She should be home any minute."

The Winstons had an adopted Japanese daughter, Kumiko, whom they adored. Ryan had met her when she had returned from music camp. She was eight years old and very small for her age. Ryan recalled how Kumiko had walked into the house and been embraced by everyone. She'd kept her eye on Ryan the whole time, suspicious of who was in her house. It was clear that she felt it was, indeed, her house, and the way she was treated did much to affirm her theory.

Everyone was chattering around her. Even Mr. Winston was home for the occasion, no doubt to see her. She smiled up at them and then glanced shyly at Ryan.

"How was it, Kumiko? Did you make friends?"

"I made a few. Bill was with me, so I didn't need to make that many."

"Who's Bill?" Ryan asked.

Kumiko turned and looked squarely at Ryan. The rest of the family looked over as well.

"That's Ryan, Kumiko. Dari's friend."

"Hi there," Ryan said and waved.

"Bill is my soul mate," Kumiko answered and walked into the other room.

Dari whispered in Ryan's ear, "Don't ask questions about it—she's really touchy about Bill."

"Is he an imaginary friend?"

"No, not really. Bill was her husband in her last lifetime. He hasn't been born yet in this lifetime."

————

Although she spent most of her time at the Winstons' now, Ryan was careful not to overstay her welcome. She would leave occasionally and return to Jill's instead of to her own house. Jill and Ryan commented little on the fact that Ryan came by so infrequently now and instead tried to revert back to their old ways. But something had changed, marring their easygoing exchange.

They watched movies together more and more to ease the tension and to avoid speaking to each other directly. Ryan lay on the couch, while Jill was spread out on the carpet with a pillow behind her neck. They were watching *Should I Dance?*

"You're prettier than that girl. You could be a movie star, you know?" Jill had taken to flattering Ryan more and more, which Ryan enjoyed, yet after every instance of praise, she liked Jill less than she had before.

"Not really. That's a little bit of an exaggeration. But thanks anyway."

"No really. You have better bone structure than all these girls in this film."

"Thank you, Jill."

"Do you want to go hiking with me next weekend? I've been dying to check out this new trail."

"No, I don't think so."

———

Sometimes Carol joined them, and that made everything somehow less awkward. Carol could sense that they had lost their intimacy and felt less threatened by them. The best night they had had in years came one evening when they were cooking a Mexican feast of fajitas and tacos with Max there, mashing up the guacamole with Carol as she sat on a stool by the counter. They had been playing Spanish music and all were laughing and peaceful. Ryan had felt a camaraderie with Carol, and the two had even joked in their old way. After eating the feast in the living room, they began watching *Signor, Don't Shoot*.

They all cleaned up together after the movie and then ate their dessert of cupcakes. Then Ryan drove Max home, took him inside, turned around, and drove back to Jill's house.

Jill was up in her "study" but came back downstairs as soon as she heard the car door slam.

"Carol went to bed," she said, staring intently at Ryan.

"Let's make drinks," Ryan said and breezed into the kitchen. Jill followed her and watched as she poured the two glasses of vodka and cranberry juice. Jill said nothing and stood near her, pretending to look through a catalog. Ryan despised Jill for her lack of spine, her lack of boundaries. She was seized with the sudden urge to do whatever she wanted.

"Let's go into the living room," she said and went into the living room before Jill answered. Jill followed her and sat down across from her on the floor.

"Why do you just keep staring at me?" Ryan asked as they sat in silence taking guzzles from their drinks.

"I don't know, Ryan."

"I'm getting another—you want?"

"No, not really."

"I insist."

"Fine, if you insist."

"You have to learn how to stand up to people, Jill," she said when she returned, handing her the full glass of dazzling bright pink liquid. She tried to say it lovingly, putting a hand on Jill's arm. "Otherwise people will walk all over you."

"You mean I should stand up to you?"

"Me, everyone. I mean, I'm sitting here drinking in your house and I'm a teenager. You should lay down the law."

"I know I seem like a doormat, but you're a hard person to say no to."

"I know, I know." Like wildfire, thoughts were catching in her brain one by one: Jill was helpless around her. Jill was weak. Jill was hers to do with what she wanted.

"Let's put in another film," Ryan said. "Your choice. Whatever you want, Jill." She crawled over to the box of films under the TV and read out names.

"These all suck, never mind." Ryan made herself another drink and lay down on the rug beside Jill.

"Do you like girls, Jill?"

"No, I don't think so."

"I get the sense that you like me?"

"You're beautiful, irresistible, and if I were a guy and not an old lady, I'd like you," Jill responded.

Ryan found her way back up and sat facing Jill with her knees folded under her. She put her hand on the side of Jill's face and pulled it closer to her own. Jill was breathing quickly and had a drugged look in her eyes. Ryan could have kissed her if she wanted to.

"Yep, it's what I thought," she said and let go of Jill's head.

———

Ryan woke up on the couch in Jill's living room and remembered vaguely the events from the night before. Shame seized her, and she felt as if she might throw up. She got up, her head still buzzing slightly from the alcohol, picked up her stuff, and left. It was just after six in the morning. She felt entirely out of control. Had she kissed Jill? She couldn't remember for the life of her. She only knew that she had gotten drunk and she remembered Jill's face looming before her intently, studying her. If she had indeed kissed that woman, it would be the worst thing she had done in her life so far.

When she went upstairs, at first no sounds were heard and she felt she could make a clean getaway. But then Jill rounded a corner and stood before her.

"I'm so sorry, Ryan," she said and reached out a hand. "I shouldn't have let you have all those drinks."

"Why are you sorry? We didn't *do* anything. Did we?"

"Well, I kissed you for a minute, I think. It's a little foggy. I think that's all. I think you got upset and went downstairs," Jill said.

"Oh, you do, do you? You think that's what happened, but you don't know. Well, thank you for explaining that." Ryan tore past Jill and out into the yard. Her first kiss was with Jill? Jill followed her out, striding across the grass. Ryan stopped walking and turned.

"I think I'm done, Jill. I think I'm done with all this. With you."

Jill stood as if bracing herself and then cleared her throat.

"But thank you for the class."

"What do you mean, thank you for the class?" Jill responded.

"Just thanks. I met someone great there. Someone young and fresh. Good-bye, Jill." Ryan got into her car and backed out, the image of Jill standing in her cargo pants, tank top, and long gray braid looming the entire time she reversed down the driveway. She wanted that image to break.

———

Ryan walked into the house and literally almost ran into her father, who was already up drinking his coffee by the kitchen door. It had been so long since it was just the two of them alone in a room together. She had avoided this moment for weeks. Why hadn't she just come home in the evening when he was in his study? She could have slipped upstairs without his knowing she had come in.

He looked at her with the strangest of expressions and said, "I can smell alcohol on you." His eyes widened, and he had the most intense look of shock on his face. In a soft, slow voice he said, "You smell like a brewery." They stood there staring at each other for what felt like a full minute. Ryan couldn't move; she was planted there, unable to say or do anything. After the horrible evening with Jill, Ryan knew she was just not up to speaking with her father.

He stared at her, inhaled, and began to speak. "You've just had sex, haven't you? You have got to stop acting out and slinking around or your life is really going to go in a terrible direction. Who is this boy? Is he your age?"

Ryan's right arm shot back, and then, without premeditation, she slapped his face.

"You're the one who's always drinking," she said through teeth mashed together into a grimace. "I bet you don't even remember biting me when you were drunk! Don't you dare lecture me on how to live life."

She did not know why, but she felt it was his fault for what she had done the night before with Jill. His brooding presence had caused her to flee their house and kiss an old woman. They both stood there, stunned, as he raised a shaking hand to touch the side of his face. Her senses returned, and she forcefully pushed past Michael, ran up the stairs to her room, and slammed the door. He was saying something in the hallway, but she could not hear it. He seemed to be mumbling it or speaking in a low and stern voice. She locked the door, but she stood and watched it just to make sure it stayed shut. She sat still, breathing hard and looking at the door, for more than fifteen minutes. Eventually, she saw his car leave but she still waited for ten minutes before leaving her room to go into the bathroom. Once inside, she locked the door, took off her clothes with trembling hands, and sat under the hot water in the shower, tears streaming from her closed eyes.

CHAPTER ELEVEN

There loomed the impression—the glass on Michael's office building was sea foam green that reflected the sunlight in one brilliant facade. The silver letters that spelled "Phairton" gleamed and stretched across that green glass. Michael remembered his first few years there, when he had been the one to recruit the talented William Young to work for them and his ideas about computer programming had revolutionized the industry, allowing Phairton to become a major company in a matter of six months. What a thrill that year had been. At Phairton no one had cared about Michael's tense demeanor; they were too busy admiring his innovative achievements.

Michael observed the tall green glass building as he parked his car, and for a split second the beauty of it viscerally took him over before he recognized it and processed it as an ordinary image and the sense of beauty vanished. He had decided to come in to the office, even though it was a Saturday. He kept going over in his mind the events of the morning.

His own daughter had slapped him today. He could laugh about it or cry about it. He wondered how such a thing could have happened.

When Michael had caught her walking through the side door at seven in the morning, he had assumed she had been at her friend's house for the night, but obviously something else had gone on. Something was different about her. Her hair was disheveled, there were ridiculous purple marks on her neck, and she had a grotesque smile pasted on her face. She had just come in the door, looking strung out and mesmerized. He was leaning against the stove, contemplating making some eggs, when she slipped in the door and just stood there, smiling to herself, guilty of God knew what.

"Ryan, I may not be the world's greatest dad, but I am your parent. It is clear that something inappropriate happened." He recalled saying something to the effect of that. "You are too young to have sex, honey. Boys at this age are really too aggressive . . ." He tried to give her a sympathetic look and thought that maybe she would open up about the experience and he would get something right as a parent. He actually could not remember if he had said exactly this or practiced saying it in his mind. He had said something in an attempt to parent.

Michael remembered the look of horror that had spread across her face as she turned to look at him. Then, the damnedest thing, she had slapped him and run upstairs. What had hurt him worse than being hit was what she had said: *You are totally crazy.* He thought he remembered her saying it, but he wasn't sure. She might not have said it. It had been mumbled. It was like those moments with his father; he could not trust that he heard correctly the insults from other people. And he could not remember how hard she had slapped him. Stunned, he had walked out to his car and drove to work. And here he was. For once he was glad to be inside his glass-walled, fluorescent-lit office building.

———

Michael walked past his secretary, Rebecca, giving her an easy smile. One Saturday a month, everyone was required to work, including secretaries—Michael had forgotten that this was her extra day. He was in go mode, and office protocol was streaming through him. He felt that people in subordinate positions, such as secretaries, seemed to love it when people of higher authority possessed a certain aura. It was a breezy aloofness that was firm yet kind, benevolent. Communication was clear, and smiles were saved up and delivered at the end of inter-actions. But, most important, everyone was crystal clear on his or her position and standing—there was no confusion in that sense. It was all laid out in simple terms, conveyed through tone and body language.

Today, because Michael was in recovery from the morning's events, he was fueled by an internal anger that was safely contained in his body, cruising on a beautiful kind of autopilot. Rebecca looked up at him, attentive, waiting, and he thought she seemed relieved that he was finally executing his role as boss and acting like a regular male. She had been waiting for this. On the days when he was meek or guilty or excessively negative, she shrank from him, automatically avoiding eye contact. Today he was inspiring her confidence in this existence they were acting out.

Rebecca was young, in her early twenties, had brown hair, and was always very well dressed in blue skirts with white silk shirts and elegant jewelry. Her face was average, though her skin was sort of milky, pasty, as if it belonged to someone five minutes dead. Her teeth were chalky, as if the milk in her skin had slipped down into the cave of her mouth, drop by drop, to hang on her teeth like stalactite rocks, or strands of mucus.

What would become of her? he wondered.

Her figure was maddeningly attractive; he was supposed to think so. The other men at the office did. She had those full and supple breasts that men become insane over, and she also possessed coy movements. Even though she had the look of the perfect woman, something about her repulsed Michael. Overall, she stank of fertility in a kind of overdone way that both disgusted and pleased Michael.

"Hey, Mr. James!" She beamed up at him as he strolled in. "How are you?"

"Just fine, Rebecca. Thanks. Good to be here, get some work done." With that he raised his eyebrows for emphasis, indicating that she was part of the team, a team that was motivated and purposeful.

Michael headed toward his office door, then turned and said, "You look lovely today, Rebecca." Oh God, he thought, have I blown it, gone too far, been too forward?

No, she was blushing and obviously pleased. She turned to her computer screen to start working, refreshed by his energy.

She did look lovely, he thought. Lovely and rank. That was no lie. With his door closed, he sat down and gave a full-bellied, shaking laugh at the ridiculousness of Rebecca, of his stupid analysis of her. Then he stopped and looked at the family picture of the four of them on his desk. Why the hell had they named their daughter Ryan? Perhaps a boy's name had made her more willful, masculine. He picked up the gold frame and turned it onto its face in front of him.

Michael couldn't bear the thought of having the picture in his office for another second. How could he get it out of there? He put it into his wastebasket and shoved some papers over it.

To have his perfect little girl become a woman, a sexual being, was one hundred percent terrifying. She could get pregnant, she could, God forbid, be taken advantage of—an older boy could get her drunk and use her. As she became more and more of a woman, her happiness seemed to fade more into the distance. It was as if sexuality were a curse and would transform even the sweetest of children into sullen monsters.

Michael remembered being young and looking at the world with wonder, expecting his father to love him, waking up every day with complete trust that it would be so. But after several years in the same house with him, he knew his father didn't love him, would never love him.

When he was young, he always knew he would have a bright future, and then midway through high school, he stopped believing it. He knew he was different from other people, but he was not sure in what way. He had learned so many things from school, and his mind became burdened with facts and he lost his sense of wonder, and more and more, people looked past him in the hallways in high school. His heart finally understood that life was cruel and people would not always give you what you deserved. He didn't want Ryan to learn that.

———

Michael got a lot of work done and made several important calls. Rebecca was in and out of the office delivering files, asking if he needed anything. The hours were just falling away. It was getting close to five o'clock, and he began to have a feeling of panic. He just wanted to stay here and keep going. There was no way he could leave the building tonight. Yes. He would stay and work. It was safe here. He could work alone, impress the senior partners. Impress everybody.

Then the thought of being here at sunset without the aid of Rebecca seemed intolerable, impossible even. How could he make her stay? He called her station and asked her to please come in for a moment.

"Rebecca, is there any way you could stay for a few more hours? We're getting so much done. I'm finally getting my workload caught up."

She looked down, dismayed, struggling to answer.

"I would pay you double for the overtime hours. You are just such a big help to me."

Her eyes lit up at that. There he was, number-one boss, his aura of authority perfected.

"No problem," she said.

"Let's order in dinner. What's your favorite food again? Thai. Let's order some Thai takeout to be delivered. What do you say?"

"Great, Mr. James." Michael was sure Rebecca was wondering who this magnificent creature was in front of her who had replaced her somewhat sulky former boss.

"I'll get right on that," she said respectfully and marched off, no doubt to email her friends and tell them how incredible he was being to her. He loved her at that moment. Then a thought popped into his head: this woman would sleep with me. It would be an awful exchange, though, and Michael shook his head, dismissing the idea.

Michael sat back down and thought of John Randolph. His family was in chaos, he was in chaos, and John was the only person Michael could think of who could calm the situation. He called his house and asked Nancy if he could speak with John. He heard her walk out onto the patio, and in a matter of moments, John came on the line with an uncertain "Hello?"

"John!" Michael exclaimed, for he was genuinely happy to hear his voice. "How are you? It's Michael James."

"Oh, good. I'm in your backyard right now, putting up some beams."

"I'm glad you're there. I was just calling to ask you for a favor."

"Okay."

"I'm going to be working late here tonight at the office. I'd appreciate it if you'd stay for dinner with my family after you're done working outside." Michael paused. "Nancy gets lonely, and the kids love you. I'd appreciate it, buddy. You could order something to be delivered. I'd really appreciate it."

"Okay. Are you sure? Should we save some food for you?"

"No, I'll eat here, and I won't be back until nine or ten. Did you have other plans for tonight, John?"

"No, I don't."

"Great. Maybe you guys could watch a movie or something too."

———

Lying on the carpeted floor of his office, Michael imagined his family seated at a table with John Randolph at the head of it. The image was perfect. Nancy would be at ease, and with his gloomy presence deleted from the picture, she would finally be allowed to just be herself. John would bring that out in her. John was devoid of any hint of pretense, of malice, and would appreciate all the simple pleasures she had to offer: food, stability, kindness, sexual pleasure, family—the very things John had sought in his own failed marriage. Michael knew that his wife had left him—he shied away from giving Michael more information beyond that, but John had admitted that much to him. He could tell that John had been an honest husband and that his wife had eventually grown tired of him, just as Michael had of Nancy. There was no doubt that John and his wife had also been mismatched from the start.

At first, he thought, Ryan will stare inquisitively at the man, wondering where her father was and nursing a constant sense of guilt for having attacked him in the kitchen. Then, over time, she'll just enjoy the new atmosphere without him. It smacked him in the face how innocent a bunch they would be with him gone. They would be perfect. He was all right, sitting here, thinking of it, as long as the family photo was no longer in sight. But he could feel the gold of the frame burning in the wastebasket, radiating in his direction, unstoppable and smug. He fished it out and carried it, picture facing down, out of the office and down the hall to the men's room.

Once safely inside, Michael relished the fact that no one would come in there. They had all left for the day or had not even come in at all, since it was a Saturday. And Rebecca would have to use the women's room. Of course she wouldn't be in here. He was safe.

Normally this room was such a purgatory—Michael would have a moment of silence in the sterile calm, his facial muscles would relax as he peed or washed his hands at the sink, no expression, nothing, and then the door would blast open and in would breeze a suited man with a doughlike face, pursing his lips and giving him the short, over-confident greeting. They would both know how much they hated the moment and hated each other for creating this awful and awk-ward scene of uncomfortable acknowledgement. Not to mention the undraping of measly shriveled-up penises that dangled tentatively over the cold bowls and emptied-out bladders, only to be refilled an hour later, when the task would have to be repeated, multiplying its demeaning effect on a person as a urination machine.

Michael stood by the metal trash receptacle and raised the picture up, then stopped. He turned it over in his hands and forced himself to look, a mistake he instantly recognized. There they were: a color-ful bunch against a shining white backdrop. His eyes turned first to Ryan. They had had this photo taken five years ago, before she had begun rebelling. She looked as beautiful as ever, silently tolerating the group, sitting there beside her mother, who looked like a cooked potato next to her. Max, hopeful and disoriented as ever, even as a one-year-old, was dressed in his white turtleneck and green cords. And then there he was. He was dressed very rigidly, in brown tones and wearing glasses, and he noticed that he looked about as smug as was possible for a human being. He could just see himself, looking out at the expanse of the tacky department store in which the photography station was nestled before the picture was taken, making his whiplash-quick judgments on Americana and then linking it to chain-store culture in general. So uptight, so haughty! The typical intellectual's dilemma caught and immortalized in one photograph.

Yes, he knew he was a cliché. Look how he even stood a foot away from Nancy as she had tried to stand closer together, he mused. He thought about how happy he could have made her if he had just put his arm around her for the photo. How easy it would have been for him to make her happy! Looking at her in her tan skirt and the blue cashmere sweater he had given her as a present when they were dating, he felt his throat tremble with emotion—how simple and good-natured she was. She loved that sweater and always wore it to show her gratitude to him for buying her an expensive gift. Why had she never gotten angry at him for withdrawing from her? he wondered. Why hadn't she stopped him, made him respect her by threatening to leave if he didn't change? Why did she trust him so completely? This trust, so complete, so perfect, was something, try as he might, he could not conquer. It waged no war and only sought to draw him in further.

Michael took one last look at the photo and tossed it into the trash. It immediately passed through the airy layers of paper towels and landed with a thud at the bottom. He imagined it beaded with moisture from soggy dripping paper left from the many pairs of hastily washed hands. He was glad that it was buried there, yet it also made his skin crawl to visualize it caught in the refuse, sad and ridiculous. Panic gripped him for a moment as he thought of the situation with Ryan. Where was she?

Something began to creep at the edge of his mind, something that had not occurred to him for a long time. It felt like a sickness and it seemed to seethe somewhere in his depths. An image was taking form. He pushed the thought away and thought about Nancy.

Michael went over the choices that made up his life again. He had gone willingly into a situation, a marriage, that he knew did not have the magic that binds two people. Yet there had been a momentum at the time; things had been set in motion, heading in a definite direction, right or not. He realized that he and Nancy must have come together to create Ryan, to breathe life into her restless soul and make her real, physical. And his thoughtful, quiet little son. Michael had been born and had married Nancy for the sole purpose of creating those two children, both unique and beautiful in their own way. That must have been it, he mused. Now Michael knew it was time for him to bow out of the picture.

He sat down on the bathroom floor at the thought, one hand wrapped around the edge of the sink. God, it was all so clear, he realized. He slapped the tiles. So remarkably clear! He sat for a minute enjoying his clear mind and then he stood up, covered his hands in the pink soap from the dispenser, and washed and dried them.

He began to recall a wonderful family trip to the Grand Canyon when Ryan was eight years old, almost nine. They had gone rafting down the canyon and camped at night with their guide and two other families. That was the year before Max was born and it had been a good one for the family as a little happy threesome. The water had reflected off the canyon walls as they drifted down, and Michael could remember the burnt salmon color of the steep rock walls alongside the river. They had of course chosen a very easy route since Ryan was little, so they all drifted along, silenced by the beauty of nature, often happy in their own thoughts and smiling at one another over peanut butter and jelly sandwiches when they stopped for lunch. At the end of the three-day rafting trip, they had stayed in a little cabin on the edge of the rim of the Grand Canyon. Their little one-room cabin had a fireplace, which Michael had lit and sat in front of, holding Ryan as the two read at night. Nancy had joined them with a novel, too, and the three had sat there together. Michael had not wanted to leave at the end of it. He had been aware that he might never be this happy again for quite some time. He remembered standing on the edge of the canyon, snapping photo after photo with his plastic disposable camera until the clicks ran out. Then he had just stood there, peering out at some eagles circling overhead the rows and rows of dazzling colored stone.

———

Michael went back to his desk and looked through the pile of papers on it. It was obvious that there was no more work to be done, and it was well after nine o'clock. There was no way he could keep Rebecca there any longer and not seem as though he were either insane or perverted. He would have to go it alone.

Michael went out to her cubicle. She was filing her nails absentmindedly while she read an email. She looked tired. He observed her. No doubt she must be as confused as he was. She must have often felt incomplete in this meaningless job. She probably wished she were famous, a movie star or something. She probably felt she was movie star material, secretly, and treasured that knowledge like a precious jewel inside her—silly women and their fantasies of grandeur.

"Thanks for staying so long, Rebecca. You were a big help. Have a great night, and see you on Monday." He tried to sound as normal as possible to conceal any trace of his insanity—the insanity he was sure everybody could see and that he never felt confident he could cover. It suddenly took all of his self-control not to reach out and pull her to him. Her loyalty and kindness that evening inspired an overwhelming need in him for the presence of another body. Even wrestling would suffice at that moment. Michael held his hands tightly together and walked back into his office, smiling like an idiot, then safely closed the door. Once inside, he began to pace around the room. He felt he wasn't hard-wired right; his nerves ran on strange impulses, as if they needed some reprogramming.

Michael contemplated going home, but that seemed entirely wrong. Home felt volatile, unsafe. Potential eruptions could happen at any time—such as a daughter rounding a corner and shoving him or delivering another awful slap. Or there was the chance that he himself might be the one to lunge out. Who knew what he was capable of, what he would do if he saw her? That satisfied look on Ryan's face—just the sight of her might send him into a rage, and he wouldn't be able to stop from hurting her or humiliating her in some way, putting her in her place.

These thoughts were really too much for him. He sat down at his desk and looked around the bleak room. Well, since he was staying, he would need to make a little camp for himself on the floor. And he would need entertainment of some kind for the evening. A bottle. He would need a bottle of some kind of harsh liquid like vodka that would burn its way down his throat and create delirium. He grabbed his jacket and headed out. This time when he returned, he would be stocked—he would have the supplies he needed for the night to work out.

Tipping back the newly acquired bottle of vodka, Michael remembered the time when Ryan was seven and had gotten the notion that she had been adopted. He figured she must have seen some movie where a girl found that information out. He would catch her hunting around his office files, going through papers in each file cabinet, crying.

"You're our girl. I don't know why you think you belong to someone else. Aren't we good enough?" He would say it tenderly. He had found the whole thing extremely amusing, and he had felt his love for her grow as he watched her distressed face.

"I'm sure of it. You don't have to wait until I'm older to tell me. Tell me now." Michael was down on one knee, and she had looked right into his eyes, searching them. One time she had collapsed into little sobs, saying "Tell me, tell me" repeatedly. He loved her strangeness and her intensely wound personality. He thanked God to have been given her. She would be the perfect companion for him, if only there weren't so much distance between them now.

The more Michael drank, the freer of his mind he became; the world was giddy and fun. He looked at the bottle of vodka in his hand. Half of it was gone. He could not believe that he had drunk so much. See, Nancy? See, world? He could hold his liquor. He felt like a boy again, sitting on the rug. The room was blurred, and he could not sit up without spinning, so he lay down and passed out drunk on his office floor.

When he awoke, it was a couple of hours later. He switched to vodka mixed with the orange juice he had purchased. At some point later in the night, after his second screwdriver, he had left for a walk and had ended up at a store that sold adult movies. Miraculously, he had made it back to his office in his drunken state, and the neon yellow bag from his half-remembered excursion sat in the corner of the room.

The night continued in a blur. He took one of his pills, which sent him to a deeper realm of drunkenness before he fell asleep and had a tortured dream of chasing something. He awoke reclined in his office chair with his feet up on the desk and the orange juice on the floor. He checked the clock and saw it was 3:05 a.m. Across the room, he saw a TV on a stand. Apparently, in his blacked-out state, he had wheeled a TV/VCR from the conference room into his office. He didn't remember doing it. It now sat unilluminated in the corner of the room. His fairly large office had a small couch and two chairs on the other side of the desk. Two huge glass windows were on the opposing walls, showing the fluorescent lights from other offices across the street and neon lights from the restaurants below. The curtains on the windows were drawn aside with a sash. Michael sat drinking and thinking about how odd it was that curtains would be hung in a corporate office, as if they were trying to make it like home. As if the place knew that he would need to stay here. Tonight it felt like home, *his* place. The glass coffee table by the little couch shone with such cleanliness and purpose that he felt even more that yes, this place had been designed for him only.

Michael looked at the bag of videos. What had he bought? He tried to remember. One was the standard, about girls and a variety of silly sex scenarios. Another one was a sampler of experimental things called *Hot Shocks*. He really had no idea what he would see on it, just that he hoped it would be weird and entertaining. But he resisted putting the video in. He just continued to sit, hands resting on his legs, gazing at the lights outside his window. If he kept his eyes out of focus, he could only see blurred white streaks or hazy patches of color. He could sit there all night, drinking and half looking. The videos really had no purpose for him, he thought, but they'd be there if he needed them, if the boredom got to be too much.

For what seemed to him like the millionth time, he went through his daily drill of thinking what his life would be like if he had become an academic. He would have had a smaller house and would probably be unmarried. He would have had students devoted to him. He would have had tenure and the summers off to write, and dinners with his friends who had stayed on and taught. He and Alex would have had their offices next door to each other, and after an afternoon of talking with students in their private offices, they would emerge tired and walk to the campus pub and order hamburgers and beers. Their students would be sitting in booths and would have waved at their favorite professors when Michael and Alex came into the bar.

He thought back to that rainy night in college when he and Alex had run from the library, a little after midnight, and stopped in Alex's dorm room to dry off. His own dorm room was farther away and the rain was coming down hard, so Alex's room was the logical place to go to. Earlier in the night, they had each worked on an essay, as the water had pounded the tall stained-glass walls of the beautiful old library. It being a Saturday night, the library had been almost completely empty, and the campus, too, was strangely vacant. It appeared that the world of other people had retreated completely out of view due to the rain. In Alex's single dorm room, they had taken off their shirts and pants, leaving on their underwear, and wrapped towels around their chests. Michael had sprawled out on the floor of the room after Alex threw him a pillow from the bed. The heater was on full blast, and both men had realized how tired they were.

Alex had been different from his usual self and surprised Michael by producing a small bottle of bourbon. He had poured two small glasses and handed one to Michael, smiling. With Alex lying on his bed and Michael on the carpet with a pillow, with only the small lamp on in the corner of the room, the two had talked about their families and finally drifted to sleep, listening to the rain. He could feel the heat from the radiator warming him.

Suddenly it occurred to him that maybe it wasn't too late to get his PhD—maybe he could still do it even though he was in his forties. But he could not imagine such a thing, could not imagine returning to grad school and sitting in the classes with young people. He saw it as too much like an admission of failure, his tail between his legs. He wouldn't try to follow another course.

Michael popped in the video of the girls and watched the plots with attempted glee. If he was going to misbehave, he better try and enjoy it. The second one was even an office seduction that tickled him. But twenty minutes into it, as he sat Indian-style on the carpet gazing up at the screen, he could not watch anymore. The girls in the video, probably all eighteen years old or so, reminded him too much of his daughter. There was a certain look in their eyes that Ryan had—a stunned kind of look, an unsure kind of invitation, vacant heated anger. He found it disgusting for a man of his age to watch such young women. It was sick, and luckily he discovered he did not get any pleasure from seeing girls in naked vulnerable positions. In fact, the sexual acts made his stomach turn. He was a father now, and this kind of nonsense was something he had outgrown. He put in *Hot Shocks* and made himself another drink. The men were really going at it. The penetration between the men seemed deeper somehow.

He had never gotten sex right. It was never right no matter whom he was with. He had been with one other woman in college before Nancy. Beth had been in his philosophy class, and he had taken her back to his dorm room one night after she had flirted with him all throughout the course of a party. From what he could remember of the night, he thought it had gone pretty well. Beth had seemed satisfied, and she had left the next day smiling with the assurance that they were an item. In class, Michael had given her cold looks. He had wanted to be the one to decide who would be his girlfriend— he didn't want the decision thrust upon him. At first Beth had been shocked, but soon she got the hint and didn't look his way anymore. He didn't like the way she dressed anyway—her printed skirts were too bright and cheery, and she was keen on wearing pastel sweaters that were the exact color of the flowers on her skirt.

———

He switched off the movie and lay back on the carpet. An intense hunger stormed in his stomach. That relieved him, as it told him what the next activity would be. He would go out to an all-night diner and get some food—something greasy and thick. He could do greasy because he was so thin. No matter what he ate, none of it ever stayed on his bones. It all disintegrated. He was the only person he knew in his forties who could eat whatever he wanted and not suffer any noticeable changes in his weight. Nothing would absorb, nothing would settle. Yet his body displeased him.

Michael stumbled to his feet and looked around the room. What if someone came in? That was hardly likely. He stashed the movies and the bottle in a drawer and left the room. He was still drunk, but he found that if he pulled it together for a few moments, he could pass for sober if he encountered another person. He walked to an all-night diner he knew of that was four blocks away.

———

Once at the diner, he sat with his eggs and fries and thought about the Peninsula. It was just waiting there forty miles away. It was a chilly night, which meant the Peninsula would be covered in fog at its desolate tip. Michael got the distinct sensation of what it would be like for him to live there alone. He felt what it would be like to be an unconnected man, like those writers who lived alone in large homes far out on the Peninsula. He could have that life—a life of no connections. It was a thrilling idea: to be a person of intrigue, a recluse, a social anomaly. Then he would not have to see his wife in their home, always waiting for something, always primed for some experience that was never going to happen.

This diner served alcohol, too, and the waitress happily brought him a hot toddy. Michael cupped the warm mug in his hands and thought of Alex, his softness, his intelligent eyes. He thought of the many nights the two of them had stayed at the college library in the big reading room, studying until they were the only ones left in the room, and they would laugh and look around themselves and finally go home. They knew they possessed a kind of dedication that none of their classmates had, a diligence that produced success, a delirious kind of pledge to their work that made them stand out. Alex always made coffee runs for the two of them and would place Michael's cup next to him wordlessly and expect no thanks. Those moments were Michael's favorite—the lack of ceremony, the respect for silence that Alex had was precious to him. Such a simple thing, yet it meant everything to him.

To be able to sit with another person and not to have to talk was the most priceless thing in the world. He had never met another person like Alex in his entire life, and he probably never would. He had never told Alex about his mental problems, but he could tell he knew. Alex saw him for who he was and accepted him—there was no need to explain anything.

And to think if during junior year he had just stayed in and studied that night as Alex had wanted to instead of dragging him to that party, Meg never would have come into their lives. When he had seen the two of them together for the first time, he had assumed it must be a silly fling, but somehow it just kept lasting and lasting. Michael had made cracks about her, for she was a mousy, loudmouthed little thing, and Alex had stormed out on him one night, making his one and only angry remark: "You are so hateful!"

Those four little words had stung, and they had made an impression on Michael's heart. After that night, a clear division had been made. They were still friends, but Meg had won. She had Alex for life from then on. That such an elegant, brilliant man could devote his life to such a mediocre little twig of a woman was something Michael would never understand. He would go to his grave not understanding, he was sure of it. Michael hoped he would outlive her and would someday be able to see her bones reduced to a pile of ash. Her laugh, her drawl, her half-hidden racial prejudices, her lack of intelligence, and her fixation on the silly details of life—all of those qualities were the most infuriating combination in one person.

Michael had once had the distinct displeasure of overhearing the two of them having sex. He had been standing outside Alex's dorm room, and he could hear the muffled sounds through the door. He stood and listened to the giggling and the shifting, and her high-pitched battle cries. That was not the worst of it. The worst was when Alex came—his moan was long and solemn. It was horrific for Michael to imagine that the moan was dedicated to this creature gripping her claws into his back.

Sex seemed the biggest joke in that it formed someone's entire life, sculpted the direction a life took. That those two polar opposites were joined as one was the biggest joke Michael had ever encountered in his life, worse than Nancy and him. He and Nancy were neutral, he felt—that was all. They canceled each other out and stood for nothing. Michael had had to stand to the right of Alex at his wedding as a groomsman, while the hideous Meg, sheathed in white, bejeweled in diamonds, grinned at her good fortune, this beautiful man who was pledging his eternal love to her. In the wedding photos Michael had looked sullen, to the point where Alex had made a comment about it, passed off as a joke and yet with a serious edge, when he and Meg got the prints back.

"You couldn't have sloughed off your melancholy ways for one day?"

"No, Alex, I couldn't," he shot back, and seriousness was permanently inserted into their friendship, as if with a syringe. The comment hurt because it was true—Michael could not do that one simple thing for his friend.

A few construction workers entered the diner as day approached—he would have to leave soon. He was still drunk, but the food had grounded him a bit. He studied one of the men who sat at the counter in his workmen boots with large, speckled hands. His gold wedding band flashed on the dusty hand, and Michael imagined that the man must have a loving wife and two daughters, all of whom thought of him as their hero.

Was there a way to fix all this with his family? He had indeed done what Ryan had accused him of. He had bitten her. He could hardly remember doing it, so when she had accused him, he had denied it. She had seemed to want him to admit to it. The problem was that in sobriety, it never seemed as though it had actually happened and so he never owned up to it. But in his drunken state, he could remember leaning over and placing his teeth gently on her neck. In that moment, he had been so relaxed that he was starting to fall asleep and did not remember who was before him or where he was. In a sober state, the memory seemed to vanish. She had stood before him, such a miraculous creation, that he felt he had to connect himself to her, and that had been his way. He was helpless to understand himself, that one decision, to take two of his pills and continue to drink, had caused him to do that bizarre thing and so to become a monster in his daughter's eyes. If he had chosen not to make another drink and take only one pill, his horrendous and baffling behavior would not have arisen in him and he would have remained a normal father, perhaps.

———

With the sun coming up, Michael knew he had to go back to his house. He wondered if John had spent the night. He walked back to his office from the diner. He locked the videos in a file cabinet, quickly tidied up the room, wheeled the TV/VCR into the hallway, turned out the lights, and locked his office door behind him. Downstairs, the security guard was asleep in his chair, so Michael easily slipped out and into the dawn.

He drove back in the half-light, swerving onto the shoulder every hundred feet or so. There weren't too many cars on the road on a Sunday morning at five a.m. He passed a few all-night diners and their lights were comforting, the rows and rows of empty booths lit up, waiting. He breezed through Orin, where the traffic lights were all switched to blinking yellow and blinking red.

When Michael walked through the side door, he saw that cookies had been left out on the counter for him, under a layer of plastic wrap. He paused in the living room by the stairs and checked the couch.

There was no one asleep there. He then crept up to his bedroom and soundlessly opened the door a foot. Nancy was curled up on her side of the bed. His space was empty, as if, even when she was unconscious and he absent, her body wouldn't dare move onto his side of the bed because she knew his place was not her place.

Michael knew it was a ridiculous moment. He didn't know what he had expected to find there. Maybe something would be out of the ordinary? Some change would have taken place. Why couldn't John have slept on the couch downstairs? To have a new body in the house, someone other than the four of them, would alter the atmosphere under their roof and would act as a catalyst for much-needed change. But there was nothing. John had probably left around ten or so the night before, as he should have. Nothing had happened.

Michael poked his head into Max's room and observed the sleeping form in bed. He then walked to Ryan's room and opened the door a crack. To his astonishment, he found her bed empty, neatly made up. It was after five in the morning, still dark out, and she was not home.

She's at Carol's, no big deal, he thought to calm himself. But he knew there was more to it than that. Something was going on. If Michael had known how difficult being a father was, he might never have done it. If he had been aware of the hours of agony that were involved with seeing a person go through every single stage of her life from birth through adulthood with little say in how it would work out for her, he would never have chosen to set this life in motion. Maybe Nancy had it right with religion. You could control more with that.

He got into his car and drove to the small coastal highway. He drove to Jill's house. All the lights were off. He did not see Ryan's car in the driveway. He passed the house and pulled over by the water.

There were several possibilities. Her car was in the garage, and she was asleep at Jill's. Her car was in the garage, and Jill let her have a boy stay there. Jill had always been a wild, tacky kind of hippie woman. She might let Ryan have her first time there. Or Ryan had taken her car and gone to be with someone, whom she was now with, and might be returning in the early hours to Jill's. It would be difficult for him to ascertain the exact reality. If the last option were the case, he could catch her. He could wait there and see if she drove back or emerged from the house in the morning.

Michael took out the draft of his novel from the box in his car and turned on the car light to read it. He had also stashed some pens in there and was pleased to find a red one. He pulled it out and began circling sentences that could be improved. The paragraph had begun so well: "The day was neither bold nor timid—it spun its wheels fairly and with neutrality, letting people come and go, but it could hardly have been called beautiful. It was a mild spring day and the grass was green, but it lacked that ripening, that opening that can be found on the freshest days of the season." But then the writing trailed off into more description and became a monotonous procession of repetition. He did indeed improve it each time he reworked it, but it occurred to him that the revisions could be endless, as it never seemed finished.

The character was a man who walked around and noticed everything, and rarely interacted with other humans. Against his better judgment, he had shown a scene to Nancy, who had gushed over it, and now Michael wanted to keep the passage hidden in his own heart forever as evidence that he wasn't just cold and clinical but could move people and create a poetic scene. His character, nameless, in first person, swims in a calm river alone at night and drifts, bewitched by the stars and freed and excited by his own nakedness. But the scene functioned independently. It was not connected to the rest of the book and was harshly beautiful in comparison to everything else he had produced.

For all his knowledge, Michael felt helpless about the idea of trying to approach an agent about his novel. He could not contact one of the two writers living on the Peninsula. He was a businessman and might be laughed at for attempting to be a novelist. He was neither a writer nor a professor. Both of those paths, if he had dedicated himself to either one, would have resulted in a stream through which he could have unleashed all the thoughts rattling around in his brain.

He tilted his seat back and let his eyes fall slightly out of focus. When he woke up it was after nine in the morning and Ryan's car was still not in sight. He drove home and parked in his driveway. All this racing around was beginning to disorient him. It was harder to remember what day it was, where he was supposed to be, and to summon the will to do the things a man of his age should do, like attend work in a normal fashion at the usual hours, use his grill, have a regularly scheduled hobby such as racquetball that he diligently showed up for.

After returning home, Michael spent the day in his study, going over bills and filing papers. His daughter was gone all day, but in the evening he heard her come in and go up to her room. When he walked past her room to his own, he heard her on the phone, laughing and talking in low tones.

Why could he not reprimand Ryan and discipline her? He felt he did not have the right; his weaknesses were so visible, and a knowing look could rouse his awareness of them all. She was stronger than he was. If he were to lay down the law, he would only be openly mocked, and he did not have the solidity or the fortitude to withstand such a confrontation. He wondered: Did she know he was crazy? Did she know? Had Nancy told her, or had she figured it out? When he acted illogically, he was a bad parent, and when he tried to be responsible and keep his daughter safe from making bad choices with boys, he was also a bad parent. It seemed he was getting it all wrong. Was there anything he could do correctly anymore?

Michael left the hallway and entered his bedroom. He felt his head spin slightly from anger and was relieved to see Nancy reading on their bed.

"I slept at the office, Nancy." He saw her weary face and knew she was about to respond with a snippy comment. He should give her something.

"Why don't I give you a massage, Nancy?"

"Okay," she said in surprise and rolled over. Michael saw the curve of her back under her green silk nightgown, the same nightgown that he had bought for her years ago. She wore it as constant proof that they were indeed linked. He loved his wife, wanted to please her, but he could not help hating that they were linked for life as fucker and fuckee, and he could not escape the fact. He saw the round curve of her butt under the silk and felt a flash of arousal, which quickly faded.

He began massaging her. He gave in and moved his hands in the style that she liked, thorough and slow, but then quickened his pace, which he knew she didn't like. He worked the loose skin on her back like dough, somewhat roughly, but she didn't complain. He was aware, on some level, that she was aroused and felt himself inevitably pulled in that direction. He didn't want to be doing this, but he would do it. It was his duty. He pulled up her nightgown, exposing her thick pale legs, and he knew she was probably anxious at having her body seen. He massaged along the sides of her thighs and then pulled down her light green cotton underwear, underwear that matched the nightgown for some pathetic reason. Maybe she had been waiting for this.

He scooped his hands under her breasts and began rubbing against her.

Michael knew he should kiss her. He would have to kiss her. Her face was turned to the side, and he leaned forward. But she remained lying on her stomach, passively ready to accept. She knew he didn't want to kiss her and wouldn't make him have to do it. He pulled down his pants and underwear and entered her, and a certain misery shook loose and began twisting in him. He knew she wouldn't come this way. She knew it too. Yet she moaned quietly for his benefit. Michael tried to pull out midway, but she pulled on his hip and sent him back in. He felt anger as he was kept thrusting by her hand on his hip. He was close, and he came, in a terrible explosion, pleasurable, abrupt. Having orgasms was deeply embarrassing for him; they always had been. In a moment of climax he felt he was writhing in the sheets like an idiot. He pulled out quickly and lay beside her. She was undoubtedly not feeling anything. The rage came back—why had she forced him to finish? She got nothing from these romps; they were childish and pointless. He looked at her face, which was looking up at the ceiling. She knew not to look at him. It hit him that she enjoyed being used.

This was what they'd come to. A strong urge to hit her seized Michael as she lay there pretending to be in a state of rapture. He wanted to slap her for pretending. Instead he got up from the bed and went to the bathroom to take a shower. He could do anything, anything in this marriage, and still she would be there, unmoving, waiting like a boulder.

CHAPTER TWELVE

Full summer had arrived. The days were longer, and everyone ached to be out of doors. Ryan's school year had ended a couple of weeks ago, and she was often absent from the house for days at a time. It seemed more and more that Michael was comfortable only in the presence of John, whom he had befriended. The two of them spent a couple of Saturdays hiking together after Michael learned that it had been John's favorite hobby when he was married.

They drove onto the mainland about forty-five minutes from Orin to a national park, and after parking the car at the trail head and walking the two-mile loop, they stopped in a small family-owned restaurant near the beginning of the trail. For those few hours, Michael was free of his family and in the company of someone who was quiet, good-natured, and actually more intelligent than Michael had initially given him credit for. Breathing the fresh air on their short hike made Michael dizzy with elation. When they clambered down from the woods and entered the restaurant, they were pleased to see that its inside was modest, basic, just as they felt it should be. They were the only customers in the restaurant, so they sat and talked after eating the greasy hamburgers. The waitress brought coffee, although they had not ordered it, and they both found that very charming because they had in fact both wanted it.

"How often did you and your wife go camping?"

"About once a month for the first year of our marriage. In the summer, we got away almost every weekend. Anne loved the outdoors. She knew more about different types of wild flowers and trees than even I did."

"You must have loved her a lot," Michael said and leaned in, giving John his full attention. He felt that at that moment, John was impressed by his concern, even though Michael's intensity seemed to catch him off guard.

"Yes, of course I did," John replied, looking somewhat bewildered, but then his face softened. "We went on wilderness retreats with our church after our marriage started to fall apart, but in the end it didn't help much."

"Was it depressing to have to go with a group after all your years of going just the two of you?" Michael asked.

John's lips twisted into a thoughtful position as he considered this. "It was for her, I think. She was always so independent. But I actually loved those group camping trips."

"It must have been a relief to appear as a couple, because when other people are around, you have to treat each other with the utmost respect. It feels good not to fall into that interpersonal hell that can be created between two people."

"Yes, it was a comfort, I guess," John replied and then stared at his hands in silence. The waitress came by with more coffee. Michael feared he was getting too intimate.

"Do they slam the religious stuff down your throat at those retreats?"

"No, it's mostly informal, more to get out and see nature.

Although there are families in crisis there. You know, kids who act out and situations like that. They say the trips help them."

"Have you noticed how my daughter acts? Have you noticed how out of control she's gotten?"

"I didn't notice that. She does seem kind of sad though, like a loner."

"Do you think she would benefit from one of those retreats in the woods?"

"I don't know. I've never had kids. I can say that it really helped other families I know."

"When was the last time you went? A few years ago?"

"Yeah, two or three years ago."

"Would you consider going again? With me and my family?" The thought was blossoming in Michael's mind, expanding into brighter and brighter technicolor—all of them in the sunshine, shaken out of their gloomy ways by the slap of Mother Nature. That was exactly what they all needed. Joy squeezed at his heart, and he felt that if John turned him down at this moment or laughed at him, he would never recover.

"I can give you the brochure, I would just be tagging along if I came. I wouldn't want to disturb you. Plenty of families go—you would meet a lot of great people."

"You aren't interested in going with us?"

"Of course I'm interested. I love your family."

As the conversation continued, Michael convinced him that the family would not be comfortable going without him, that on some level he was proving indispensable to them. John seemed to warm at this, a modest smile playing about his lips and eyes. Michael hadn't felt this content for quite some time. He felt that if he could just depart and lose himself in some random location with John's gentle, honest company, he would be able to make it through his life.

He had been going over Alex's essay when he had free moments, writing his best feedback in the margins of the piece. The act of reviewing his essay had kept Alex much on his mind lately. Alex had shepherded him through his college years, allowing for some happy memories to fill the album of Michael's life. What solace was found in the company of someone like Alex, someone elegant, dignified, yet full of good nature despite all the snobbery his good breeding implied. Shockingly, Alex was the furthest thing from arrogant or snobbish, although Michael somehow always felt he should have been or deserved to be. Michael realized that he had found the same sense of solace with John. When they spent time together, the hours flowed along seamlessly and his companionship did not irritate Michael's mind but allowed for some calm to enter.

———

That same day, John and Michael drove out to the retreat center, passing run-down sections of Rhode Island with above-ground pools and houses in need of a good painting. Elderly folks sat on the porches as they whizzed by, and off the highway, on the smaller streets, kids stood at the side of the roads, footballs in hand, and waited for their car to pass since their own lawns were too small to play on. They eventually got out to pure wilderness, with occasional houses with old rusted trucks parked in the drive. Michael met the couple in charge of the center, Bill and Joy Dover. They were hefty, ugly people, but they had a shine to them, no doubt the result of a kind of inner peace that he himself had never felt. The center consisted of a scattering of basic yet clean cabins and a small lodge where meals and evening meetings were held. Michael could imagine John and John's wife walking those trails. Then they would fall asleep after pushing the two twin beds together, his arms wrapped around her small frame, listening to the insects moan as they tried to keep their bearings in the wind. Michael was fascinated by the idea of John clinging to his wife and his marriage while she got more and more distant until she left him for good. Why would any woman want to leave a man like John? He was not the most exciting person on earth, but he was trustworthy, available, kind, and handsome in a rudimentary way. Wasn't that what women wanted?

The cabins were sparsely decorated, but what decorations did line the walls reminded Michael of Nancy. One was a wooden board, painted to show smiling faces framing the words "Home Sweet Home." For once Nancy would not feel oppressed by all the fanciness of his world but would be surrounded by what she loved. If John's wife had been around, Michael knew there was no doubt she would have liked Nancy. They were both religious and simple-minded—basic, good people. They were all good in a way he felt he could never be, and he was beginning to envy their easy ways and straightforward desires. His own desires were intangible, located in a realm that was constantly out of reach.

Michael was quickly learning that this was the very thing that had made him fail as a parent. To be unable to get strength from what surrounded him was a failing that weakened both himself and his offspring. If only he could have started over.

He put down a deposit for a weekend three weeks away at the start of August, and he and John went on their way. As they were driving back, Michael asked if he could finally see where John lived.

"Can we stop by? I'd like to see your place."

"It's nothing compared to your house. It's about the size of your garage. And I haven't cleaned yet. I was going to do that later today."

"That doesn't matter. Believe me, if I were still a bachelor, I'd keep my place messy. The only reason our place is clean is because of the ladies. My natural tendency is to keep things out of order." That wasn't even true, but he enjoyed saying it.

They pulled up to the house, which stood on a plot of grass about a hundred yards from the other houses nearby. It wasn't quite a house but resembled a hybrid of a house and a trailer. It was white, one level, and rested a little unevenly on the soil below it, so that the right side seemed a little higher than the left. Flower beds surrounded it, a cheery ring of purple, red, and yellow flowers. A flaglike banner waved in front of the door, depicting cartoonlike flowers, a cottage nestled in their midst.

The inside of the place was quite different from the happy exterior; it was poorly lit and consisted of only two rooms, in addition to the eat-in kitchen and the bathroom. Michael was a little shocked when he first saw it, but the feeling quickly began to wear off. The two couches in the living room were a drab color, somewhere between olive green and beige, and the material was shabby, worn-out corduroy. The bedroom door was open, revealing a small bed next to a dresser, with a gold cross on the wall. An old green carpet covered the entire inside of the "house." A couple of dishes sat in the sink.

John was clearly embarrassed by his place and sat down in a resigned, uncomfortable posture. He offered Michael a beer from the fridge, and soon they settled into drinking. They talked about the plans for the tree house John was going to build for Max.

"We should put it on the edge of the yard in that big sycamore tree. You know, I've been meaning to take a week off of work for a while now. I could help you build it," Michael offered.

They were on their third beers when the light had almost completely faded outside the window. John's back was slouched into the couch opposite Michael. His face bore no expression as he stared out his window. It was the first time Michael had ever seen him completely at ease. The fuzziness of the alcohol gave a soft quality to the objects in the room.

"I should turn on that lamp to get some light in here," John mused, but he didn't get up. "Shouldn't you be getting back to your family?"

"They don't need me. I hardly even exist there. It's like I'm living there, but I'm not really there. It's like I go to my office, but nothing really needs to get done that's that important. I feel I'm disappearing. . . ."

"Now come on, that's bull, man." John looked indignant, and it occurred to Michael that the man had no idea how bad his family life was, that he had a completely false conception of how their house functioned. That seemed to be a good and safe thing.

"Yeah, you're right. I just feel sometimes like things are so solid, like they have a will of their own, and I could just as easily not be there, and the machine would keep on turning. You know what I mean?"

John smiled. "No." They both laughed and took sips of their beers.

Michael realized that John and his wife must have had many good nights together in this place. Cramped though it was, it was enveloping, stabilizing, and close to nature. Michael wondered if he could drink enough so that he would be allowed to stay the night and not have to drive back to his hell. He got to his feet and made his way over to the fridge. There were only three beers left—that was borderline. It was probably not enough to get him fully drunk. He took another and gave one to John, thinking if he offered it it would give John the chance to say no.

There was a long silence, and then John said, "You're lucky to be living on the Peninsula."

"We moved there when Ryan was only five going on six." Michael thought of what else he could say about it. "That summer there was a hurricane, and she and her friend Carol ran out on the yard with umbrellas and were lifted up off the ground. It was so windy they seemed like they were flying for a second."

"Weren't you worried they'd be snatched away?"

"It wasn't that bad of a storm; mainly just the wind and fast-moving clouds. They were only lifted about one or two feet off the ground." Michael felt foolish after saying it, as if he were a neglectful father. Here he was sitting in John's living room on a Saturday evening, drinking, talking about flying kids in hurricanes, with no plans of returning home to his family.

"Why didn't you and your wife have kids?"

"We were only married for a couple of years. Anne was different, anyway."

"Different how?"

"She wasn't a normal type of woman. She hated cooking and cleaning, and while she did like children, she liked *other* people's children. Sometimes I felt she was the man and I was the woman."

John pressed his fingers a little tighter around the can, causing the aluminum to make a little cracking sound. Michael looked into his face to see if he was in a state of anger or frustration but found only a detached melancholy there instead.

"She was raised around boys—I think that's where the problem started. She was a tomboy, a mismatch."

Michael couldn't really envision what this woman had been like, but he liked knowing that another pair had been through this. He let his mind drift back through a series of corridors. It was windy outside, and now the darkness was complete. John got up, switched on a lamp that sat on a table across the room, and went into the kitchen. Michael knew this was it. He would have to leave shortly.

Then miraculously, John said, "This house is depressing. I know a bar near here. Do you want to get out of here?"

CHAPTER THIRTEEN

More and more the image kept returning to Michael's mind—that of himself living in a house devoid of other people. As he drove with John that evening, out of nowhere the image returned and took over his thoughts. The stillness of no other living beings, the absence of expectations, decisions, desires. There would be a kind of peace to his living, and his reclusive life would set him apart from other people.

The two men drove fifteen minutes to a local bar that sat on the edge of a creek. Across the street stood a campsite in the state park, where backpackers stayed before they started off onto the nearby trail. The bar had a mix of backpackers in fleece jackets as well as regulars, old men who worked nearby and came because it was the drinking spot closest to their houses or to work. The bar had multicolored Christmas lights tangled in lines a few feet above the rows of bottles. It was dark, and over the years the wooden bar had been carved into with words or initials.

Another source of light was the squat jukebox in the corner, which glowed a light yellow color as it played a small selection of fifty CDs. *Greatest Hits* was written in gold script across its side. The songs were mostly country, with some classic rock. A group of four young men sat at one of the two tables by the door. They wore their camping gear, fleece jackets and rain pants, and two of the men had dreadlocked hair.

John and Michael sat at the bar and ordered some beers. The group of campers would occasionally erupt into fits of laughter over their conversation and then settle back down into talking. The bartender was a woman, older than he and John, with bleached dirty blond hair and a wrinkled face. She seemed to know everyone in the place, including the backpackers. She had a mellow cheerfulness, as if nothing made her happier than to float from one end of the bar to the other, making chitchat with the customers.

Patsy Cline was singing "I Fall to Pieces" on the jukebox as they drank their beers. It began to rain lightly, and a girl walked in, dressed in gear similar to that of the hikers. She sat down with the group of men, and they immediately became even livelier in her presence. When she took off her coat, Michael saw that she had on a lavender-colored turtleneck and had brown hair pulled back into a ponytail. She was attractive, there was something about her. Michael saw John watching her as they talked, and all the men at the bar would turn and take her in from time to time.

Michael studied John's profile and imagined all the nights he must have spent in the bar since his divorce. "So, is this your hangout?"

"I have been known to come by, but I'm definitely not lumped in with the regulars yet." The alcohol had settled John, and Michael studied his completely relaxed face. He was actually quite a handsome man—it just took a while to see it. Some people were like that. They would hide and then suddenly appear in their own faces, reshaping the contours and owning what was theirs.

"Are you close to your parents?" Michael asked John, and as John began to speak, Michael again studied his face, half listening to his words. They had the bartender keep the drinks coming, and they shared stories from their childhoods. John had been the youngest of four brothers and had been continually escaping their teasing and pranks. Michael had begun to tell John of his own battles with his close-minded sister when a man named Steve sat down with them and interrupted their conversation. Steve seemed to know John well. He had a beer belly, and his face was crudely drawn from the extra weight he wore.

"John and I worked on the same house together last year," he explained to Michael. "Man, look at that girl. Why the hell is she in a place where it's all men and then her? Attention hussy."

John held up the brown bottle and watched the little lights reflect off its surface, then looked over at the young woman seated with the hikers. She was sipping her drink from a stirring straw, her big eyes peering up at the men around her. How could women do that so easily—display a kind of innocence? Michael wondered. It was confusing for men to witness.

"Man, you better quit staring or those hippies will beat your ass," John said to Steve.

"I can't help it," Steve said with resignation. "Besides, they won't do shit. They have no idea I'm even here, let alone looking at their girl. Rich fuckers. What do they know anyway? Their parents pay for their damn trips up into the woods, their cars, all their shit is given."

John nodded—he was more intoxicated than Michael had realized. His speech was slurred, and his eyes were less and less able to focus on one thing.

"Do you think I'm a rich fucker?" Michael said with a laugh, although he was curious to know the answer. Despite his many problems, Michael had always had plenty of money. He had accumulated much from his own job and through inheritance; he had an excess of money in the bank. In that regard, he was stable and could take care of himself and his family for the rest of his life.

"It's okay for you—you're a dad, and dads need the goods," John answered. "A father can never have enough money—there is always something to pay for with kids. Not that I would know. I haven't produced shit in my life. My damn wife wouldn't have kids with me—good for nothing. I mean, people can't live together for years and years just the two of them—they need to at least make something. If not, someone gets bored."

Suddenly Michael wanted to see John completely unravel, fascinated at what he would uncover. He ordered two shots, and they downed them.

The hiking girl was standing beside them at the bar, ordering herself another drink. She had a rather large chest and a delicately crafted face. To Michael's embarrassment, both John and Steve were blatantly staring at her.

"Here, honey, let me get this one," Steve said, fumbling in his pants pocket for his wallet.

The girl's face clouded over, but she handled it well.

"Okay, then," she said and gave him a small smile. Clearly, she pitied the three of them, yet her good manners prevented her from saying what she was really feeling.

"What'll it be?"

"Screwdriver, please." She looked over at Michael and John to see what else she would have to deal with.

"Please sit down—here, have my seat," Michael offered. He cared for neither Steve nor this girl, yet he wanted to see the situation continue, to see what the punishment would be for such a ridiculous kind of flirting—the girl was probably not even twenty-one.

"No, thank you, my friends are waiting," she replied. Michael felt the sting of rejection. Even though he had not wanted anything to do with her, it was still hard to be refused.

"You don't have to pay for my drink," she said, turning to Steve.

"Don't be so fussy. Don't make it into such a big deal. Can't a man even do *that*, I mean, are you so above me that I can't even buy you a drink?"

She stood there stunned, and her cheeks flushed, which, paradoxically, made her more beautiful.

"I never said I was above you, I just don't want you to have to pay for my drink when I'm going back to my table." She looked over at Michael, as if hoping he would diffuse the situation.

"I mean, why are you with these ragamuffin guys anyway?" Steve persisted, his voice louder than John and Michael were comfortable with.

"Steve, quit it, man. Leave her alone," John intervened.

"Oh, are you in love, John? Are you going to court her now?" He twisted up his face and, laughing, leaned over close to John. "I know it's been a long time since you got laid, but do you really think you have a shot with someone like her, just because you hang out with big bucks here?" He gestured toward Michael.

The girl took a couple of steps away from them.

"Come back. Can't you see us is fightin' over ya?" He said in a mock country accent.

Two of the backpacking guys came over and stood behind the girl. One was shorter, with a compact body and shaggy brown hair. The other was extremely tall and lanky, with pale skin and red dreadlocked hair.

"What the fuck is going on over here?" the tall one asked.

"Teach your fucking girl some manners." Steve was shaking slightly, and his eyes had the wild look of a cornered dog.

"Oh, *she* needs manners, old man? What are you thinking will happen here? You'll score? You fat old loser?"

Steve sprang to his feet and lunged at the taller of the men. As his elbow knocked into the girl's chest, she hit the wall. John wrapped his arms around Steve and pulled him a few steps away from the backpackers.

"Who do you think you are, the sheriff of this bar? You useless tree-hugging freaks?" Steve shouted at the men.

The two men stood near him, a smirk on their faces.

"What, did you drive here from Brown? Just up for the weekend from Yale? I bet you told her: we can go to a hick bar to see some local culture tonight, honey. Soak up some of the local culture on some of Mommy and Daddy's money."

Instead of being offended, the men laughed and looked over to their friends at the table, who also began to laugh.

"Get off of me, man! Whose side are you on?" Steve demanded of John, who was still trying to hold him back. His voice sounded momentarily hurt, as if he really felt John had turned on him.

"Let me go, you pussy bastard! Why don't you go after *them*?"

John struggled to hold Steve, but Steve eventually got loose. Steve, clearly drunk, swung at the tall man again, and his fist hit the man's neck. The man was hardly affected by the punch, but Steve fell backward, his face red and twisted into a grimace. Then Steve turned and grabbed John by the collar of his shirt and punched him in the nose. It was a weak punch and didn't draw blood, but it was enough to make John clasp his hand to his nose as he winced in pain.

Michael watched the scene before him with his heart pounding. It was all happening so fast, he felt paralyzed. Do something, do something, he thought. He reached out and tried to push Steve away from John, and succeeded in moving him a few feet before Steve slammed him into the bar stools. As he fell between the stools and onto the grimy floor, piercing pain shot through his shoulder. Steve looked down at him and shot out in a fierce whisper, "You fucking homo—

you can't do shit." Michael stumbled to his feet as Steve turned his rage onto the backpackers once again.

The tall man easily knocked Steve over, and then he and the smaller one dragged Steve toward the front door, his legs writhing pathetically behind him. The girl looked on, tears welling up in her eyes. Steve was deposited outside, and the two guys came back in. Michael waited to see if Steve would burst back in, but he did not.

John put a hand on the girl's arm. "I am so sorry about that. I hardly know that guy, I swear."

The "sheriff" came over to the two of them.

"That guy just sat down with us—I hardly know him. I am so sorry," John said.

"You sure about that? You sure you're not out to get us, too?" the red-haired man said and laughed. He seemed relatively calm. He appeared to be like some big exotic bird, his gnarled red hair like feathers. "No biggie, guys. Come have a drink with us—we can put two tables together."

They bought several rounds and sat at the tables by the windows. John sat next to the girl, Heather, who had relaxed and was now giving easy smiles. The kids were indeed students from Brown, down for the weekend camping at a Rhode Island state park nearby, as Steve had guessed. The group was talking about hiking and comparing stories about camping trips gone bad. Michael sat facing the window and past the lights in the window, saw the blackened bark of the trees and the thick masses of leaves against the sky.

"We got flooded—I had to stand on my friend Laura's back in the middle of a stream of water to get our bear bag down from the tree!" Heather exclaimed.

"That's not so bad," John put in. "My wife and I both got hypothermia once and lay around useless when it was snowing, instead of making our dinner and unpacking our sleeping bags. We almost froze."

"Camping schmamping, have you guys ever tried going to the bathroom during a three-day rock climb while you hang in your harness? What about when you have to ice climb down a crevasse to get your water from a glacier because you have to perimeter camp in a blizzard? Ever been stuck on a glacier?" The man to the right of the "sheriff" interjected.

"We couldn't afford to do trips like that. The Himalayas are not so easy to get to," said John.

"Forget the Himalayas, man, I'm talking about the Rockies. Or heck, go up to Vermont or Canada and you'll be set. You don't need to go far to have extreme weather, man. We'll take you, man. Come with us, we go all the time. You don't need much equipment." The "sheriff" was animated but otherwise seemed unaffected by the many rounds of alcohol. Everyone else was floating around him, getting sloppier, while he remained solid.

Michael would lose himself in the pleasant drinking but then suddenly, the image of his crumpled body on the floor between the bar stools would snap back into his mind and anxiety would course through him. Why didn't I do more? he asked himself, and a feeling of deep anguish seized him as he realized he had not helped John, had sat there stunned for most of the fight. He wondered what John thought of him—did he see him as less of a man? Why do I care so much about what he thinks? Michael wondered.

———

The rest of the night was a blur. When the bar closed, John and Michael left and sat in John's car and drank from a bottle of whisky. They reclined their seats back as far as they could.

"I should have done more to help you. I could have punched Steve if I just focused more. It shouldn't have gotten to that point—I should have done more." Tears were streaming down Michael's face, but he saw, with relief, that John had his eyes closed and had not noticed. He felt his hands shaking, due, no doubt, to his not having taken his medication. He pulled it out and slipped a pill down his throat without John seeing him.

"Naw, man. Don't worry about it, seriously," John said. "You did what you could. Steve is a real bastard, but he is strong. He's bull-headed too. It's hard to stop him from doing anything."

"Does your nose hurt?"

"No, not really. God, it feels good to be fucked up, to be a fucking mess like this, doesn't it? I am so tired of having my shit together all the time and pretending to be just fine. I am so tired of pretending to forgive my wife for leaving me, for gypping me out of a great life, and for not giving me children. She wouldn't know how to be a wife if her life depended on it—it's like she was missing that gene. My parents never liked her. My mom warned me not to marry her, and in the end she was right. My mom said, 'That woman is cold as ice,' and she was right! Why didn't I listen to her?"

"You didn't know, you just didn't know," Michael said, his head spinning and his fingers curled around the cool bottle. Remembering it, he lifted it to his lips and took a swig. A few drops splashed onto his collar.

"Are we both crying?" John asked as he looked at Michael. John's eyes were watery. "Maybe we are homos. Filthy homos, like Steve said." That set them off laughing. Michael kept turning to study John's face as they laughed, looking for something, waiting for some other comment. He suddenly wished he weren't so drunk—he could barely move. In this moment, the only people who existed were John and himself. He had no responsibilities, other than to be here with John and enjoy his company. Michael suddenly felt he was a young man, as was John, ageless, two young men getting drunk with no one to answer to. In this moment, nothing was defined yet, no big decisions had been made as to what the course of life would look like. Michael laughed until his guts started to cramp. He felt himself sliding off into unconsciousness and then bursting back. They continued taking drinks from the bottle, and eventually both passed out in their seats.

———

They slept the night in the car seats, passed out drunk. In the morning, Michael woke up with sweat on his forehead. He could feel the alcohol still oozing through his veins. It was sickeningly hot in the world both inside and outside the car, though the world inside the car was plagued with stagnancy, while outside squirrels were running around from tree to tree and life was bursting with verdancy.

"Fuck, man, oh shit," John mumbled as he groaned back to life. Whenever John spoke in this vulgar way it both disappointed and thrilled Michael. He wanted the softness of his friend's personality back, although the softness did bore him. Michael went off into the trees to pee, and, while he was walking back to the car, hunger ripped at his guts. He asked John if there were any fast-food joints nearby. He didn't want to have to get out of the car to go into a restaurant. They drove to one and ate the greasy food in silence. Every once in a while John would exclaim an obscenity and bring his hand wearily to his forehead.

Michael thought about the fact that John had been mesmerized by the young girl at the bar. It was unlikely that he found Nancy attractive if he was preoccupied with superficial charms. He also remembered, with horror, his own conduct at the bar, how he had let Steve knock him into the bar stools, how he had not done more to stop him. Shame gripped his heart, and he regretted that he had not dived into the action more. He felt he lacked normal impulses and secretly suspected he was a coward.

When Michael said good-bye and got into his own car, they chatted while he started the engine. Both of them were unsure how to part or how to comment on the previous evening. Michael was beginning to feel nauseated from the food, the alcohol, and the prospect of going home. Yet he knew he must go home.

Before he left, a thought struck him, and he turned to John, who was standing beside the car window.

"Want to come by tonight for dinner with us?"

"Sure. Should I bring anything?" John said it with ease, as if he were already part of the family, and relief spread through Michael, calming his nerves and stormy bowels. This wasn't really a parting— there would be dinner later. No need for panic. His friend was coming back.

———

When Michael arrived back home, no one was there. Nancy had taken Max somewhere for a Sunday outing—her car was gone—and Ryan was out as usual. Maybe Nancy had left him or had at least stormed out, her patience with him worn thin at last. Michael showered and kept turning off the water to listen for the sound of car doors slamming, but he heard nothing. After he had finished showering and put on fresh clothes, he went to his study and sat down at his desk but could not sit still. Had Nancy driven to her mother's house? It was possible. Michael went down to the basement and shot some pool. He could not fully relax, as someone might burst into the house at any moment. He went up to Max's room and lay down on his bed, instantly recognizing his son's distinct smell on the comforter. Each of his children had a particular smell that hadn't changed much over time. He wanted this to be his room. He wanted to be a little boy and not have a damn thing to worry about other than sleeping, getting up, being fed, and playing in the yard. This tranquil room should have been his room, and he would lie in it now and pretend that it was.

Michael slept deeply, and when he awoke, it was dark out and Max's tiny lamp with the swirling seahorses was on, glowing blue and pink in the corner of the room. Nancy must have turned it on when she came home and found him there. He could picture Max whispering "Daddy's asleep in my room" and Nancy saying "Shhh" as she held her finger to her lips, gently turned on the lamp, and left him in there. He thought, what a foolish thing for her to do. That he had been caught in such a childish and vulnerable position and had been treated, accordingly, *as a child*, angered him. The lamp with its swirling colors continued its idiotic rotation as Michael flipped on the harsh light of the overhead to drown it out. Why could Nancy never get mad at him?

When Michael came downstairs, Nancy was standing at the kitchen counter, her back to him, chopping something. Max was sprawled out coloring in the other room.

Nancy turned around when he walked in and said nothing. He saw in her eyes sadness but no anger.

"We went to a movie at the mall," she said.

"Last night—"

"I don't want to know." Her voice was firm, firmer than Michael was used to.

"I was just out with John."

She wiped her forehead with her left hand and leaned against the counter. "It's obvious I have no control over anybody anymore, whether they come or go. You, Ryan. You could have called me. Nobody seems to respect me enough to place a simple phone call."

Michael studied her. She had aged visibly over the years and wore a lot of weight around her middle. Her arms had never been slender, but they had lost what little definition they once had. Her face, too, had lost most of its angularity and it saddened Michael to realize it was all his fault. Her body was losing its form for him, and the daily disappointments were crowding over her skin, stretching everything out. Grotesquely, he was going through the opposite process and seemed to be hollowing out, losing weight and becoming more angular as the years went by. It was as if each body, repulsed by the other, had made a decision to change in an opposite way—she expanded while he contracted. Michael felt more and more like a pencil or a razor blade, while Nancy's extra weight seemed to swim around her, unsure of what it was supposed to be doing.

"Max had an asthma attack this morning. He saw me crying and it triggered his anxiety, and then he had an attack—one of his worst ones in years. It might have been a red-zone attack." She rubbed her forehead. "I don't know, maybe it was yellow, he had to lie down after it. Then when he got up, I took him to the movies because I didn't know what else to do with him. I think it might have had something to do with the fact that two of his favorite family members are never here."

"Oh Jesus, Nancy. I'm sorry."

"I hate it when you say 'Jesus' like that."

"What can I do to help?"

"Now? Nothing. I needed you before."

"I feel terrible."

She raised her eyebrows over an otherwise deadpan face. "Dinner will be ready in an hour."

"Where is Ryan?"

Nancy slammed her hand down on the counter. "I don't know," she said, her voice hoarse. She grabbed a bottle of wine and went outside. Michael followed and found her sitting in a wicker chair. He and Nancy sat on the patio, not speaking, drinking wine. Nancy had a resigned look on her face, a sternness that scared Michael.

"Well, I've got some news," Michael started. "I have a trip planned for all of us. I've got it all arranged. Should I tell you or keep it a surprise? What the hell, I'll tell you. I've scheduled us to go on a wilderness retreat. You will love me for this—it's with a Christian retreat center. John told me about it, he used to go there with his wife. It's in the mountains, and there's hiking and cabins. Max will love it because there are kids' activities—other kids will be there. Ryan may not love it, in fact, I know she won't, but she'll deal with it. *You* will love it—I thought of you when I was there."

"That does sound nice. I don't know why you don't think to ask me before you just go ahead and do things. What I could really use is a massage. This place doesn't have that, does it?"

Michael wrinkled his brow. Nancy was starting to sound like the local Peninsula women. She was acting uppity—he had never seen this side of her. He didn't know what to think of it.

"No, this place is a spiritual center. If you want that, you should head down to the day spa. I have always encouraged you to pamper yourself—why don't you just go and do it instead of talking about it?"

"I was partly kidding."

"No, you deserve it. I'll call them myself for you, give you the works. How about today?"

"Michael, I was kidding. We don't need to spend all that money. I can just soak in a hot tub upstairs."

"No, why do I make all this money," his voice coiled low in his throat, "if we're not going to spend it on things like this? I mean, isn't this why people have money, so they can treat themselves? Why do you act like we live during the depression or back in Castleton, *West Virginia?*"

"Don't talk to me in that maniacal way of yours."

"I am just saying you don't need to make everything into such a big deal—get your freakin' back rubbed by some Korean lady who needs the money—what the hell do I care?"

"How do you know it will be with a Korean person?"

"Oh, for Christ's sake."

"Why are you getting so worked up over this? I just mentioned I needed a massage, and I wasn't even being serious. It's like I'm talking to a crazy person sometimes—" She stopped herself in mid-sentence and covered her mouth with her hand. "I didn't mean that."

"You shouldn't blame anyone but yourself, you knew what you were getting yourself into when you married me. I didn't hide a thing."

"I know. I'm sorry, I never should have said that." She went to him and put a hand on his arm, a gesture that only made him angrier.

"Stop pitying me. God, your whole life is so depressing, taking care of messed-up people—me, Max—between the two of us, I don't know how you have the will to live. I know you think of yourself as a modern-day Mother Teresa, but martyrdom is not all it's cracked up to be. Get a day job."

"Calm down, it's all right. I'm sorry I got you all worked up. I just wish you would consult with me about things first so they don't come out of left field."

"I can't even stand the sight of you." Michael said it and waited for the anger to appear in her eyes. Nancy said nothing for a moment, and a look of defeat, one he knew well, registered in the features of her face.

"I know. I can't stand the sight of me either, so we have something in common." She smiled as she said it, and he laughed and softened. Michael looked into the living room, overcome with the desire to pound a glass of cold vodka on ice. The urge left as quickly as it came.

"Let's go upstairs. I want to . . . fuck you," Michael said and pulled her to him. He was going to give her what she wanted because he could not bear her expectancy for it for another second.

"Really? Now?"

"No, next month. Yes, now." Excitement lit up her sad brown eyes. They scampered upstairs, and Michael pretended to ignore the two minutes when Nancy was in the bathroom "freshening up."

She came out of the bathroom, a devilish smile on her lips, pulled up her shirt, and quickly stripped down to nakedness.

Her confidence aroused Michael, and he kissed her and planted himself into her, as they gazed with wicked pleasure into each other's eyes. He then turned her over and continued, feeling lightheaded and wild, and then yelled out when he came and collapsed next to her, giggling.

"Turn over," Michael instructed her.

"No, you don't have to, I enjoyed it. It's fine."

"Goddammit, Nancy, will you let me make you come? For heaven's sake, get over it. I don't care how long it takes."

He worked on her body until she finally began to shake and clutch at the sheets. She looked up at the ceiling, embarrassed, while he, proud, scooted up off the bed and trotted into the bathroom to take a shower. He could still successfully screw someone, despite all his problems, and he was happy to know that. He was still a man, for Christ's sake. He would never understand why she became so ashamed after having an orgasm and didn't try to. It could all be easy as pie if he just kept it light and simple. He could do this. He could do it. Light and simple was the name of the game.

———

When John knocked on the door around six thirty, Michael yelled for him to come in and John did so, a bouquet of flowers in his hand. He brought them in for Nancy, a carnation mix, and Michael smiled to himself at the tacky choice in flowers. Such were the choices Nancy would have made when they first married. It was endearing now to see it play out again.

When Ryan skipped into the house and turned to see them all sitting in the living room, John playing with Max, she furrowed her brow at the scene. It was the first time she and Michael had seen each other since their altercation a few days ago. She looked to Michael to see if he would say anything about the slap. He smiled meekly to show her he would not.

"Hope you'll join us for dinner, Ryan," John said, and now she couldn't say no. Michael had averted his gaze from her, and John was saying the words he couldn't say. She went up to her room and then came back down and drifted in, sitting by Max. When John asked the questions, the right things happened. The TV was playing a comedy film, and they were all half watching it. Michael had initially wanted to pour some gin into his seltzer water before John arrived, but now the urge had lessened into nothing. He sipped his water and politely watched the film. Nancy, too, sat in a chair and kept her eyes on the screen. She was undoubtedly in amazement at the scene before her, as seen in the little looks she stole at the kids on the floor with their books and Max's toys and of John occasionally joking with Max and laughing at the movie.

Michael wanted to blurt out: See? I knew it! A different man was needed for this house. John's normalcy seeped through their home like a great fog of goodness, allowing all of his family to relax. Michael felt that John protected them all from Michael's sick mind, his cold demeanor, his complete and total inability to be a normal father to his children and a normal husband to Nancy.

Instead of saying anything, Michael remained seated in the yellow chair across from Nancy's blue one, John between them on the couch, the teenage girl with her tan legs sprawled out by the little brother. Nancy got up to put the pasta in boiling water, and when she returned, she looked relieved to see them all still there as she cautiously took her seat again.

Ryan had not looked at him, but he wasn't hoping for that much to happen. She did turn to her mother and say, "Mom, this movie's good. Can we bring trays in here and keep watching when it's ready?"

"Okay, but then dessert at the table, like a normal family?" Nancy tried her bargaining, and it worked. Ryan looked back at the screen and nodded.

With John here, things were normal. He was the glue that held them all together. Michael could not share this with him. Best to try to pretend to be normal. Best to take what they could get and not demand more. Nancy wasn't stealing worried glances at his glass. She knew he hadn't visited the liquor cabinet. In gratitude, most likely, she rose and left the room silently. He knew why. She would prepare the trays for all of them, so that when the pasta and meat sauce were done, they could just put a large serving on each of their plates and get back to the movie.

They ate ravenously, all eyes on the screen watching Steve Martin, dear old Dad, handle each of his children's issues with aplomb.

"Can I have more, Mom?" Max asked, and Nancy swept across

the room, smiling, and took away his tray, reappearing with more food. Michael relaxed.

"Me too, Mom. More for me?" Ryan asked. Both parents hid the pleasure that had washed over their faces.

"Sure thing," Nancy said, taking her tray and disappearing into the kitchen.

After the movie ended, they went into the kitchen, where they made ice-cream sundaes on the kitchen table. Nancy had spread out the tubs of vanilla and chocolate ice cream, the rainbow sprinkles and brown sprinkles, and the hot fudge sauce. While the kids were laughing and drizzling the chocolate sauce on their ice cream and John was busy scooping his ice cream, Michael turned to look at Nancy. She was watching her kids with quiet pleasure. She turned to look at him, and when their eyes met, Michael was overwhelmed with appreciation for her and a tear came to his eye. He mouthed, "Thank you" to her, so that no one else could see, and then smiled. She stood there stunned; a tear appeared at the corner of her eye, and she wiped it away in time to offer Michael a bowl and take one for herself.

They sat for a few minutes, and then Max asked, "Another one?" and they all settled back into the sitting room and put on another Steve Martin movie, a relief to be back with him and his "Dad knows best" antics.

Nancy would tentatively turn to Michael every once in a while and smile to see if the love she had seen was still there, and he would return her gaze, out of sheer appreciation for everything she was and every tiny thing she did for this family. If there was goodness in this world, it was surely found in her.

When the second movie ended, the tired kids shuffled up to bed. Nancy looked to Michael for what to do now. She was as desperate as he to preserve what was happening. He took control as the man of the house.

"John, stay over. It's a long drive home for you, and it's late." John looked at Nancy, and she nodded. "We have a guest room all made up. It's no inconvenience."

"Great, thank you."

"Want to have a beer first on the porch, admire our work in the yard?"

"Yeah, sounds good."

"Nancy, honey, I'll be up soon to bed. I'll see you in there, sweetheart."

She smiled and nodded, taking the bowls in and then heading up to bed. He had done a good job tonight, Michael thought. He had made love to his wife. He had pleasured her. He had brought his family together. Now he had good company while his family slept. It was a different sort of night.

They sat out there in the warm, muggy evening, heavy in their chairs, not speaking much and enjoying the cold beers. He might wrap his arms around his wife tonight in bed. He knew what it felt like to have a wife and be a husband—to be proud of what she did and who she was, her loving qualities reflected in the happiness of the offspring, the family. He opened the door to John's room, delivering him there, said an awkward good night, and ascended the stairs. John would be there in the morning, he thought over and over as he climbed the steps. With John asleep below him in the beautiful house he had bought, he felt like a real man. He put his arms around his wife and held her while she slept. He let her hold his hand, and he held her tight. At a certain point, sleep took him. It was easy and natural to drift off; John was there.

CHAPTER FOURTEEN

Ryan and Dari made milk shakes and went upstairs to Dari's room. Both wore silk pajamas they had picked up at the discount lot in Orin. Dari's were a lilac color, Ryan's a baby blue. Dari's younger brother was having his sleepover party in the basement, a group of twelve-year-old boys excitedly watching movies in the basement. They could hear a steady murmuring of voices and loud exclamations. The house was alive with voices.

Ryan had slept over the last five nights at Dari's house and had no intention of leaving if Dari and her family allowed her to continue to stay. Last week they had spent the Fourth of July at Dari's family's house, grilling hot dogs as they all sat on wicker chairs outside. Far off, they had watched fireworks in the sky over the bay, and the brothers had put on a horror movie and they had all lain around watching it and clutching each other with fear. It had been a perfect day.

The girls lay on Dari's bed and flipped through a *Glamour* magazine that they had bought to go along with the theme of girlie sleepover parties. They had decided to buy the most raucous colors of the cheapest makeup and do their faces up for glamour shots from the neck up. Ryan finished covering her cheeks with rouge that resembled burn stains, picked up the dainty plastic eye shadow brush, and began to color in the space above her eyes with the glittery light blue shadow.

Kumiko gave a light little knock, a timid tap near the door handle. She pushed open the door and stood there, a despondent and quizzical look on her face.

"What's up, little bud?" Dari asked.

"Nothing." Kumiko stood by the door, her tiny hand on the knob, staring shyly at the floor. Ryan had been to the house enough times to know that something was clearly wrong.

"Okay, what's wrong, little bean? Come sit on the bed and tell us." They moved over, and Kumiko sat down in between them.

"Nothing. I'm just feeling calm, that's all."

"Okay, but if you are ever upset and need to talk, we're all ears," Ryan said and picked up her eye shadow brush.

"What are you guys doing in here?"

"Glamour shots. Want us to do your face too?"

"Yeah, but I want the electric yellow eye shadow."

Ryan finished her face and turned to Kumiko.

"Look up," she said, and the small dark eyes darted up to the ceiling. Kumiko had the flawless skin of a young girl, smooth and fine. Ryan tried not to smile, but she was enamored of the girl's pretty face and delicate features: her little nose and the jack-o'-lantern smile. She spread the yellow shadow over her lids, and when Kumiko opened her eyes, they flashed with an eerie brilliance. She seemed more of an otherworldly creature than ever.

"No rouge for you—you are perfect already as you are. I don't need to do anything else."

Kumiko went to her room to go to bed. Ryan and Dari snapped a few photos of their painted faces and then washed off the makeup with warm green washcloths.

They lay on the couch before bed watching television. Ryan lay with her head near Dari's lap, and she could feel the atoms buzzing on Dari's thigh, only inches away. The TV voices hummed and murmured before them, and when a certain program or image grew tiresome, Dari would flick the remote and something new would light up. Everyone else in the household was asleep, and the moment seemed endless.

Dari clicked the remote, and they saw a woman gliding along an old castle corridor, holding a small candle, looking desperate and afraid. It was a black-and-white movie, ancient. The movie's image would flicker, momentary visual static undoing its integrity. The grittiness appealed to both of them, and Dari remained on the channel for a while as they watched in silence.

In one swift movement, and without thinking, Ryan slid up closer to Dari and rested her head on Dari's thigh. After she realized what she had done, she lay there paralyzed and stunned by her own bizarre recklessness, not daring to move again. Surprisingly, her friend's leg did not tense against her, nor did she speak or move away. Her thigh muscle was relaxed under the weight of Ryan's neck and head, and as they continued to watch the screen, Dari gently laid a hand on Ryan's hair and stroked it absentmindedly. Heat exploded up Ryan's neck, yet she kept still.

Dari finally spoke. "Should we go to bed?"

They got into Dari's bed and lay in silence. Ryan had felt drowsy earlier in the night, but now that she was under the covers, her eyes snapped open. Her body was tensed and her breath was shallow and strained, as if she were pushing each breath out. They seemed to lie there forever, and Ryan assumed her friend must be asleep and wondered what she'd do. She didn't trust her body, she didn't know if her hands would move of their own accord if she were unconscious, acting out their secret wishes on her sleeping partner. There was a summer thunderstorm booming and flashing outside the window, occasionally sending down sheets of rain that drummed on the roof. She wondered what the gulls did in this type of weather; did they burrow down somewhere safe, or did they sit proudly on the sides of the rocking boats in the harbor, excited by the growling clouds and the electrified sky?

"I'm not tired, are you?" Dari's thin voice surprised her, and she became aware of something shifting in the chemistry of the room. She had her. It dawned on Ryan that she *had* her.

"No, I'm not." A few more minutes passed, and suddenly Ryan felt a small cold hand touch her arm and the little fingers wrap around her wrist. Ryan buried her face into Dari's neck and breathed in the smell of her hair, her lips moving. A slow, aching feeling started turning its mechanism in her gut, and she knew the deal was sealed—they wouldn't be separating. Ryan hardly had time to notice the relief she felt at the reciprocity of the feelings, so lost was she in wanting to slam herself into this body. They embraced, their lips came together, and they pulled their bodies together as close as possible. All clothes came off, and Ryan moved her mouth over every area of Dari's body, down to her bony knees and back up. After several minutes, it became clear to her that Dari wanted her to stay in one spot until a terrific spasm released itself. They drifted off, and Ryan woke up to Dari's mouth moving over her. Giggling, she found it easy to give in as the little mouth dutifully worked on her until she felt the surprising tremble and then the powerful release.

"Was that your first orgasm?" Dari asked.

"Yes."

"I gave you your first orgasm? Wow, lucky me."

The two began laughing as they moved their hands over the soaking wet sheets. Ryan felt herself surging with power—that was what had been missing from her life, and now she was completed.

They played a game with each other where one girl began to doze and the other would quietly begin to work on the other's body until she awoke full of desire and then came. It was the easiest thing in the world, and she was pleasantly surprised to know that Dari tasted like honey. The almond scent was still on Dari's skin, and she had the softest skin of anyone in the world. They eventually wrapped themselves up together tightly in the quilt and slept deeply.

At three in the morning, Ryan woke up and Dari was not in the bed. She waited a moment and heard the door open. Dari entered, carrying carrot slices and two pieces of chocolate cake on a tray, as well as a large glass of milk. They ate the carrots first, then the cake, and then shared the glass of milk. Then they dressed, tiptoed down the hall to the bathroom, brushed their teeth, returned to the bed, and undressed. They kissed until it felt as though they were blue in the face, and then slept until a quarter past seven.

CHAPTER FIFTEEN

Michael had received the invitation from Will and Mary Campbell two weeks ago, right after the Fourth of July. Will was hosting a dinner party for the Yalies, and he included a special note letting Michael know that Alex would be there and they both hoped to see him and hear his comments on Alex's essay. Will lived five minutes away on the Peninsula, and Michael and Nancy had been to his place before. It was a pretty little house, and they had a chicken coop in their yard and a stream running behind it. Four couples were attending his party, all former students and their wives. Alex and Meg were making the trek down from Massachusetts and staying the night at Will's place, or so Will told him.

On the day of the dinner party, Michael tried to feel excitement, but instead he felt terror. He had not seen Alex in fifteen years. After Alex's wedding, they had seen each other once at a mutual friend's cocktail party a few years after college, but their interaction had been strained and with his move and new marriage, there had not been much to bind them together over the many years.

His hands were shaking more than usual, and as he dressed in their bedroom, he kept getting distracted and forgetting what he was doing. Going to the bureau to get his socks, he paused in the middle of the room and looked around, then sat down on the bed, wondering what he was supposed to do.

His chest felt as if it were pulled tight in a vise or a corset, and his mind kept repeating the comments he would give on Alex's essay when asked. There was too much textual support from other scholars. He needed to add more of his own opinions around the quotes. Yes, that was it. He tried mouthing the words aloud in the empty bedroom and pretended he was telling them to a classroom of students to make it really feel official.

He couldn't have a drink now. He would be driving Nancy, and he would never put her life in danger. He had two small bottles of vodka in his jacket pocket, though. When they arrived, he would say he had to use the bathroom and go in and drink one of the bottles to calm himself down.

With shaking hands, he pulled out the familiar tan plastic bottle and wriggled a pill loose. He returned the bottle to his pocket and walked to his bathroom, filled a glass of water, and let the water slide the pill down his throat. He had on a brown tweed jacket, and he felt he looked like a British detective from another era. It was as if he were wearing a costume for an academic, which showed how much he had abandoned that identity. His brown hair showed no signs of balding, though it was thinning. He did not look right, but the thought of selecting a new outfit was an exhausting effort he could not entertain.

Alex and Meg had children, he thought. Yes, he knew they had children, two girls. But he wouldn't have to see them; the party was for adults only. He sat back down on the bed. He suddenly felt very old. His thinness, a physical quality he had been so proud of, now seemed only to indicate frailty. Signs of age were showing in his face, particularly around his eyes and in the wrinkles on his forehead. He sat on the bed in this way, observing his reflection for several minutes. Nancy had run out to get a bottle of wine and a pie to take with them to offer as dessert. She would probably be home in fifteen minutes. Michael was relieved that she was taking care of it. She really was a good woman, he reflected, and shame flooded him yet again for not loving her enough.

He looked like a tired teenage boy; an old one with some disorder that caused advanced aging on a body that clung futilely to youth. He heard the front door shut as Nancy returned and then kitchen cabinets slam downstairs. He would have to go down soon. Did he have to go down? No, he could shut the bedroom door and remain locked inside for a few more minutes.

"Michael?" Nancy called up the stairs.

Before he and Nancy left for the five-minute drive to Will and Mary's house, Michael made himself a hot coffee with brandy mixed in and put in vanilla flavoring to hide the scent of the alcohol from Nancy. He could sip it as they drove, and it would settle his nerves.

————

Michael and Nancy were the second couple to arrive, after Philip and Jane. Philip had been good friends with Alex at Yale and was friendly with Michael, though he never seemed to know quite what to say to Michael. Philip had gone on to become a tenured professor at Wesleyan, and he had married one of his former students, Jane. Jane was a pretty blond woman who had come from an upper-crust family and always wore pearls on her ears and whose tanned skin glistened around her catlike eyes.

When Alex and Meg walked in the front door, Michael beheld his old friend. His tall stature was immediately impressive, as it always had been. Meg clung to his side, her tiny bird hand clasped on his sculpted forearm, and her little heels clip-clipped across the wooden floor as they made their way inside. Michael saw that Alex had put on a little weight, but not much—he was still beautiful, but something was missing. He was wearing khaki pants and a plaid starched shirt, no doubt selected by Meg. The colors were too bright and the fit too boxy for Alex to have picked them out himself—the button-down shirt had pink and purple squares. As Meg gave Mary the bottle of wine they had brought, Alex turned his great curly head and he and Michael looked at each other. His easy, tranquil smile appeared, and Michael responded in kind and rose to his feet. The two shook hands and hugged briefly. Michael was startled to realize that he remembered Alex's smell and it was the same as it had been—pleasant and strong, like the forest.

One more couple arrived, and everyone exchanged hugs and admired the house. A sickening feeling crept through Michael as he kept an ever-watchful eye on Alex. He could not, in fact, keep his eyes off of him. Even when he was standing across the room talking to Ken's wife, Sharon, who had been a student in their class along with Ken, Michael watched Alex.

It was as confusing as seeing a diamond shrouded in silver tinfoil, something pure and beautiful muddled by a tacky imitation of beauty. His beauty kept disappearing and being lost as Michael studied him. Meg had dulled him down in the end. This was not the normal effect of aging; this was something sinister. His laugh was different. Michael had never seen a person go into and out of states so quickly, from shocking truth and beauty to falseness. Yet when the real Alex emerged in disparate moments, Michael drew in his breath every time. He was magic—yes, he was magic. He had a deep voice, one of tenderness, and he imagined Alex with his daughters and pain gripped his heart knowing how good a father Alex undoubtedly was: tucking them into bed, buying them ice-cream cones, ushering them safely into the waves hitting the beach, protective as a father should be. Would the girls turn out false like Meg or refined like Alex? There was no telling. At that very moment Meg clicked across the floor in her little black-and-white polka-dot dress, dropped her diamond-laden hand onto Alex's arm, and turned to Michael. He felt he detected cruelty behind the smile playing at her lips. Maybe Meg knew she was taking the life out of Alex, moment by moment.

———

During dinner, everyone ate the turkey and Alex commenced to talk about his daughters using the Slip'n Slide.

"You should have seen them," he said with his gentle mirth. "I went out with them, and they were jetting across the lawn so fast and then landing on the grass with such force I thought they were surely hurt! Mud everywhere! And you should see the grass—"

Meg interrupted. "Of course they weren't hurt. We would never let them slide anyplace dangerous."

"Oh, no, she's right," Alex said, growing flustered at his mistake. Michael imagined reaching across the table, taking Meg's face in his hands, and smashing it into the dish of green beans Mary had prepared. A designer gold watch flashed on Alex's beautiful wrist when he cut his meat, one he would have never picked out for himself. The light from the chandelier above the dining room table hit it every time Alex turned his hand, and it made Michael's head begin to hurt.

When Michael and Alex spoke to each other, the softness and gallant refinement returned. Then Meg would begin to hover around Alex, and his smile would become uneasy and his manner changed to one of false pleasantries. After dessert and while everyone moved to the living room to enjoy their coffee and have more wine, Michael whispered to Alex that he needed some fresh air and would he like to accompany him to the backyard? Alex's face lit up yes, and Michael realized that Alex had been lonely for his company as well.

"I'll grab one of the bottles of wine and meet you out there," Alex said in an uncharacteristic moment of mischief.

They walked through Will and Mary's yard to the little stream and remained standing, as there was nowhere to sit. They passed the wine bottle back and forth. Michael was in that perfect stage of drunkenness in which he had lost all feelings of self-consciousness yet still felt clear in his mind and could probably walk a straight line. He gave Alex his comments in more depth for the essay on the permissiveness of the unreliable narrator in the three novellas.

"You know, Michael, I have been working on that essay for over two years now, and I could never figure out why it wasn't a slam dunk when I sent it out. Will couldn't either. We give it to you, and within a month, you know exactly what to fix to make it perfect. You have a gift, my friend."

Michael didn't want the evening to end. He thought of his gazebo, newly built, just a ten-minute walk away.

"Alex, I'd love to show you all the new things we added to my yard. It's only a few minutes away. Let's go over. We can sit in the gazebo and keep talking."

"Well, Meg will probably kill me, but we never get to see each other, so why not? Let's do it." Michael tucked the bottle of wine under his jacket and they walked on the grassy sides of the windy roads, talking about college, about doing road trips up the coast on weekends, going to local bars in newly discovered little New England towns. Still talking, they walked past grand old Cape Cod–style houses, past the pond, through a wooded area, and finally to Michael's yard.

The two crossed the lawn to the gazebo, which was mostly finished, except for the ceiling latticework. The yard was immersed in dusk, and the lightning bugs were out, slowly waltzing from bush to bush. Michael and Alex sat in the gazebo and talked.

"Your house is stunning, Michael," Alex said as he took a sip of the wine. "I can tell from out here that it is gorgeous." The house was lit up, as Max was asleep inside, the high school babysitter sitting somewhere inside, probably talking on the phone to a friend.

"Thank you, we put so much into it and were lucky to get this property."

"Our house is nice, too, but it doesn't have the character that yours has. Meg is a good decorator, but she is very 'by the book' in what she chooses. It's fine, though," he said and waved his hand to dismiss the turn the conversation was taking into negativity.

"You know, I miss you sometimes," Michael said and waited, his old friend shame grinning wickedly next to his heart.

Alex smiled sadly. "I miss you too, Michael."

"Those days in college were the best of my life, I think."

"For me, too. Those and fatherhood. Holding my daughters when they were born and watching them grow up has been something I never imagined would be so wonderful." And the lines on his face appeared, lines he was happy to have. The exchange for him, the loss of freedom to Meg, was worth it.

Alex was happy. A hollow feeling inside of Michael became emptier still, and he did not know he could feel so entirely empty of all the meaning and experience in the world.

"Still," Alex continued in his sensitive way, "if I were to compile the greatest hits of my life, in terms of memories, my time with you would be up there. You know that. My time with you, fatherhood, and my life with Meg. My job is, whatever, it's a means to an end. My daughters mean the world to me, and our time in Connecticut meant the world to me too, friend."

Michael suddenly recalled the morning after that one rainy night in college he had spent in Alex's room. He remembered waking up on the floor around five a.m., still drunk from the bourbon, and putting on his dried pants and shirt to leave the room for the bathroom. Before he had left, he had turned and looked at Alex in bed. One of Alex's muscular legs lay exposed to the air, and his hand was on his chest. The blanket covered all of him except for the single exposed leg and his upper chest and face. In sleep, Alex's face took on another dimension of beauty Michael had never had the pleasure of seeing before. His wavy brown curls fell loosely over his surrendered pale face, the full lips, the strong jaw. A sudden urge to lie on top of Alex seized him, a desire to press himself hard against the solid figure. Just as strong as his desire was to kiss that mouth, the desire to have those strong arms wrapped around him, was his desire to hold himself back, which he did as he gazed at the sleeping figure with burning intensity. After he stumbled to the bathroom, calming his arousal and his pounding heart, he returned to the room and fell asleep on the floor once again. When he woke again, he recalled some sort of bizarre passion and dismissed the moment as the insanity that came from drinking alcohol and having no female companion.

In the gazebo, the two men locked eyes and passed the bottle back and forth. Michael was getting up his nerve to ask the most important question of his life.

"Did you love me?" The words had come out, but Michael now felt he might choke. The air in the gazebo was heavy, pregnant with musky night air and illuminated bugs.

"I did," Alex responded.

"Did you want me?" Michael asked.

"I don't know." There it was—a better answer existed, but that answer contained within it the seed of all possibilities, the seed of potential. Something had been there; Michael had not been crazy to imagine it. He burned all over, he quivered, and he stood up with the bottle and turned to look at Alex. There was the deeply handsome face he had admired so much, the strong jaw, the dazzling green eyes. There was the beautiful neck. For the moment, all the damage Meg had done vanished, and the face of a younger man was before him. Alex held his gaze, and for the first time Michael saw a flash of lust in his eyes. It was utterly intoxicating and paralyzed Michael where he stood, his eyes locked on Alex's.

At that moment he saw a figure crossing the lawn toward them, a horrible blur to Michael's right. Moving like an inevitable tide, the polka-dotted dress whooshed through the night. "Alex?" she asked in their direction.

Wearily Alex responded, "I'm in here, honey." She stood before the steps of the gazebo and eyed Michael with clear disdain but said nothing to him.

"I'll be back in a little while, honey."

"I drove over, Nancy said you might have wandered over here . . . I didn't know where you went."

"Sorry, honey. Go on back, and I'll join you in a while. Michael and I need to catch up." Surprisingly, she obeyed, and, giving the dark space where Michael was standing one last look, she turned on her white heels and clipped across the grass as gracefully as she was able to with her heels sinking into the dirt.

Michael sat back down beside Alex, desperate, as their time together was drawing to a close. He felt a feverish desire, confusing for his system to process.

"Alex—"

"I know."

Michael reached out and placed his hand on Alex's strong arm. The sensation was like stretching out on hot sand after a cool swim— perfect heat.

"We can't," Alex said and rose. "I don't know if we ever could, but we are too old now, that's for sure." He placed a hand on Michael's shoulder, a resigned hand, and smiled his soft smile. He was clearly very drunk, and he stumbled a bit. Then he made his way down the steps and strode across the grass away from Michael.

"Alex, can you find your way back? Do you know the way back?" Michael called out to him before he disappeared.

"I remember, Michael. I can find my way back. I'm sorry. I loved talking to you tonight. I loved talking to you . . ." he said as he disappeared around the side of the house.

Michael sat in the gazebo for more than thirty minutes. He could not bring himself to return to the party. He went inside and called Will to say he had had a wonderful time and had too much to drink, so sorry! Then he wandered out his back door with a bottle of gin, down to the old pond he and Ryan used to walk to. He sat on the sandy bank in the dark, taking swigs of gin, then took his shoes and socks off and walked barefoot and fully clothed into the lukewarm water. With the water up to his shoulders, he held the bottle to his chest possessively with the bottom half of it submerged and the bottleneck exposed to the air so he could take occasional small swigs and look around, keeping watch on the surface of the water and the brush around it.

Things could have turned out differently if Alex had never met Meg. Alex would not have gotten married, or would at least have put it off until he was settled as a professor. Yes, they would have been poor, but poor and beloved. And they would have had each other's company for all these years as they watched the students come and go from the university together—youth entering, while they slowly aged on the beautiful campus. Michael would have published in the academic world, and Alex would have helped him edit his pieces before Michael sent them off. Perhaps they could have moved next door to each other or, if the house was large enough, have shared a house. Michael could have taken the upstairs and Alex the downstairs, and before bed they might have read together in the living room before a roaring fire. Complete peace would have been the makeup of that house.

Nancy wouldn't find him out here, and if she did, he would just sink below the surface. The little fox emerged, walked to the side of the pond, and stuck its tongue into the water, lapping up a few little gulps. It sensed him there, floating in the middle, and raised its head, looking squarely at him. Michael looked back, happy for this nonhuman company. He hoped it would stay. He tried to compel it to stay with the intensity of his gaze. The fox stared back, unable to make sense of what Michael was doing in the middle of the pond at night; this was usually his terrain for nighttime drinking. Then he quickly turned and scampered off, out of sight.

———

When Michael walked into his house through the back around midnight in his wet clothes, still partly drunk, he was surprised to see Ryan in the kitchen making tea, having just gotten home herself. She looked at his wet clothes and concern washed over her face.

Utterly defeated, Michael dropped his normally stern countenance and just stood there.

"Is everything okay?" Ryan looked again at his wet clothes and the mud on his knees. "Dad, I'm sorry I hit you."

"Ryan, I'm sorry for everything. I'm so sorry for everything."

"Is everything okay?" she asked again, her face softening.

"No, it's not, but it has nothing to do with you. You're my special girl, Ryan, you always will be." He found he was close to tears. "I want the best for you." Embarrassed by his sudden emotion, he quickly went up the stairs and locked himself in the guest bath for a shower.

CHAPTER SIXTEEN

Packed to the brim with sleepy, distracted bodies, the car headed west on Interstate 20. It passed dunes topped with dried-out weeds, and the sun flashed brilliantly, reflecting off everything—off the windows of other cars and the restaurants they passed, off the pavement, and off the ocean that glittered in stunning blasts when it appeared around a bend. Ryan and Max sat in the backseat, Ryan looking less miserable than she had in days past. Nancy and Michael had gotten her to come along only after Nancy had threatened to take away her weekly allowance if she didn't, something that would have forced her to find part-time work for spending money. She had one condition that they had granted: she wanted to bring her friend Dari along.

During the drive, Michael thought about the dinner party he had attended a week ago, and he wondered if going had been a mistake.

Alex had still been the most poised of anyone in the room, but his elegance had faded, like an old painting too long neglected. Meg had become more grotesque, a cartoonish bleached-blond nightmare. Michael had never before been so repulsed by another human being, although he had disguised it well for the sake of the party. Meg was the most unnerving, most gut-wrenchingly soul-killing woman he had ever encountered. Recalling her jokes made him wince with pain; remembering the sound of her voice made him want to split the earth apart.

Michael pondered all of that as he drove the car to the retreat center. Whenever he recalled his questions to Alex, asked with a vulnerability that he didn't know he possessed, and remembered the responses, his stomach turned and then tightened, as if an internal fist were keeping a stranglehold on him, a grip on his spine, lest he collapse and spill all over the world. Images were hitting him in a series now: Alex's lips saying "I don't know," Meg crossing the lawn in a blur of white and black polka dots, Alex looking like an ordinary man when placed beside Meg.

Michael had been up all night, and his hands were full-on shaking, though he was able to drive. He kept pouring more coffee down his throat and wiping the sweat from his brow. Everyone in the car kept talking, their voices disrupting his thoughts. His family was packed into the family van, and John was following in his own car. Michael had spoken little, and he could tell that every once in a while, his family members and the girl would steal a worried glance at him. Michael couldn't bring himself to utter a single word, and he drove clutching the wheel tightly.

———

When the car arrived at the center, the place was even more basic than Michael remembered. The pine cabin he would be sharing with his family and John had four bedrooms, but each of the rooms had only bunk beds, and he was shaken with embarrassment, for this was all his idea.

There was afternoon prayer in the Solstice Chapel, and the group made their way over to it. They sat in a pew, all in one long row, and Michael realized that there were no other families in the chapel with them. It was the middle of the day, and it was just their family with the landscaper and Dari. Every once in a while, everyone looked at Michael, waiting. No one talked, and Ryan and Dari appeared to be smirking at each other. Ryan's little mouse of a friend hadn't said much to Michael but seemed to have become best friends with his daughter overnight.

Max leaned forward and turned to look at Michael, and his eyes looked slightly frightened. Even Nancy, ill at ease, was sitting very upright, and it was clear to Michael for the first time that everyone present thought he had lost his mind. Nancy did not seem to be enjoying herself, although she was trying for everyone else's sake, and John was especially quiet. This was supposed to be the kind of thing that would light Nancy up—she had been waiting years for something like this, or so Michael had thought. The skin on the back of his neck began to itch. When the owners of the retreat center, Joy and Bill Dover, came out and began talking only to their row, as they were the only ones present, the group bristled and stiffened under their kind gaze. Michael felt that if he did not remove himself from the room immediately, he would indeed lose his grasp on keeping the lid firmly pressed down.

"It is so good to have John back with us again. And he's found new friends. It is amazing to see such a large and beautiful family— two beautiful sisters, and the little boy and a couple here to reconnect away from the hectic world, get back to 'the stuff of the earth,' as we like to say." Bill held his hands together in front of his rather large belly, drawing everyone's attention to it while he spoke. He turned to his wife, who smiled and began to speak.

"Bill and I have been here for over twenty years, and we've seen a lot of families come and go. People come because at home there's always the television, there's always something to pull you away from the people you love the most. People feel weak these days, weaker and weaker as they have too many obligations, too many movies, video games, laundry lists, school papers . . . I could go on and on. That's why my husband and I came here and started this retreat center. Our marriage was in a rough patch, and we didn't know if we were going to make it through. But we did, and we're here, and our family is the stronger for it."

Both had on matching lime-green T-shirts and stood under the stained-glass windows in dazed serenity. Had John told these people of his troubled marriage? Had they tailored their speech to fit what they felt was a troubled dysfunctional family? Michael had no idea whether or not John had told the Dovers anything about his family's problems. He remembered his sister, Sarah's, awful grin in the photo she had sent of herself and her gaggle of children. It was a grotesque, hearty grin, one that seemed to show either transcendence of the problems of the earth or utter disregard for them and rapture for her own private world.

"Bill will read a welcome passage, adapted from the Bible, and then we'll have a period of silence." Michael thought of Alex as he had seen him at the party; there was a lost wildness, something crucial had been rubbed away—a slow killing. The way he held a cup of coffee was different, the way he sat in a chair was different. But in their time in the gazebo, Michael had seen the hidden beauty of his character emerge, and it had taken his breath away. The moment was beautiful, but to have Meg march across and snatch it away filled Michael with anger, and to see Alex leave with Meg, once again an ordinary, uninteresting man, made their exchange in the gazebo seem to be a fantasy. Meg got to lie down with him every night in bed and hold him. What had she ever done to earn his hand? Michael wished above all wishes that he had never gone to the stupid dinner so that he could instead remember Alex as he had been in college: fresh, innocent, respectful, lanky, intense.

Every time Alex made love to his wife, she took another part of him for herself, she stole a bit of his preciousness and pulled it into her feverish vagina for her own purposes. She was the most horrible person he would ever encounter in his life—Michael knew it. And if it had been medieval times, he would have enjoyed nothing more than to kill her. But he would never be able to put an end to her. The thought that she could outlast him made him physically ill, that she might live to see him reduced to nothing but a pile of ashes would be a horrible fate. Alex was gone; it was blasphemy, and no one saw it but himself. He was the only one who had really known Alex and seen him for what he truly had been—a perfect human being, his beloved.

Through sheer force of will, Michael made it through the rest of the meeting in the church, back to the cabin, and set out his toiletries in the modest bathroom.

———

They went into the cafeteria for dinner. Some hippie boys working at the retreat center kitchen eyed Ryan and Dari with interest. They were probably fresh out of high school and had come here on the work exchange program that was advertised on a flyer on the board in the registration building. They might have driven down from a state like Vermont to escape drug-addicted parents and attempt to clean up their lives. Pea-green plastic tables filled the room, and the family sat on orange plastic chairs.

There was an evening bonfire and everyone went, including a new couple that had arrived shortly after Michael and his family. The three scrawny cook boys were there, and the Dovers, of course, ever present, unstoppable in their gladness. They all sat on wooden benches with wooden backs, and when Michael stretched back, he suddenly found himself very relaxed in the night air with the fire burning and crackling before them. Joy Dover told a sad Native American story about a man who had been killed protecting his lover from the bad intentions of other men, and in her sorrow after his death, his lover had stood high up on that rock ledge—Joy pointed to the one on the mountain behind her—and she had jumped to her death. It was said that she had become an eagle that flew around the mountains and forests looking for the other eagle. The sad story quieted everyone, and a serene, introspective mood lay heavily on the group. Joy and Bill went on to sing a Native American song, and then they told stories from the Song of Solomon. Michael's eyes were closing. With his head nodding forward, he slept.

When he woke up he was alone, and the first thing he saw was the campfire, still burning before him but smaller in size. The stars filled the sky above him, and Michael found he was wrapped in a blanket. He had been lying on his side on the bench, passed out asleep. It might have been the deepest sleep of his life. He heard the hoot of an owl, and the fire crackled every few seconds. He forgot where he was, and he pulled the Native American blanket more tightly around him and dozed off again. It seemed his systems wouldn't allow him to stay awake. He actually tried to wake himself at one point and open his eyes fully, but they kept shutting. He could hear the fire, feel its heat, and hear the wind moving through the trees, the side of his face surrendered against the wooden plank, but he could not keep his eyes open.

The trees above him were tall, and they swayed gently and bowed their green tops judiciously over him, making friends with the mild wind. At one point he heard the sound of a little animal moving under the platform below him—a mouse, chipmunk, or some other ground animal. It did not startle him, and his eyes remained glued shut, listening. It seemed an enchanted forest. He felt as if he were having the sleep denied him for forty years. He was the wood. He was the fire and wind. There weren't any dreams, only the quiet world of the deepest levels of his mind, the world of shapes and primordial sounds and movements. His bone marrow was having a "conversation" with the elements, and more essence was being negotiated.

At dawn, Alex's original young face appeared in his mind and Michael's body began groaning awake. The face was expressionless, then that smile, enough to begin the familiar twisting pain around his heart. Michael's eyes snapped open, and his body began to tense once again.

A memory emerged from somewhere deep within him. It was from that drunken night in college, when he had gone to the party, found his arms around somebody, heard laughter, awoke remembering nothing, and walked around the campus ashamed afterward for the rest of his college career and, in fact, the rest of his life. The memory was about five seconds long, but it was the key. Before he blacked out, Michael remembered, his arms had been around the strong torso of a crew boy, the captain, Skip Brenner, the great rower for the university team. Skip was over six foot three and had bright short blond hair. Skip was looking down at him with disapproval and seemed to be moving around with the parasite Michael attached to him, perhaps as part of a joke since Michael would not let go. Michael remembered enjoying the ride of clinging to this man, and then he suddenly reached up, trying to climb up Skip to reach the handsome face. His mouth made it as far as Skip's neck, and he pressed his lips firmly down. He heard noise, shouting, and he was hit hard in the face, and then blackness. He remembered nothing else until he woke up alone on the lawn the next day.

No wonder he had put such a memory out of his mind. It was the truth of a desperate man. The day after that terrible party, and all the days thereafter, Michael felt a growing dread at the thought of staying at the university to get his PhD to teach. Instead he had a desire to get away. He began taking business classes and knew that upon graduation he would go for his graduate business degree at another school in another city. He had gone to the party in the first place because Alex had had his second date with Meg that night, and she had very quickly become his steady. It all fell into place as one gigantic debacle that had reached its tentacles across his life this far.

He had clung to Skip as a lowly barnacle clings to a ship. He had wrapped himself around the body of a man, ridiculed by all around him, exposed for the lunatic he really was. The party guests must have all laughed and pointed at Michael for a good while, until the joke got tiresome and Skip got really fed up and shook him loose. But no, Michael had come after him again, a predatory, primitive version of himself hell-bent on getting what he wanted, contact. Until he had been punched in the face and dropped onto the lawn, ultimately harmless, a nuisance no more. A man. To do that to a man! How could he have forgotten the details of that night?

He remembered being so disappointed that Alex could not accompany him to the party, as he usually did, because he had a date with Meg. Michael remembered drinking and laughing with the crew team, but he had somehow completely repressed the rest of the night, his embarrassing lack of control, his parasitic desire to be close to Skip, the tall, impressive form of a man. He did vaguely remember his sore jaw when he woke up on the lawn and ran back to his dorm, utterly ashamed before others saw him, but even then he did not know why he was so ashamed, that even then, so close to the events, the memory was gone.

His shame at recalling this memory now was so large that it silenced him, and he walked along the retreat's lake in that silence, letting the memory slip back to its dark place in his heart. He was washed out, drained of all feeling, drained of all desire. His anxiety was on hiatus, and a sense of hopelessness took its place. He remembered the men who had stood in his father's court for conducting illicit activities in a men's bathroom on the outskirts of town. His father had dealt with them with the same even-keeled approach he gave to all his criminals, but once home, over dinner, Michael's mother had asked him how his day had gone and he had mumbled, "Faggot perverts."

Michael walked back to the cabin in which they all were staying and looked in the window to John's room. The curtain was half drawn, and he could see John in deep sleep curled on his side, the room shadowy in the first light. The walls of his room were light blue, and there was a crucifix on one side. Michael looked down modestly at his own hands that he held together, not in prayer but as people do with each other, palm to palm. They were nice hands, he thought, as his mother had always told him. He looked in the room at John's hands, which were folded in front of his chest. More gnarly, more character, those hands had.

Michael walked through the grass by the lake that had clear emerald green water in it, shimmering in the early dawn light. He would recommend swimming in it to his family. He walked up the steps to the old wooden chapel beside it and tried the handle. It opened, and he entered. Bill was sitting in the first pew, his eyes closed and his hands at his sides. Several candles were lit on the altar before him, and other than the candles and the light streaming in through the stained glass, reds, greens, oranges, and blues, creating a swirl of color on the church walls, the room was mostly dark. Michael sat next to Bill, a few feet away, and when the man didn't open his eyes, Michael closed his as well, joining him in full darkness. His hands were shaking lightly, but he allowed them to buzz at the end of his long arms.

He remembered his father's constant looks of disapproval and his irritation when the two would find themselves alone in the hallway. "Oh . . . " his father would always say when he found himself confronted with his son at the other end of the hallway, and then his father would force a smile when he remembered his manners. Michael would smile back politely and then look down, to show respect, to show reverence. But now, he was aware, the smile had been coated in shame. The two bone marrows had had a conversation while they both slept in the house, father and son, and the father had not liked what was in his son. His father was proud of how he loved women, loved their bodies, loved their style, and he had been most proud of the wife he had selected for himself, the embodiment of femininity and grace and style. He must have hoped he could have at least shared that appreciation with his son, the womanizing trait, the desire to devour the female flesh that walked the earth.

Michael allowed the thoughts of his father to slip away in the silent church, and thankfully, Alex slipped away too. He remembered his mother in her bed at home, and he knew he must see her soon. He had to see how she was doing and to be under her kind gaze again. He opened his eyes and saw that Bill was staring at him and smiling. Bill didn't say anything, he only waited.

"I'd love some counsel," Michael began.

Bill nodded. "I would be happy to help, Michael."

"I am having issues delivering on my obligations as head of the household."

"A family needs a strong leader. Are you having issues with fidelity?"

"Not exactly that."

"Well, that's good. That type of betrayal is hard to fix. I'm so glad it's not that. What can you not follow through on? You are obviously feeling troubled, and your family looks to you to be their leader. Women are the weaker sex, more powerful in some ways since they are creators of life, but they look to us for strength and leadership, to show them the way, not to mention the children."

"I know," Michael said and looked down, sighing wearily. "It's being married that's hard."

"Marriage is hard. It's a long road. There are times when you hate the other person. Every couple experiences this. But you have to stay the course. Remember why you fell in love with your wife, and let that glue bind you back to her."

"I was never in love with her, Bill." The words just came out, and both men were shocked and silenced by the hideous, helpless reality that they created.

Bill struggled for something to say. "Can you fall in love with her now?" He turned to look at Michael. Michael saw that his face was desperate and that he truly cared about Michael's predicament. A kind man, devoted to helping others. But Michael and Nancy could not be helped.

"No, Bill, I can never fall in love with her."

Bill seemed to accept that after a minute of sitting. "Okay, then, if you can't honor her, you need to let her go and let Christ take her in his arms for comfort. She at least needs that."

Michael spent the day swimming. The water was deliciously cold, and there was a wooden floating dock that the girls swam to and lay across. Ryan even swam Max out to the dock, holding him in her arms, laughing. Nancy sat on the shore with her cover-up on, wearing a large sun hat, but at a certain point she took out a book and seemed to relax. Michael had taken one of his pills, so his hands had stopped shaking and he was getting that familiar foggy feeling in his mind, the thoughts were dispersing, and everything was slowing down to place him in the moment. He swam halfway around the lake, occasionally darting down to the bottom, where round granite rocks and a few lone dark fish sat, and swimming back up to the surface. It was a beautiful, sunny day, not the slaughtering kind of heat but merciful, with a breeze. He remembered swimming this way a few times as a child, with his father watching from the shore. He would show off and dive dramatically down to the bottom in order to attract his father's attention. His father had smiled at his brazen swimming, especially when he was younger.

He saw John waving to him, and then John entered the water and swam out to him.

"I'd like to swim around the lake too, if you don't mind," John called out, his face gleeful as he paddled to keep his head above water. So the two thin male forms moved through the water toward the other side of the lake with Michael leading, and when they rounded the bend, Michael saw that there was a small private beach, attached to a little yellow house. No one was around, and the house seemed to be shut down for the time being.

They lay down in the grass just above the little beach with their feet in the dazzling gold sand. John's chest was thin, but it was attractive—pale, not too much hair, with nice trim arm and shoulder muscles. He realized that John's body was not too different from his own. He could get used to this company, he remarked to himself as he had so many times about John. His silence helped Michael make it through this life because the crowded thoughts dissipated with no additional chatter. The wind picked up and made little ripples on the water and sent a small stream rushing to the shore.

Again Alex's solemn young face appeared in Michael's mind, causing his heart to flutter. He cleared his throat. "John, you've come to mean a lot to our family."

"I feel the same. You guys have brought me back to life. It's so nice to be around children, too. I always wanted kids, but it might be too late for me now."

"If anything should happen to me, I want you to help out and be part of things—whatever's needed . . . would you consider that?"

John sat up, alarmed. "Are you sick? Did your doctor say something?"

The word "sick" stabbed Michael like a knife, but then he realized that John didn't mean it in an accusatory manner. He was only concerned about Michael's health.

"I don't want to get into the details," Michael replied, "but if anything should happen to me, I would need to know that Nancy and the children are taken care of. I need to know that."

"What are you talking about? You are sick, aren't you? Does Nancy know?"

The word "sick" could mean so many things, Michael mused. He was sick, in a sense. "I might be sick," and when the words escaped his mouth, it was such a relief to say them. "I have a malignancy—"

"The doctor found a malignancy?"

"Yes, they found it. It had been there for a while." Off in the distance on the other side of the lake, a red kayak drifted by with a young couple paddling—the woman paddling in ineffectual strokes, hitting the water with little chops. The man was trying to paddle forward in smooth strokes and he was carrying them forward.

"Oh, Michael, I'm so sorry. I'm so sorry."

"Nancy doesn't know anything, and I would like to keep it that way."

John sat stunned. "Okay."

It was such a relief to tell John of his inabilities, to tell him that something was wrong. This conversation felt entirely honest, though it was not technically true. It felt truer than much of what he said to other people, and it was as far as he could get with the truth.

"That's why you brought me here to the retreat center, isn't it?" John said. "To tell me this?"

"Yes, John." Sleepiness was flooding his mind, and the day before him seemed real and then not real. "John, can we just sleep for a little bit? The sun is so nice—"

"Yes, let's take a nap. I didn't sleep so well. Let's rest. You will need your strength, so let's rest."

Michael smiled to himself and sank into sleep. He was being treated with sympathy now . . . something was wrong with him, and he needed the sympathetic response of a kind person, which he was being given. When he awoke, it was cloudy and John was lying on his back with his hand over his face, not asleep but trying to be. Michael tapped him on the shoulder, and the two eased themselves into the cold water.

Swimming back, at around the halfway point, Michael's body felt heavy again. It was hard to move his arms through the water. The tiredness was creeping back into his bones. He realized that it might be nice to fall asleep in the water, be pulled under, and allow the water to seep down his throat. He could slip to the bottom of the lake, life could leave him, and he could be food for those sleepy black fish that surely hadn't had a good nibble for a while. It would be a peaceful way to go. He stopped moving and opened his mouth slightly. The water started to go in, and his body fought him instantly and he began to cough out the water, preserving himself. He did the slow crawl through the darkening water, as more and more clouds formed overhead. Drops of rain hit the top of his head and the water around him, but he barely noticed. Eventually his feet hit the sand. John exited the water behind him. The rain was coming down hard now, and the two men ran up the side of the hill laughing, getting their feet muddy. They had no towels, and they ran across a field to the cabin and sprinted inside.

After showering and wrapping himself in a towel, Michael heard the shower turn off downstairs, too. The two men were mirroring each other in different parts of the house. He felt they were the same person, almost; different versions of the same man, and one day the one below would be the one above. John would be showering and climbing into bed with Nancy. John would rub her back at night while she fell asleep. It would be better, and her time with Michael would fade away as if it had never really happened at all. Michael slid into bed beside Nancy for the last time. She was asleep, enjoying her nap. He fell asleep, too, with his arm slung over her. She nestled in closer to him without waking.

———

After dinner there was evening prayer, and everyone looked happy during it, quite a change from when they had arrived at the church. Nancy was relaxed, and the kids were sun-kissed. Ryan was getting the freckles she got when her face tanned. John was solemn and gave Michael loving, sympathetic looks. Other than that, the group was a portrait of happiness. The longer he stayed, the harder it would be to leave, Michael realized. It had been a relief to tell John that something was wrong with him, but it had also set forces into motion. He would be leaving the family, and as much as he had desired it for years, now that it was here, he realized he loved Nancy's dear face, he loved to see his children beside her. But he had to leave. He had never belonged here. His hands began to shake, and his heart pounded. Again the face of Alex and his lips saying "I don't know" and again his father's disapproving eyes as he studied Michael. He must leave, or he would never be able to rip himself away. He must go now.

Michael bent forward in the pew and whispered to Nancy, "I'm not feeling well, sweetie—I need to lie down."

"Let me come with you." She moved as if to get up.

"No, please stay here—don't cause a scene. Just let me slip out, okay?" He rose to his feet and shuffled past the two girls and Max and John, ignoring their inquiries, and made his way out the door and into the night.

He staggered to his room and lay on the bunk but sprang up instantly. Someone would come find him. They would surely be back soon.

He gathered up his leather travel bag and left a note with the woman in the office, trying to word it with special fervor: "I need to be alone right now, Nancy. I'm not feeling well and just need to rest. I am going home. Please don't come after me. Please stay as everything is already paid for."

"Please don't let them leave—tell them to enjoy the trip. I just need to lie down." Michael walked down to sit by the water of the lake behind the chapel. He was shaking, and he knew he had to leave immediately. His stomach was growling with hunger, yet he felt nauseated at the same time. He wrote a note that he taped to the door of the closed office door of the Dovers: "Make sure John and Nancy get married." Then he found his car in the darkness and began the drive back to his house.

———

As he drove, he thought about Alex. If he could have only gotten one kiss, one kiss from those full lips, perhaps he could have had one moment of passion in his life and died a happy man. It would have been so easy for Alex to have given him that one moment, something true he could have savored.

The tiredness began to set in. His eyes kept closing as he drove. He stopped at a parking lot at a beach he used to go to with his family, turned off his car, and crawled into the backseat to sleep. His dreams were twisted all night. He saw candles lit by a bed and a man and wife in it. Joy Dover lay under her husband, Bill, as he moved over her. In nakedness, their bodies were exactly the same size, thick and rotund, the only differences being the two parts that were now engaged in this tender battle, interlocked as they worked slowly into each other. Bill would lower his head occasionally to kiss his wife, but they never stopped their rocking movements.

Michael tried to turn off the image and felt the itch for it to be over, for them to disconnect and once again be separate, but the dance seemed to go on forever, as if they were postponing returning to their distinct selves for as long as they could. They resembled to him two earnest round beetles, who were harmlessly enjoying the simple pleasures allowed them below the spout of a watering can. Their skin looked coarse over the spread of their backs and arms, but they had a secret center hidden below their movement that was delicate and soft like a wound, a part shown only to each other and with the utmost reverence. The obscene thoughts made his stomach churn.

He awoke a little after midnight, his eyes snapping awake as the wind howled outside his car. A strong desire to go home one last time seized him, but before he left, he went out onto the rocky beach on a jagged edge of the Peninsula and let the wind blast him on all sides. The wind was moist and slapped the side of his face lightly. It was chaotic out here and very alive. Water churned below him, and air raced over the rocks aggressively. After a few moments of standing with his eyes closed and feeling the elements have their way with him, he got back into his car and drove home.

CHAPTER SEVENTEEN

After he returned to his house just before one a.m., the dark hours wouldn't let him sleep. Michael studied the rooms that made up the structure. The living room had acquired a salty smell over the years. Its sterility was giving way to the constant mist and rain that hovered over the land. He could smell the traces of sea air on the pillows, and the wood, originally fresh and light colored, had become darker. It was possible, he thought, that someone entering the house might not immediately know which room was an addition and which was the older, more authentic part of the house.

He called the retreat center to assure them that he had made it back safely and was resting at home. Relief rushed through him upon reaching an answering machine—he wouldn't have to talk to an actual person but could just leave a message.

Michael's plans slowly started to reveal themselves as he found himself imagining living in the empty rooms of his mother's house, without her, and if the phone were to ring now, he anticipated that the call would be an announcement of her death. The thought terrified him and also gave him enormous relief. For nothing was clearer to Michael than the fact that he had failed both as a husband and as a father. Once he had fully admitted it to himself, he could no longer stand living among them. He had not been cut out for any of this and knew there were others who could have done it better.

The past twenty years of his life seemed to him an illusion or a distant dream, a life someone else had lived, and he could not remember how he had actually done it. The births of each of his children had had an intensity to them that now seemed unreal. His father's death and the months of depression that had followed it, when Nancy had patiently cared for him and put up with his moods and naps, seemed to belong to the realm of dreams. Michael now needed that phone call from his mother's caretakers more than he needed anything else in the world, to be shoved finally into an existence different from this one.

He saw that he should have not abandoned Alex; that had been a mistake. Instead, as painful as it might have been, he could have shared Alex with Meg. Alex would still be a magnificent being if he had been there for him. Michael would have helped preserve it in him. Now he was aware that he had another chance at closeness with John, one that was quickly retreating. He did not have the strength to claim what it was he so desperately wanted. His life had been woven into a tapestry of fear and desire that was finally unraveling, and he was not sure he had the energy to do it in this life. He was too weak, too fractured.

With horrific irony, it became clear that if John married Nancy and became the father of his children, Michael would never again be able to spend time with him as he did now. His new friend would be gone, and he would be truly alone.

How badly he wanted to lie down by himself in his own house, but it was never safe. What if they all returned home? The intruders would come in for him from all angles. There would be nothing more pleasurable for him than to lie down on the living room carpet with a pint of raspberry sorbet and some vodka, watch the house get dark, and then fall asleep with his head on a soft pillow. But he felt he didn't even have the right to do so, as none of it was truly his. He wanted to lie down with John and say inconsequential things to each other.

Michael realized what he was thinking as he stood examining his house, his desires to lay down with a man here, and he bolted upstairs and got his sleeping pills. He found a dark corner in the basement on a couple of old blankets, a place where he surely would not be discovered, took three pills, and went to sleep.

———

When he woke up, he looked at his watch and saw that it was after five p.m. Had they come back? He went quietly up the basement stairs. He heard no signs of life in the house and saw they had not returned—no bags, no car in the driveway. Relieved, he packed two suitcases of his things, took a box of important papers and documents from his study, and loaded them into his trunk. He had a sense that he would not be returning to his job in Providence. At dusk he walked into the woods behind his house, sat behind a large rock out of view, and watched the darkness begin to overtake everything. He did not want to be home when they all drove back in John's car. They had probably had breakfast and lunch at the retreat center's mess hall. He imagined Max, Nancy, and John sitting at a round table and three other families scattered around them, eating solemnly and occasionally raising their heads and talking.

He remembered the green plastic tables and orange plastic chairs, and the terrible glare of the overhead fluorescent lights, beating their ugliness down on the hunched-over families. Michael's heart began to race once again with the realization that they were all more than aware of how faulty he was, how unfit and unsound. How badly he wanted to join them, and how ridiculous he suddenly felt. When he got hungry, he ate some nuts he had brought in a bag, and when it was dark, his mind began to race. Had they stayed there or had they come home? What would home look like now?

When the night was truly in bloom, he walked around the side of the rock and beheld his house, two hundred feet away. The house was shockingly pretty in the moonlight, so large, such an impressive accomplishment, being able to afford a house like this. He walked up to it, cautiously, a new knowledge taking hold. It was not his house anymore. He got to his knees, crawled into the underside of one of the larger hydrangea bushes by his house, and found he could be completely concealed if he lay in a ball. He would stay here because it was safe. His heart would flutter with panic, and twice he took a pill out and put it in his mouth to calm him, and so he lay, half awake and half not. Suddenly he heard tires on the gravel driveway, car doors slamming, and Max's sweet voice calling out to his mother in the dusky night. John said something to Nancy. The two girls laughed as their feet drummed up the steps and into the house. Through the branches of the bush, Michael saw the lights inside go on one at a time, as outside the light poked little holes into the darkness and illuminated the bugs dancing in the air around the bush.

He heard a click at the back door and went around and crouched to the left of the back patio, just out of view, and listened, his heart pounding. It was Nancy and John coming outside, Michael could hear from their voices. The screen door shut behind them.

"Yeah, he called the retreat center office and said he made it home okay, but I called home several times and he didn't answer. I'm not supposed to tell you this, but he has a paranoid condition and a lot of anxiety. They call it neurotic paranoia. We've dealt with it our whole marriage. It's nothing new. He would not want me to tell you this, but I have to have someone to talk to, and I know I can trust you. You and Michael are quite close, anyway. Did he ever mention any of this to you? John, I am really worried."

"I had no idea. I mean, he is an eccentric guy, but I didn't know he had troubles like that."

"Please be discreet about it."

"I will, of course. Why do you think he wanted to come to that retreat place?"

"I think he may be going through one of his fits, and I think he really values you and what you suggest. I know you recommended this place, and I think he trusts that."

She paused for a moment. "Do you know that when I first met him at Yale I thought he didn't like women? I thought maybe he was above all of that, someone who couldn't be bothered, who is too intellectual to bother with any of it. I was surprised when he asked me out. But now I know that it's not that, it's just the mental issues. But he's worth it."

"I can tell that you love him very much."

"I do. He can be quite cold and closed off, but he has a heart of gold. Geniuses are always troubled, I think. My bet is he is sleeping at his office or a hotel. I know he'll call me in the morning. Right, he'll call? He'll come back?" Her voice sounded panicky, and it took on the tone it had when the tears began. He knew that poor tone all too well after years of marriage.

"Oh, Nancy, I'm so sorry," John responded, his voice genuinely sympathetic. Michael hoped he might comfort her with a hug, but he couldn't see anything. They lowered their voices, and Michael could make out a muffled mention of Ryan. He heard Nancy's tearful voice.

"Oh, just normal teenage rebellion stuff, I think. They used to be quite close—she adored him when she was little, and they just drifted apart. It's a mystery to me, I guess."

He heard Nancy pour wine into a glass and then silence for a minute.

"Did you know that I was planning on moving sometime this year?" John asked.

"Really, to where?"

"Colorado. My brother lives there, and there's so much contracting work to be done in the area he lives in. Plus it's so beautiful out there, and it'd be nice to get a change of scene from all the memories of my marriage and my divorce. Now I'll be staying here though. I decided not to leave."

"Oh, wow. Well, I'm glad you're staying. Michael will also be glad. He's gotten very attached to you." With that Nancy's voice wavered with emotion. "I'm so glad you're here now. I don't know what I would do—"

"Definitely. I'm glad to be here, Nancy. It has been a long day. Should I drive back home or stay?"

"It might be nice to have you in the house until we locate Michael. I really am a bit worried; I'm trying to stay calm. I'm going to attempt to go to bed, though I might not be able to sleep. Good night. Do you need anything?"

"No thanks. I know where everything is. Thank you. Everything is going to be okay, Nancy. Good night." Michael thought that he detected hints of love in John's voice; he had used a loving tone.

"I will poke my head in on Max to make sure he's fallen asleep— would you like that, Nancy?"

"Oh yes, thank you. Thank you so much." Nancy sat out there alone, and Michael carefully went back to his bush, plugging his ears to stop hearing the simple sobbing of a woman alone on a porch. She eventually sighed and went in.

———

The lights in the house switched off one by one as Michael sat in the grass by the house. In the large hydrangea bush, he startled a rabbit that poked its nose in to hide there. It darted into the middle of the lawn, waiting to see if it would be pursued, and when it was not, it shot into the forest. He sat looking into the tangling matrix of roots and stems that created the foundation of those colorful round blossoms.

No doubt everyone had settled into his or her own room. He let what felt like enough time pass for one person to get restless and find the other. The right person would find the right person. Order had to be restored. His hands shaking, Michael inserted his key into the back lock and went inside. He stood there once he had shut the door, waiting for someone to be startled by him. Nothing moved. The house was bathed in silence and shadows. He took his shoes off and slid across the clean wood floor. Seeing the house as if for the first time, it looked beautiful to him, as though it were out of a catalog. His heart ached as he knew he would never stay here again. *It was not his house. It had never been his house.* It was time for him to see what it looked like with a real man of the house.

He went up the staircase and stood outside his former bedroom with Nancy. He just had to see, a final confirmation that his plan had been appropriate. He flung the door open and turned on the light, bracing himself for what he was about to witness. Nancy sat up aghast in her blue silk nightgown, alone in the bed. He stood there, and she looked around in terror. He realized she was concerned for her safety. *Where was John? Where was he?*

"Michael," she said in fear and with that ever-present concern that was rightly placed on him but that he could not bear to hear one more time. An inner part of him broke to see the empty bed. His plan had not yet worked, but it would work. It would work. He slammed the door to his old bedroom shut, stormed down the hall and flung open Ryan's door, to say good-bye or to apologize, he wasn't sure which. He saw her in bed, but she was not alone. He saw she was in a tangle with the girl Dari. He saw their tan limbs, so carefree, wrapped around each other, and they were midkiss. Alarm flashed over both of their faces, identical looks to Nancy's, concern for their safety, it seemed. His mind felt as though it would explode from sight after sight in a now foreign and incomprehensible environment. *Was she drunk? Did they know what they were doing?* Before the girls could speak words of concern, words he certainly could not bear to hear, Michael stalked down the hall again and down the stairs, rapid-fire, and out of the house, leaving his shoes behind by the glass doorway.

The hours and hours of time spent creating the perfect features of a house, perfect glass doors, perfectly decorated rooms, and all the effort, the trying, faded behind him as he ran to his car.

———

He ran past houses with TVs on, sedate adults lounging in front of the flashing sets, past empty basketball hoops waiting for young men to stand below them and give it a try, give the game a chance. Crickets churned their endless song around him, grinding their melody into the night. Just before he reached his car, Michael heard a rustling in the bushes and knew an animal was in there. He had a feeling it was the skinny fox with the bright eyes that haunted their neighborhood. Was it hunting something? Did it know Michael was leaving, and had it come to say good-bye? Would it skulk around his property once he was gone, or would it lose interest and wander off to another place? Maybe it would starve in the winter months. He didn't know.

In his car, he passed the turnoff to Jill's house, a turn he had made a thousand times when he dropped his daughter off to play when she was young. He passed Sammy's and the video store where they had gotten all their rental tapes for years and years, then sped off of the Peninsula and onto the mainland.

———

When Michael arrived at his mother's house in Greenwich two and a half hours later, it was after midnight. Her night nurse ran into the hall at the sound of the door opening and gave Michael a frightened look. Even after he explained that he had lost his shoes in an emergency, she still looked at him with wariness. This he was used to, as every person he now encountered seemed to be onto him and his secret. He would never be normal. He was insane and was in love with a man, and not for the first time. He had been helplessly in love with Alex, an adoration that would never die, and now he was falling in love with John. John was no Alex, but he had a surprising appeal that couldn't be denied and that was growing stronger the more Michael was around him.

He felt that his insanity had infected his daughter, no doubt, and out of desperation she too had turned perverted and sick. It was probably due to the fact that he had bitten her several months ago while drunk and had transmitted his diseased state into her in what he must have felt was a harmless playful moment of affection. Or perhaps he had passed along a faulty gene? His behavior was something that was utterly incomprehensible to him. When he was drunk, a monster emerged, a monster bent on destroying his life. Michael could not be trusted, he felt, to be the caretaker of any person, of a wife or of children, and he would remove himself.

———

In the morning the night nurse was gone, and his mother was slow to wake up. Her health had become worse over the months as her bones became more brittle and her curved spine increasingly pressed into her lungs. She had not made it clear just how bad her health had become when they spoke on the phone, probably not wanting to burden him. As if she could be a burden! But now he saw her rapid decline clearly before him in her crumpled form. She slept longer into the day. When she was awake, she smiled to see him there, sitting in an easy chair with his legs up, sipping a cup of tea, finally peaceful. She gazed into his eyes and seemed to know him, his thoughts, every last bit of who he was, and she loved all of what she saw. Her gaze would continue for long periods of time, understanding and kindness quietly burning behind her tired eyes as they met his. He fed her breakfast, and then they both napped and later watched a golf tournament on TV in the afternoon.

———

During this time, the room was the stillest it had ever been. This, the dining room of his youth, was now converted into a makeshift bedroom or sickroom. Michael remembered all of the family dinners that had taken place, all so formal; even with casual food like macaroni and cheese, good dishes had been used and candles had been lit. He had always felt such an excitement eating here, knowing that he would soon be able to return to his room, soon be able to be alone in relative silence. The anticipation that that salvation was coming allowed him to eat in peace, listen to the lifeless conversation, a smile on his face. Michael thought his mother always assumed he was smiling due to the food or the family time, and there was no reason she had to know the truth behind his pleasant expression. It would have only hurt and confused her, but maybe it wouldn't have, as she certainly knew him better than anyone else and accepted his odd ways.

———

Michael stayed with her every day, and the days began to lose a sense of differentiation from one to the next. He turned off the ringer on his mother's phone and without its insistent sound took comfort in sleeping in the easy chair next to her bed. Several knocks were heard on the front door, but he didn't answer them. It was Marilyn's friends who were coming to see how she was. Finally, he spoke through the closed door to them, claiming it was a bad time for a visit and he would call them when they could again come by.

Marilyn spoke occasionally and slurred her words often. Michael only bathed her twice a week, as the pain it caused her hip showed in her face when he would lower her into the tub. Her fingers would grip his arm and she would look up into his face, caught up in the pain of moving and ashamed of her nakedness. He spoke soothing words to her and tried to bathe her as quickly as he could. When Michael handled her this way, he could feel viscerally the brittleness of her structure, the sense that the bones were collapsing inside, that all was giving way. He could hardly bear those excruciating moments when he had his arms around her and could feel her fragility and sense her desperation, her complete helplessness. Every time after he had bathed her and she had fallen asleep, Michael went upstairs to his room, shut the door, and cried.

After a week of this, Michael washed her only with towels in her bed, as the nurses had shown him before he let them go. She soon started to reject his offerings of soft food, claiming she wasn't hungry. She began to eat only ice chips and slept longer. Michael sat in the room, eating canned soup and drinking his cups of tea, and when he was sure she was dead, when he saw the hardened form up close that appeared so solid, yet so fragile, as if it would shatter upon touch in its brittle, contracted state, the form that only vaguely resembled his mother, and he could tell that he was no longer looking at her, he made himself very comfortable in the chair, took twenty of his sleeping pills, and began to make his way out of his body. The parameters of the room began to blur.

CHAPTER EIGHTEEN

When he woke up, the room was dim. He was lying on his back, looking up at squares on a ceiling. A nurse walked by the room and then back to the entryway when she saw he was awake.

"You're up," she said matter-of-factly and sat down in a chair next to him. She was uncommonly young looking, with wavy brown hair and a pretty face. It occurred to him that she must have been loved by someone.

"How did I get checked in here?"

"You called us."

"What do you mean?"

"You called the ambulance to come and save you, so we did." She was remarkably calm about the whole thing, a half-amused smile on her face, as if it had all been just a silly prank, and for a moment, he felt that it was. He had saved himself amidst the throw-up and the frothy spit that had been on his face and his shirt and in front of him on the carpet.

There was something else he was supposed to remember. He remembered it: mother. He fell silent. She saw his face change. "Yes, the coroner came and took your mother's body away. I am so sorry."

"Why am I not in a psychiatric ward with restraints on my wrists?"

"We didn't think it was necessary since you called us before you blacked out. What a wonderful thing to do." She seemed genuinely in awe of him, as if he were heroic, and since one felt compelled to believe anything she said, so confident was she, he felt he had to go along with it.

"You'll stay here with us for a few days until you get back on your feet, and then you'll be released to the world."

"I don't want you to call my wife. But I would like you to mail a letter to her in the next day or so, once I write it, okay?"

"Whatever you want, Mr. James." And with that she left.

———

In the privacy of the small yard behind his mother's house, he lay stretched out on a lawn chair, the late-afternoon sun full upon him. It was quiet back here, the old carriage house fifty yards ahead of him, the compact bushes framing the little squares of grass. The air was still and pregnant, heavy.

He would not be returning home. The thought of returning to his old life was impossible; it was an idea so awful and so heartbreaking as to cause him physical pain at the thought of it. It caused his body to sink even deeper into his chair in a kind of revolt. His body would not let him get up if he did that. It would not drive back. His life with Nancy was over. Though the weight of his failure as her husband was crushing, he knew with the utmost clarity that they would get a divorce. That at some point, months from now, his children would begin to visit him here. He could take them out into the stillness of this brick yard and have dinner with them on the patio overlooking it.

Ryan would understand. She was stronger than he was and so might be able to get what she wanted out of this life. Maybe one day she would once again ask for his advice on books or writing. Perhaps somehow she would want to rejoin herself to him or ask him for advice when she hit a wall in her life. It was up to her. He would be naked here with them, a strange man living alone, and the thought of such a family gathering was horrifying, but it was less horrifying than the idea of ever going back to that house and inserting himself back into that prism of expectations. It was an absolute impossibility.

Would Michael ever have a true lover, one who took his breath away? He didn't know. He knew he had never had one. The malignancy, the unstable mind, all of it, came from this lack and from nowhere else. A life of pretending had spawned an evil twin who would not leave his side. Until now.

———

Nancy had undoubtedly gotten the note he mailed to her a day before trying to kill himself. He could imagine her walking to the mailbox and opening it, her hands trembling upon seeing his handwriting. It read simply, *"Please marry John. You always deserved better than me. I am not sick in a physical way, but I am sick in more ways than you know."* Would she ever understand? She would undoubtedly blame it all on his mental problems. She would never understand him fully, though she had tried. Even after receiving the letter, she would not believe him, but she would cry and cry, attempting to understand; John would be there for her, and she would fall into his arms while she cried. John would be furious with Michael for lying to him and so would feel okay with taking his wife. Perhaps Nancy would be furious, too, and so she could move on. They could bond in their fury, it could bring them together. Michael might never see John again, and the thought, strangely, brought a tear to his eye. Then the sadness sank in deeply and for that moment dissolved. He had given her John as an offering, an offering he would have loved to receive. The two would grow old together in that house, and when they were buried, their headstones would remain side by side in the graveyard, proof of life, proof of love. So many years later, Michael might not really be remembered at all, for John and Nancy would have so many wonderful family memories between now and their old age. Perhaps Michael himself might have some nice memories, so that the forgery of his life could somehow be undone. The future stretched ahead, unclear.

There were no phones here. He had unplugged them all. He would call Nancy in a few days and have the agonizing conversation of divorce. Until then, he had this: sunshine on his face, his tired surrendered body, solitude, quiet, pouring into his soul like a stream of goodness. He had this at least. He would answer to no one and betray himself no more. If Nancy came to the house, he would let her pound on the door but would not open it. The door had been locked in three different places; she could not get in. She could not access this yard except through the house; it was deliciously private. He felt nothing for her but endless neutrality, with points of deep sympathy for her plight but no bitterness. More than for her, he had sympathy for himself and a desire not to have to think. There was the quiet yard with the busy insects floating over the flowers, there were the still bricks sheltering him in a contained space, there was the solidity of the empty house behind him. There was the dazzling beauty of his mother's young face captured in the photographs in the house, her eyes hopeful for a romantic marriage, for a bright future, for joy. Housed in those eyes, he saw himself reflected a thousand times in unnameable points of light. The poisonous bitterness he had held all his adult life had died when she had died, and now there was just this: endlessness, mercy, stillness, the body free from restlessness. This would be a good place to settle.

ACKNOWLEDGMENTS

I would like to acknowledge the years of support and love I received from my mother, Harriet, and my father, Richard, as well as their belief in my novel. I would like to thank my husband, Dexter, who has been there for me through the highs and lows of life and the writing process and has loved me the whole time.

I would like to thank my brilliant agent, Monika Woods, a diamond in the rough, whose intelligence and abilities as an agent are second to none, as well as the great team at InkWell. Your eagle eye gives me chills, Monika! A huge thank-you to my editor, Karen Kosztolnyik, the editor of my dreams, who is warm, generous, sensitive, and is both savvy and intuitive. Karen, thank you for having a genius ability to carefully preserve a writer's voice, while also finding and teasing out the places that are yearning to come out more fully in the story. Any writer is truly lucky to work with you. Thank you, Monika and Karen, for your passion for the book. Go Team Shark! I also want to thank the amazing team at Gallery Books/Simon & Schuster for their tireless hard work and their enthusiastic support: Jen Bergstrom, Louise Burke, Jen Long, Jen Robinson, Meagan Harris, Liz Psaltis, Wendy Sheanin, Lisa Litwack, Anna Dorfman, and

Becky Prager. Becky—thank you for answering countless questions and being a great guide along this path. I am truly fortunate to work with this team of dedicated and skillful people who truly nurtured this book. Thank you to Lynn Cullen for your kind presence during the editing phase and for your friendship.

I want to thank my fiction writing teachers. First, my early mentors: Tom Drury, David Plante, and Jaime Manrique, all of whom made a huge impact on my style and made me feel valued as a writer from a young age. David nurtured this book in its infancy and Jaime worked with me on it years later. I would like to thank Mark O'Donnell who spent a whole year working on this novel with me. I owe a lot to the generosity of Tom Perrotta, who years after our workshop at Yale together, always made himself available to me despite being extremely busy. Thank you so much! A big thank-you to my Columbia professors: Jonathan Dee, Nathan Englander, Alan Ziegler, Mark Slouka, and Binnie Kirshenbaum. I would also like to thank Nancy Zafris for sharing her knowledge of craft and for her great workshops at Kenyon.

Garnette Cadogan: you're an absolute angel! Thanks for believing in this book before others did. Also, John Freeman, thank you for your advice and support while I made this dream a reality. Thank you, Diane Zumer, for your powerful belief in my work.

Thank you to Karen Russell, Molly Antopol, and Elyssa East for your kind words and unwavering support. Thanks for always being there, Jamie Pietras, through all the long years. Thank you Eva Wylie for letting me use your image for my website, and to Dr. John Wylie for allowing me to consult with you in your area of expertise, psychiatry. Thank you to Deborah Kelley-Galin for listening to me throughout it all. Thank you, Scooter Jones, for being my writing companion.